the problem with second chances

PIPER RAYNE

Cover Design: By Hang Le

Cover Picture: Wander Aguiar Photography

1st Line Editor: Joy Editing

2nd Line Editor: My Brother's Editor

Proofreader: My Brother's Editor

For Rylan Greene and me, it was simple. Love only got us so far.

I've known him since we were six, long before he became the professional soccer star he is now. We've weaved in and out of one another's lives as rivals, teammates, friends, and lovers. Until three years ago, when my life took a hit and I ran back to my small Alaskan town, Lake Starlight, away from anything or anyone that could hurt me.

He's never far from my mind, a constant pining ache in my heart, but I've convinced myself I'm better off. But now, my best friend announces her engagement and that means Rylan will return home to stand as best man to her fiancé.

He'll be back in my orbit for three whole weeks... but I can easily keep my distance. Sure, we'll have to walk arm in arm down the aisle together, he'll hold me close during the bridal party dance and we'll stand for pictures next to each other. Nothing I can't handle.

I'm so naïve though because he's not in town for more than twenty-four hours before he knocks on my door. I should know by now, that the two of us will never be finished business.

The Problem with *Second Chances*

CALISTA

Spring

A knock on the café window startles me as I'm about to sip my coffee and a drop spills on my pants. I look out the window and Aubrey's waving with a huge smile.

My best friend called first thing this morning, insisting I meet her here, that she had huge news. And since most of my clients in our small Alaskan town are family members, it was easy for me to reschedule my appointments.

She rushes through the front door, waving and saying hello to everyone who also decided to come to Brewed Awakenings this morning. You'd think she's running for mayor.

But she's not. I already know why I'm sitting here, and I've been dreading this day for almost a decade, although with each passing year, I knew it was guaranteed to come.

She shrugs out of her coat, slides into the seat across from me, and picks up the latte I ordered her with her right hand. Aubrey is left-handed. "Thank you so much. I needed this."

"So... what's going on?" I play the part of dumbass so I don't spoil her surprise.

Aubrey beams and bites her lower lip, her blue eyes flooded with happiness. She sets down her coffee, pauses dramatically, and raises her left hand where an engagement ring now rests. "I'm getting married!" she squeals.

And I match her squeal because that's what a best friend does when her number one announces her engagement.

I spring out of my seat, and she stands from hers. We wrap our arms around one another, not caring who we might be bothering.

"Let me see." I hold her hand to get a better look at the ring. Her fiancé does well for himself, so the lucky girl scored herself a three-carat diamond. "It's gorgeous."

She's giddy, barely able to leave her hand in mine before lifting it to appraise the ring in the light of the dim coffee shop. I hug her again. I'm happy for my best friend, I am. I'm just upset about what it means for me.

We slide back in our wooden seats, and she sips her latte. "OMG, Calista, can you believe he finally proposed?"

It only took Declan five years too long, but he was busy working his way through law school so he could take over his dad's practice in nearby Anchorage. He had goals he wanted to reach for himself before giving Aubrey everything she wants.

"And you wanted to give him an ultimatum." That was two years ago. Most of our other friends were getting married and Aubrey couldn't stand that he hadn't proposed.

"I know. I just needed to trust him."

Sure, everything's great now. Where was this casual attitude after the trips she came home from, depressed because she was sure he was going to ask her, or the anniversaries where she demolished desserts and inspected the bottoms of champagne flutes?

"So, give me all the details." I smile at her.

She tells me how they were at his parents' cabin, arriving late on Friday. He made an excuse about having to check something inside and left her standing on the porch. So far I'm not impressed and would like to go wring Declan's neck for leaving her outside to be a bear's dinner.

"He texted me to come in. So I walked through the front door and there was a line of lights with rose petals that led me to where he was on the back porch. I opened the French doors and white string lights were strung all across. 'Adore You' by Harry Styles was playing and he was in the middle of a heart made out of petals and lights, bending down on his knee and holding the ring. Oh, Calista, I thought I was gonna pass out. After all these years..."

I smile, knowing how happy she is.

You are too, I remind myself. *Stop being a selfish bitch.*

"I strolled over to him."

"I'm surprised you didn't tackle him and yank the ring from his fingers, screaming yes over and over again."

She laughs. "It's what I wanted to do, but..." She wiggles in the chair and sits up straighter. "I had years to practice what I would say and how I would act."

Once our laughter slows, I say, "Go on."

"He had this whole speech that..." She cringes. "I don't really remember, but it was about how he loves me and living together until we're old." She waves. "You know the typical stuff about being side by side with him forever. And then he said, 'Marry me?' And I said, 'Yes!' He slipped the ring on and I jumped him, and we toppled to the ground."

I laugh because that's totally Aubrey and why I love her so

much. She doesn't hold back when she's excited about something.

She continues, telling me about how they had sex so many times she was sore. And that they don't want to wait long, so the wedding will be in October.

October... my stomach plummets.

"That's so fast. What about next spring? Spring is so nice. And it gives you a full year to plan the wedding of your dreams."

She looks at me over the rim of her coffee cup.

I hate that look.

The pity look.

The "it's okay to be upset, but you're going to survive" look.

She sets down her cup and squeezes my hand. "You'll be my maid of honor, right?" I nod, pushing back the tears threatening to spill.

"Even though..."

I nod.

"I knew you would and that's why I love you so much. It'll be painless. Well... not painless, but I already told Declan that there will be no dance with the bridal party. And you'll walk down the aisle yourself—he'll be standing next to Declan at the end of the aisle already."

"Perfect, so I can actually enact what it would be like to walk down the aisle to him as if it were our own ceremony."

She tilts her head and frowns.

"Forget I said that. Sorry." I wave away my petty words.

"The only thing you have to do together is walk back down the aisle after the ceremony. Stand next to him during the receiving line, and that's it."

I squeeze Aubrey's hand. "Don't worry about me. I'm a big girl. He's a big boy. Everything will go great. I'm your maid of honor, so I'll make sure of it."

She smiles, but still looks a little hesitant. "Thanks."

"Has Declan already asked him?"

If I'm lucky, maybe he won't be able to make it. Maybe he'll have some big professional soccer player thing he's committed to. But I know nothing would keep him away from his best friend's wedding, just like nothing would keep me from Aubrey's side.

Damn us and our loyalty.

"He called him this morning before I came here."

"And?"

"He's going to be Declan's best man."

I sigh.

Rylan Greene.

I can barely think his name without it feeling like a knife turning in my gut, but in six months, my arm will be hooked around his.

God, my entire life has orbited around that man since the age of six. For a brief moment in time, I thought we'd be where Aubrey and Declan are now, but I couldn't have been more naive. For Rylan and me, love wasn't enough. Pure and simple. We wanted it, we really did want us to work out, but love only takes you so far. Sometimes life gets in the way.

"Calista?" Aubrey waves her hand in front of my face. "See, I told Declan we should just elope."

I squeeze her hands. "No, Aubrey. This will be a great day and we need to celebrate. You need to be happy. And it's been so long coming, I want it to be everything you ever dreamed."

"You sure?"

I nod. "Let's talk colors. What are you thinking? And where are you having it?"

I bombard her with questions to stop my heart from beating out of my chest over the fact that a small part of me is excited he's coming home.

I'm such a glutton for punishment where he's concerned.

CALISTA

October Present Day

y heart races and sweat drips down my temple even with the chilly air that arrived in our small Alaskan town this morning. The path around the lake isn't as busy as it usually is, which I'm grateful for because today is not a day I can field nosy townspeople's questions about the wedding of the decade that's happening in only three weeks. Everyone is abuzz about my best friend Aubrey's wedding to the hot young lawyer who grew up in the neighboring town of Sunrise Bay.

As I move from a jog to a walk to head back to town, I spot my old soccer coach, Uncle Jamie. I try to turn around quickly to do another lap to avoid him. Besides, it'll help with all this anxiety I have about Rylan returning to town.

We have a big family. Now that all the original nine Bailey kids have married and have their own children, I can't walk through the town square without running into at least one of us.

"Calista!" Uncle Jamie shouts with his Scottish accent and waves before I can sneak away.

I take out my earbuds. "Hey, Uncle Jamie."

He goes in for a hug, but I wave him away since I'm so sweaty. "How's the knee holding up?"

I shrug.

"Do you want me to grovel?" He doesn't bother with chitchat, but if he did, I'd be more suspicious.

Uncle Jamie's new quest is to persuade me to coach soccer at the sports complex he co- owns. He wants the girls to have a female coach and thinks I can help them develop their skills and give insight on what it's like to be a female athlete. It shouldn't be any different than being a male athlete, but no one's naive enough to believe that. Take Rylan and me for instance. We trained together since we were six and our paths went two very different directions with two very different opportunities.

"I told you, I just don't have the time."

He holds out a box of Sweet Suga Things donuts. "Here. Last box."

"Aunt Sedona will kill you if you give it to me."

He chuckles. "Probably. But it's worth it. There's no one in the area even close to as qualified as you are."

I blow out a breath. "I'll tell you what. Let me get through this wedding and then we'll talk, but don't get your hopes up."

"Man, after everything I've done for you." He winks and opens the box.

Damn, they look delicious. I shake my head. "Nope. I have a bridesmaid dress to fit in."

"And a lad to show what he's missing?" He arches a dark eyebrow.

I think Uncle Jamie feels comfortable talking to me about my issues with Rylan because he's been entwined in our story from the beginning.

"Those days are over."

He looks at me with kindness I want to scratch off his face like a feral cat. "We both know the two of you will never be finished business. Even if…" He shakes his head. "I look forward to you letting me know after the wedding." He opens the donut box again. "Take one."

"Nope. I need to work on my willpower. I'm going to jog another lap."

"Yer gonna give yerself a stress fracture."

"I'm good. Promise. See you later, Uncle Jamie."

I jog away, knowing my uncle means well, but I haven't kicked a soccer ball in almost three years and my life is perfectly fine. Sure, it hurt like hell when I figured out that the game I've loved all my life gave me the middle finger, but finding my backup career was hard enough. Yeah, I went to school for accounting, but I never thought I'd use it. I intended to play soccer until I retired. But life didn't go that way.

I slow my pace and wonder if I should just start running in nearby Winterberry Falls where no one really knows who I am. It's a newer town in the midst of modernizing from a fishing and hunting town, rebranding to bring in younger people. At least that's what Buzz Wheel said when they reported about it.

I'm finishing my run, still worrying about having to face Rylan in only two days, when I spot a pair of women waving in my direction. Upon closer inspection, I recognize them as the grandma gang—Jean and Alice from Northern Lights Retirement Center.

I'm not in the mood for them. Don't get me wrong, they're sweet ladies. Alice is Aubrey's grandmother and still dyes her hair red in an effort to make herself look younger, whereas Jean is full-on gray, but the darker gray. But even though I don't feel like dealing with whatever they're bringing to my doorstep, I promised my great-grandma Dori that I'd visit them once she was "dancing in heaven with my great-grandpa."

It was hard for the whole family the day she passed. Of course, she made it to one hundred years and one day old—she was adamant that she'd be over one hundred years old when she went.

Everyone was upset, but Uncle Kingston reminded us all of a conversation he'd had with her at her ninetieth birthday party. She said that whenever it was her time to go, it was okay, because she'd had a good long life full of love and was ready to spend eternity with my great- grandpa.

My family The Baileys had a big celebration of her life, and it was as if a queen had died. But I guess in a way, one did, because Great-Grandma Dori was like the queen of Lake Starlight. My family went into overdrive donating to the city on her behalf, so you can't go anywhere without coming across a plaque that says the item was donated by her and my great-grandpa.

When I reach Alice and Jean, you'd think they were the ones who ran five miles from how out of breath they are.

"Oh, thank goodness we found you," Alice says, her age-spotted hand holding out an envelope. "We'd been waiting by your apartment, then went over to get a donut at Greta's and got sidetracked because she was out. By that time—"

"For Pete's sake, just give it to the girl." Jean takes the envelope out of Alice's hand and shoves it into mine.

There's some weight to it, so it's not just a letter. I look at it. "Is this something for Aubrey? The wedding?"

They exchange a look.

"Just read the note and follow the instructions. You'll get more answers tomorrow," Alice says.

Then they hightail it, fast walking back to the streets of Lake Starlight—or as fast as women their age can walk.

I stare at the envelope. It has my name written on the front. I walk over to a bench that has a dedication to my grandparents on it, sit down, and slide my finger under the flap to open the envelope. The heaviness I felt inside is a key. There's a small notecard-sized letter with it. I'm pretty sure it was typed on a typewriter, or at the very least is in the font of a typewriter.

I hold up the card to inspect it further. I'd bet money it's from an actual typewriter.

Tomorrow 9am

27 Cottagewood Dr.

Lake Starlight, Alaska

Cryptic much? If I weren't fairly sure the grandma gang was trained by Rylan's Grandma Ethel and my Great-Grandma Dori before they died, I'd be worried I was going to be murdered.

Shoving the key and the note into the side pocket of my workout leggings, I walk through town. Instead of heading to my apartment, I go to my dad's restaurant, knowing he's open for lunch and will be there.

I walk in the door off the back alley and smile when I see Dad at the cutting board, chopping away while the television above is lit up with a soccer game. The man was all baseball and still is, but my playing made him a soccer fan, which always means he has to choose what to watch in October, baseball or soccer playoffs.

"Hey, Dad."

He drops the knife, scurrying to find the remote. I rise up

on my toes and kiss his cheek. I notice the gray around his temples is more prominent these days as I'm pulling away.

He grabs the remote, but I put my hand on his. "Leave it. It's okay."

Rylan plays for Chicago, but they were kicked out of the playoffs the first week, which is why he's now going to be here three weeks before the wedding instead of two days before. I had hoped he'd pop in and out of town like he did for his grandma Ethel's funeral last year when he never even spent the night.

"Are you sure?" my dad asks, looking concerned.

"It's exciting, no? The underdog Charlotte is still up there, but Chicago lost first round." I shake my head and prop myself up on his counter.

He goes back to chopping onions, not one tear streaming down his face. Must be years of conditioning. "I couldn't believe it. I thought Chicago was a shoo-in, but they didn't seem on their game. No one was really commanding them on the field."

What he means is that Rylan wasn't commanding them. He's the center midfield and he was really off his game the other night.

"Yeah. I wonder what could've thrown him off. I mean, the man played the day after his grandma died and scored the most goals and assists in one game in the history of the team."

My dad shrugs. He likes me to think he doesn't care about Rylan, that after we broke up, Rylan was put on his shit list, but we both know that's not true.

He puts the onions in a dish and starts on the peppers. I jump down to join him, heading to the sink to wash my hands. After I've put on my apron, I take a few of the peppers and grab a cutting board and knife. I can't cut as fast as my dad, but any help is help.

We work quietly for a minute, my mind wandering before I ask, "When Great-Grandma Dori arranged for you and Mom to get together, what did she do?"

He momentarily stops cutting and I regret asking because talking about my great-grandma always brings a tinge of sadness to the room. I'm about to tell him to forget my question when he starts chopping again.

"Don't go thinking I didn't fall in love with your mom the minute she arrived in town with you." He winks, and I roll my eyes.

I'm the product of a one-night stand. My mom had to track down my dad when I was eighteen months old. They were strangers to one another, but they fell in love. It's like a one-in-a-million story, considering they lived happily ever after.

"I know. The minute she set foot in the restaurant, you knew."

He points his knife. "Exactly. But G'Ma D just... she had this sly way of making sure you never tripped over your own feet." He places the knife down and turns around to lean against the counter. "I can't speak for my siblings, but losing our parents as young as we did... all of us were in different stages of our lives when the accident happened, and I think we each developed our own hang-ups. Mine was that I never wanted anything serious with a woman until I was completely established. Figured I had so many years and my career was the most important thing to me. It's not like G'Ma D locked us in rooms until we fell in love, she just gently pushed and then she'd..."

A smile comes to his lips. It makes me smile, remembering her too.

"She'd tell you a story about her and Grandpa, or maybe my mom or dad, something that turned on the light bulb and made you get your head out of your ass." He stares at his feet for a second then turns around and chops peppers. "Why do you ask?"

The letter and the key practically burn a hole in my pocket. I'd love to be forthcoming with my dad. He's my number one cheerleader, but I need more information first.

I shrug. "Just wondered."

He turns off the television as if knowing soccer reminds me of Rylan. He probably assumes I want to get back together with him, that this wedding will be another shot after how many before. Another press of the button and his hard rock music belts out of the speakers. I guess that's the end of our conversation.

RYLAN

I get déjà vu on the escalator down to the baggage claim. I was just here eight months or so ago when my grandma Ethel passed away. At least then I was able to fly in and out without having to spend the night. I had hoped for the same short visit when Declan called me six months ago and told me he was going to propose to Aubrey, but I promised him I'd return here as soon as my season ended and unfortunately that was earlier than I'd hoped. Declan should be happy she stood by his side all these years. Anyone who knows Aubrey knows patience isn't one of her virtues.

My bag is the only one riding the conveyor belt since I stopped upstairs to eat before coming down. Every one of my family members, including my parents, asked to pick me up, but I told them I'd need a car, so I'd drive myself to Sunrise Bay.

Three weeks.

I knew this day was coming, but I still find myself unprepared to see Calista again.

It doesn't help that it feels impossible to get my head together since we lost in the first round of the playoffs, and I can't listen to any sports commentary without the subject of my piss-poor performance during the playoffs coming up. Coach said to flush the year, flush the game, but I keep replaying how the opposing players got by me.

I grab my suitcase, bigger than I normally bring home because I haven't stayed for longer than a week in years. And I can't really give a reason for that. Or at least one that I'll admit.

After grabbing a rental SUV, I couldn't be happier to be driving into Sunrise Bay on my own. Instead of taking the highway, I extend my drive another half hour by taking the back roads, needing time to prepare myself.

Calista and I cannot have a repeat of last Christmas. It's like having to rip a Band-Aid off a festering wound afterward. When I leave town this time, things between us have to be finished for good. I need to do some soul-searching.

A surge of emotion hits me when I pass the sports performance building that Jamison Ferguson and Kingston Bailey own. I spent all my youth there, and so did Calista. From the time we were six, we trained together under Jamison since he'd played professional soccer in the US and Europe. He's the entire reason I am where I am.

But my first real memory in that place—other than my annoyance at Calista when she'd beat me to the goal—was when we were fourteen. It was a big tournament and Calista was playing with us because Ian Porter had broken his leg that week. The problem was that by that point, Calista was playing with the girls' team and since we were both center midfielders, Jamison decided to have us take turns playing center. I laugh, remembering how stubborn she was then and still is.

"Uncle Jamie, you know I'm the better player." She put her hands on her hips. She'd started wearing shorter shorts and only sports bras by midpractice when she got hot. My juvenile self could barely keep my hard-on hidden.

"You're kidding. God." I sighed and shook my head.

Jamison was her uncle and I sometimes felt his loyalty went her way, or he had a soft spot for her because she was a girl.

She kicked the ball out from under my foot and dribbled it around. "See?"

She got the ball up in the air and bounced it on her knees, then bopped it on her head to her feet again. Not about to be shown up, I kicked it away from her.

"You guys," Jamie whined.

But I was busy kicking the ball downfield, Calista chasing me. She got in front of me, her eyes focused on my footwork. We were the best in the club, but that wasn't good enough for Calista. She had to be better than me too.

She kicked, and I pushed the ball the other way, laughing.

She groaned and followed, almost getting the ball from me before I stopped and kicked it the opposite way. Sometimes I wanted to put her in her place, show her I was the better player; other times I wanted to kiss her. My body was at war with my mind and was so fucking twisted back then.

"Go, Calista!" Declan said from the sidelines. He'd come with me because we were going to the high school football game after practice.

I scowled at him while Calista's forehead crinkled. "That's your friend? What's his name again?"

"Declan."

"What kind of name is that?"

"What kind of name is Calista?" I kept drawing her closer to me, making her think she had a chance to get the ball.

Declan liked Calista. He'd been on me for weeks about setting up a double date with her.

Her labored breathing cooled the sweat on my neck. Our hands brushed as she stepped into me, but I kicked the ball to the right.

"Come on, you two," Jamie hollered across the field.

"Not fast enough," I taunted.

She groaned and got closer, then her breasts brushed my arm and she got a toe on the ball, shooting it out from under me. She ran down the field and I sprinted to catch her, but I was still processing that her breasts had grazed my arm. I figured that was exactly why there were always separate men's and women's leagues.

She kicked and scored, shimmying her hips left and right with her arms raised above her head. I bent over to catch my breath.

"She got you, Greene!" Declan screamed and I flipped him off behind me.

"It's her perseverance. She never gives up." Jamie clasped me on the shoulder. Calista kicked the ball toward Jamie and he caught it flawlessly. "Okay, you two. We're done for today. I'll see you at the game, and let's remember that yer on the same team tomorrow."

Calista giggled and grabbed her bag. She'd shower, then Jamie would drive her home while I was headed to the game with Declan.

In the shower, all I could think about was Calista and the way her nipples had poked out of her sports bra when she stood in front of the fan to cool down earlier. My dick was starting to grow hard, but I wasn't about to knock one off in a public bathroom, so I turned the water to cold. My older brother Jed always made comments about needing a cold shower, so I figured that might help. Thankfully it did help enough that I wouldn't be going out with a boner. Declan would never let me forget it.

I walked out wearing jeans and a Sunrise Bay High School sweatshirt, my hair still damp from my shower. Throwing my bag over my shoulder, I stopped when I heard Calista's giggle, hating that someone else was making her laugh. I had to get over this crush I had on her. It was making me insane.

"Awesome, tomorrow night then." Calista nodded and walked away from Declan as I approached.

"What happened?" I whispered to Declan since Calista was standing by the glass doors—waiting for Jamison, I assumed.

His face lit up with the same look that had gotten me in trouble so many times before. "Double date tomorrow night after the game." He ran his palms together.

"Who's the other couple?"

He laughed because Declan didn't always care how what he wanted affected others. "You and her friend Aubrey."

The only thing I knew about Aubrey was that she came to some soccer games and always had Calista's number painted on her cheek. That and the worst part, was that she wasn't Calista.

"Thought we were gonna..." I looked around. "You know, the Netflix thing."

He nodded and scoured the area too. "Relax, they're coming with us."

"What?" I snapped.

Calista glanced over, her usual smug look on her face.

"They're going to get us in trouble."

"No, they won't." He waved away my concern, but I knew it wasn't a good idea...

The next night, my brother Fisher walked me into the sheriff's station after we were caught sneaking into other people's houses, watching things on their Netflix accounts as a joke so that it would change the algorithm and suggest they watch weird stuff.

Declan leaned forward and looked at the girls, then at me. "Just relax, my dad is a lawyer. They have no proof."

"No matter what, I'm screwed. My brother is the sheriff, and my dad and mom are probably already on their way down here." I crossed my arms and glared at Declan, but beyond him was Calista, and she offered me a soft smile as though she felt bad for me. I inwardly rolled my eyes.

The entire night, Declan had been trying to impress Calista and it'd been getting on my nerves. We should've been done two houses sooner, but he'd insisted we keep going. Then Mato, another officer, found us sneaking out a window.

A while after he'd left us to stew, Fisher came out and pointed at the other three. "You go with Mato. Rylan, you're with me."

"Told you," I mumbled, following my older brother.

Fisher rambled on, saying pretty much what I expected from him. "How could you do this? It's disrespectful to our family."

"Declan likes Calista," I admitted, and Fisher's face fell. My whole family believed I liked her, and unfortunately, they were right, but I wasn't about to tell anyone that.

Minutes later, my dad and mom knocked on the door of Fisher's office and he pried it open. "Here's your felon. Going to check on the others."

He left and I got Dad's disapproving glare while Mom was glancing at Calista talking to Fisher.

All in all, our parents came to get us, which was humiliating. On the way out, Declan shook his head at me while his parents talked to mine.

"What?" I asked.

"Her friend said Calista likes you. Of course she fucking does."

"Bye, Declan," Aubrey says, her dad glaring over while he had one hand on her upper arm, leading her to their car.

"See you, Aubrey."

Calista was already in her dad's truck. She sat in the front seat, looking stoic as her dad kept turning to talk to her. I gave her a small smile and she shared her own with me.

"Aubrey's cute, right?" Declan interrupted. "She's hot. Do you like her? Because if you don't, then..."

My gaze stayed on Calista before her dad turned at the light. "Go ahead, Declan. I don't like her."

He clapped me on the shoulder. "Awesome. Thanks, Ry!"

By the end of the week, Declan had gotten Aubrey's phone number and asked her out.

I shake my head from the memory when my phone buzzes on the console.

Declan: Best man duty #1 - get your ass to Lucky's in Lake Starlight.

Instead of continuing to Sunrise Bay a few exits down, I get off in Lake Starlight.

I park and jog across the street of their small town that is quaint and touristy like my own. Declan hasn't shown yet, so I take a stool at the bar and ask for a beer. Any one of Calista's relatives could walk in here. Hell, maybe even she could. My heart leaps with hope, which makes me a very stupid man.

"What's up?" Declan says from the door. You'd think he was a Lake Starlight lifer the way he seems so comfortable here. He comes over and we shake hands then hug. "Damn, it's been too long. You've been slacking on your best man responsibilities."

I nod, feeling a little guilty. "I'm all yours now."

"Oh, before I forget, Aubrey's grandma Alice wanted me to give you this."

He hands me a small envelope. It reminds me of one that would accompany a bouquet of flowers.

I run my finger under the seam to open it. The card reads:

Tomorrow 9am
27 Cottagewood Dr.
Lake Starlight, Alaska

What the hell is this all about?

CALISTA

I pull into the driveway of the address on the note. The trees surrounding the house are thick and it resembles what I pictured when my mom used to read me Hansel and Gretel when I was young—a small cabin set in the woods in the middle of nowhere.

Parking in the gravel driveway, I secure the key in my palm and start up the brick walkway toward the front door that is painted a pretty sky blue. The top of the door is rounded with a circular window at the top. The mat at my feet reads, "Hello. Now go away." I chuckle, wondering what the hell is going on. If I walk in there and Grandma Dori is on the couch because she faked her death, I may lose my mind.

I unlock the door then slowly turn the handle, opening the door. I release a relieved breath when I don't find an axe murderer waiting for me.

The space is small but cozy. Walking around the tiny cabin, I find that it contains one bedroom separate from the rest of the open space, which has a full kitchen, living area, and a small kitchen table and chairs. I want to curl up on the couch with a blanket, a tube of cookie dough, and veg out while bingeing a show.

When my eyes lift to the walls, I see framed pictures of Great-Grandma Dori and Great- Grandpa Philip. I've never seen these shots of them before—them here outside the cabin, and again at an ice rink. There are pictures of them in the town square, and it looks so different than it does now.

This cabin was theirs.

I take that in for a second because I'm pretty sure no one else knows about this place. I've never heard anyone mention it.

It must be some kind of hideaway from the world.

A knock on the door surprises me, and I startle before I walk over to answer. I swing the door open and there stands a tall man with gray, slicked-back hair, dressed in a three-piece brown-plaid suit. I recognize him from the Lake Starlight Retirement Center.

"Calista Bailey?" he asks.

I nod.

"My name is Gilbert Berry, and I was a friend of your great-grandma."

I nod.

"Anyway, I wanted to get here before the others arrive." He glances behind him, and I spot a small car he must've driven over. "Mind if I come in?"

"Not at all." I step out of his way.

"I don't want to delay this any further. The fact is it took two years of me praying I didn't die before I got the chance to give this to you, but here." He hands me a letter. "From your great- grandma, as you probably already assume. This wasn't part of her original will and no one else from your family knows about this cabin—Dori wanted it left to you."

I stare at her handwriting on the letter. "But why not do it in the will?"

He smiles and glances at the envelope. "I'm pretty sure you'll find that answer in there." His gaze ventures over his shoulder once more. "I want to give you some time before they arrive and take over. I'll see myself out." He turns on his wingtip shoes and leaves before I can ask who they are.

Desperate to read anything my great-grandma left, because I miss her every day, my finger slides across the opening before the door even shuts behind him. My eyes well with unshed tears seeing my name in her handwriting across the top of the letter.

My dearest Calista,

If you're reading this letter, I've flown up to heaven to meet the love of my life.

A TEAR SLIPS down my cheek and I wipe it away.

Don't be upset. I lived a long and happy life. I saw every one of my great-grandchildren born, unless your dad and mom decided on a few more after I passed. Ha ha. More than anything, I wanted my grandchildren to find the loves of their lives, just like I did with my Philip. Yes, sometimes I meddled to make sure they didn't stand in their own way, but I was blessed to witness their love stories firsthand.

This cabin is where your great-grandfather and

I loved one another. Oh, the stories those walls could tell. It was our getaway, our seclusion from the world, our hidden sanctuary. And now it's yours to do with as you wish. If you want to tell the family? That's fine. Share it with your cousins? That's fine too. You don't have to keep it to yourself. There is no stipulation on how you use this special space.

I do have one thing to tell you though—you're getting this letter and this cabin now because it's time. I told Gilbert to deliver this when he thought you might need it most. So, I'm going to give you a piece of advice I think you've needed to hear for a long time, and I hope you're finally ready to hear it… sometimes the right person comes into your life at the wrong time. But at some point, it will be the right time and the love they'll bring into your life will be worth the wait. Be open to receiving it.

Farewell, my first great-grandchild. Enjoy the journey, it goes by way too fast. But if you're lucky like me, it's one heck of a ride.

Love you always, Great-Grandma Dori

PS: I'm missing a specific tape somewhere. If you find it, could you kindly destroy it? That was for me and your great-grandpa's eyes only.

A shiver runs down my spine. Please tell me she isn't talking about a sex tape. I'm pretty sure she is.

I fold up the letter when the sound of a car driving up the gravel catches my attention. I throw the letter in a drawer in the kitchen filled with silverware and rush over to the door.

I open it, assuming it's Alice and her gang, but I'm wrong. So wrong. And I'm not even close to prepared for who is there.

I slam the door shut before he sees me and pace the room.

Why is Rylan here? I stare at the ceiling, but really, I'm throwing dagger eyes up at heaven.

"What did you do?" I whisper-shout.

I can just see her smirk and shrug, nudging me to answer the door.

The knock on the door is loud and startles me even though I expected it. With one last deep breath, I open the door and Rylan's eyes meet mine.

"Calista," he whispers. He clearly wasn't expecting to find me here.

His gaze travels down my body. If I'd known I would run into him today, I would've improved on my outfit—yoga pants and an oversized UCLA sweatshirt that's seen better days. Mindlessly, I lift my hand to my ponytail. Great. And if my memory serves me right, I'm not wearing a stitch of makeup. What a way to reconnect with "the ex."

"Rylan?" I don't sound nearly as surprised as I should.

He leans forward and peeks in. "I was given this note." He pulls a small piece of paper out of his pocket and hands it to me. "What is it?"

Sure enough, he was given the same note I was. How is Great-Grandma Dori pulling this off from the afterlife?

I hand him back the note and open the door farther, allowing him to come in. "My great-grandma Dori owned this place."

He walks in, and my eyes drift closed briefly when his scent hits me. It's a scent that's only ever been Rylan's—a combination of crisp cologne and fabric softener. He's wearing jeans, a blue sweater, and brown boots. As he ventures inside, my gaze soaks him in. God, every damn time he looks better than the time before.

"And you just found out."

Guess I shouldn't be surprised he put that much together. He knew our grandmas' antics and was probably given the card about the meeting from the Grandma Crew 2.0.

"Yeah." I lean on the counter, watching him inspect the space as I did before finding out I own it, which I still can't believe. "She left it to me."

He swivels around and his eyebrows shoot up. "Wasn't the will already read?"

"Two years ago, but some guy from the retirement center was just here and gave me a letter explaining it all."

His lips widen into a big smile. "That's great! I bet it was good to hear from her."

Rylan knows how close I was to my great-grandma. His grandma, who was Dori's sidekick, meant a lot to him, but at some point, he decided he wanted more out of life than small-town living.

"It was." Silence thickens the air in the small room. "I'm sorry about the playoffs."

He nods, looking at the floor. "Can't deny it doesn't suck. First round." He shakes his head, and his eyes lift to meet mine. "I'm going to figure out what the hell is wrong with me this off-season. Jamie's meeting me over at the gym later this afternoon."

"That's good."

God, how is our conversation this awkward?

"Do you go there a lot?"

I shake my head. "No." Only when I have to do my uncle's books and never when anyone is playing on the field is what I don't add.

Silence fills the space once more.

"So do you know why I'm here?" He looks around for a clue as though we're in an escape room or something.

"I don't know. She didn't say anything in the letter. I'm kind of surprised she wanted you here since she said I could keep this place a secret from my whole family if I wanted."

He stuffs his hands in his pockets and leans on the back of the couch. "Your secret is safe with me."

I smile. The sound of gravel crunching is the perfect distraction from this awkward situation, and I practically run to the door, where I see the Lake Starlight Retirement Center shuttle coming up the driveway. Alice waves to me from the driver's seat and presses hard on the gas, then she slams on the brakes right before she's about to plow into the cabin.

My hand flies to my chest. "Jesus."

"Is that Aubrey's grandma?" Rylan asks over my shoulder.

I glance to the side and there he is, his face inches from mine. The strong jaw and hazel eyes that haunt me almost every night.

I slide to the side to give him space. "Yes. Alice, along with Jean."

"I don't think they should be driving that thing."

"And why's that? Because they're women?"

He draws in a breath at the bite in my tone. I don't care though. This feels better than pining.

"More because they almost killed both of us and took down the entire cabin. Also, because they're, like, eighty years old." Rylan turns to face me. "I see you haven't changed."

There goes the fragile peace we'd formed. I scowl. "What are you talking about?"

"Everything is a man or woman thing to you."

"Because it's defined my entire life. The men's league gets paid so much and the women's league gets next to nothing. In college, how many scholarships went to the men's team versus the women's? And how much better training equipment and resources in general did they get?"

He raises his hand. "We don't have to talk about this. You've already done your presentation on the topic."

I stare at him with cold eyes.

"Knock, knock," Jean says in a singsong voice. She's a taller woman, at least compared to Alice who I'm not sure is even five foot. Jean walks past us, holding a box that she places on the kitchen table. "Sorry about that. Dori might've descended down and killed me had I ruined this cute little cabin." She looks around and sets her gaze on me. "Isn't it beautiful?"

I nod.

She looks back at Rylan. "Glad you got my note. Declan's a good boy."

Rylan smiles at her, but it's not his genuine smile. "Why am I here?"

"Oh yes, I was told you like to get right down to business," Jean says.

Rylan's eyes find mine over her shoulder.

Jean pulls out a round thing that, if I remember correctly, holds slides.

"I want a slideshow for my granddaughter and her groom that can be shown at the reception," Alice says. "We already did a lot of the work and wanted to see what you thought. Pete at the center used to own a whole photography company and made all the slides for us."

"PowerPoint slides?" Rylan asks.

Jean and Alice look at one another in confusion. Jean picks up a slide. "No, like slides."

I purse my lips to keep from laughing because I'm not sure these machines have been used for decades.

"What? We thought we were helping." Jean looks at Alice. "What did the instructions say?"

And there it is. Someone else is pulling the strings to make sure Rylan is here with me right now in a cabin my great-grandma and grandpa used to get freaky in. I wouldn't doubt that Great-Grandma and Ethel planned this years ago, thinking they knew us better than we know ourselves. Suddenly, my great-grandma's words about "wrong time and right person" make more sense.

Rylan's and my eyes catch across the room. I'll always love Rylan, but at some point, you have to throw in the towel, and I did that three years ago when I walked out on him.

five

RYLAN

lides. They cannot be serious.

I catch Calista's eyes over Alice's bird's nest of red hair. She's trying not to laugh, which only causes my laughter to bubble up in my throat.

"Pete said this is what you do for weddings." Alice's concerned look ping-pongs between Calista and me. I don't have the heart to tell this poor lady that Pete is about forty years behind on his information.

"Well"—I know Calista will never say anything to be mean —"let's have a look."

Jean takes out the projector and Alice puts the slide circle on it. It strikes me as funny, since usually it's the younger generation showing the senior citizens how to use electronics, but I'd have no idea how to use that thing if my life depended on it.

I close the drapes while Calista takes pictures off a wall to use as a makeshift screen. It's dark enough, thanks to the over-grown vegetation around this place.

"You guys are gonna love this. There's even a few of you two." Alice winks at me.

I nod, stuffing my hands in my pockets. I need to suffer through this because Declan wouldn't stop giving me shit last night and he's right—I've done nothing to help with this wedding and I promised that as soon as my season ended, I'd be home and help with whatever he needed me to. I'm the best man. Even his bachelor party was more planned by his dad than me, but Declan isn't a Vegas-and-stripper kinda guy. We went up to his parents' cabin up north and fished and chilled out. At least for that I didn't have to come into town at all. I flew into Anchorage and drove straight up to the cabin.

"You guys ready?" Alice beams and presses the button on the slide machine.

The thing makes a loud sound as it flips to the first picture, which is of Calista and me on the soccer field around the age of six. It must be the first time Jamison was coaching us. Our shin pads look bigger than our legs and my hair is sticking up in the back. Could my mom not have given me a cooler haircut? Calista's hair is in braids and she's smiling at the camera while my mouth is half hanging open. She's so much more photo-genic than me.

"Huh," Alice says and glances at Jean, who shrugs.

They press the button for the next slide, and I know without discussing it that Calista will never let this slideshow happen at Aubrey's wedding.

The next photo is again Calista and me, but this time we'd won a game and we're high- fiving one another. I think it must've been when we were eight, when our hatred dulled slightly because our team won so many tournaments that year.

"I hope Pete didn't get all this mixed up?" Alice bites the inside of her lip, clicking to change the picture again.

The third slide is us at a soccer banquet. It's probably the first time I saw Calista in a dress, and I remember how mad she was when her mom said she couldn't play in it. Eventually, her dad went home and got her shorts to wear underneath because she pouted while all the boys used the empty field to play. Her hair was long and straight with a barrette holding back the front, showing off ears that she'd gotten pierced that year. I only remember because she kept trying to get past the refs and every time we were about to start, we'd have to wait for her to take out her earrings. I was a jerk of a kid to always razz her about it.

"Oh, dear." Alice presses the button over and over, streaming through pictures of Calista and me... at prom, high school graduation, college days, college graduation, the day I was drafted. Grandma Dori's ninetieth birthday where I took a shot and kissed Calista, not knowing what would happen.

I suck in my bottom lip, watching all the years of our intertwined lives flash before me on a bare wall.

"Excuse me," Calista says and walks out of the room, closing a door a second later.

Alice doesn't stop, like she's expecting something to change, but the only pictures of Aubrey and Declan are them with us at a dance and when we went on a trip years ago. "Okay, we need to go ask Pete about this." Jean stops Alice, thank goodness.

My stomach sours and I feel queasy from watching all these reminders of my time with Calista. I'm about to go and get Calista when she comes out of what I think is the bathroom, her eyes slightly red.

"We're going to the retirement center to talk to Pete," Jean says.

"I'll go with you." Calista grabs her purse and keys from the counter. "There's been a mix-up and I'd like to get my hands on the ones he has of Declan and Aubrey. I appreciate all the help so far, but I can take it over."

Like I said, I knew she wouldn't leave it to these two.

I'm ready to say goodbye—but then guilt coats me. After my conversation with Declan last night, I should help. Plus, Calista's probably done so much for this wedding already.

I clear my throat. "I'll join you."

"Not necessary." Calista raises her hand.

"More the merrier. Come on, I'll take you all in the shuttle." Alice and Jean walk out the front door.

I glance at Calista, who has her eyes narrowed on me.

"I'm going." My tone brooks no argument.

She huffs and stares at me some more.

"You either ride with them in the shuttle or hitch a ride with me."

She narrows her eyes. "I'm not sure which is worse. Doesn't matter. I have my own car."

After I squeeze my eyes shut for a minute, I work up the courage to say, "Don't you think we should talk?"

I'd planned for her to be one of my first stops when I got into town, though I'd gotten sidetracked by the text from Declan last night and the mysterious note. I don't want a repeat of what happened last Christmas, and we have no choice but to be around one another for the next three weeks. Might as well get all our shit out on the table.

"Come on, you two." Jean peeks her head in. "Pete takes his nap every day at eleven thirty. If we miss him, then you'll be hard pressed to get a coherent Pete until tomorrow. He's always a little funny after his nap." She taps her temple.

"Fine," Calista says, sounding like a petulant child, "but I'm driving. You can ride with me."

A sharp chuckle leaves my lips. "Whatever makes you happy."

Jean shrugs and turns around to make her way back to the van.

Calista heads to the door but stops short and turns toward me. "What does that mean?"

"Go. I didn't mean anything by it. I just mean that I don't care which one of us drives."

She whips back around, the end of her ponytail hitting me in the chin. Damn it.

After we explain to Alice and Jean that we're going to take Calista's car, so they don't have to come back out here, I file into her small SUV. She quickly tries to pick up all her crap—fast-food bags, empty coffee cups from Brewed Awakenings, even some clothes are strewn on the back seat.

"Did you get kicked out of your apartment?" I ask, glancing around the vehicle.

"No. I'm just on the road a lot. Some of us don't get transported by private jets, you know?"

I shake my head. "I just meant this isn't like you. You were always so clean and organized."

She turns the ignition and slams on the gas, gravel spitting up and hitting my rental that's parked beside her.

"Fuck, take it easy. I didn't buy insurance." I see all the nicks from the small rocks as we pass.

"Whoops. Sorry. Good thing you got that great contract a couple years ago, right?" She smiles at me, but it doesn't come close to reaching her eyes.

"Jealousy never did look good on you."

"Ha, I'm not jealous. I'm perfectly content with where I am right now." She throws it in drive and winds through the narrow roads as though she's driven on them her whole life.

"Working a desk job where all of your family members are your clients and living in a small town where you can only hope to meet someone during tourist season because you've known everyone your entire life?"

She grips the steering wheel harder and shakes her head before turning up the music. "Don't worry about me, Rylan. Oh, that's right, I was never much of a concern for you."

I turn down the radio. "That's bullshit and you know it."

She doesn't say anything, concentrating on the road ahead, her hands at ten and two on the steering wheel. "Is it?"

"Fuck, Calista, you were my everything."

She sucks in a burst of air and lowers her window to let a stream of fresh air flood the car. "Let's just get through this wedding, okay?"

"Deal." Maybe there's nothing to talk about.

"And if you want to bring a date, it's no big deal, I'll be fine. I mean, if you were even concerned," she says.

I wasn't because I have no plans to bring a date. Even though I know there's no chance for us, a small piece of me has always hoped that one day would be our time. That maybe she'd change her mind.

"Fine. Same goes for you." I say it out of spite. I'd rather take a fork to my eyeballs than to ever see her with another man.

"Thanks. I'll consider it then."

She drives crazy as usual, and we end up beating Alice and Jean to the retirement center. Instead of waiting for them, Calista gets out of the car and walks right in.

I slowly exit, feeling a little hesitant because I haven't been here since Grandma Ethel lived here. I miss my grandma, but she led a long and happy life, which is pretty much all we can ask. Plus, I'm sure she's up there with my grandpa Jim, living her best afterlife.

When I came home last Christmas, I noticed Grandma was walking a little slower, and my mom told me how much she missed Dori. It was like a domino effect. Dori passed, then Grandma Ethel, and the third member of the grandma gang, Midge, passed away only two months ago. My dad thinks they didn't want to be here without the others. After losing their husbands, they found one another, and their friendship was everything to them.

My feet grow heavy the closer I get to the sliding doors because a part of me feels like she should still be in there, meddling in my siblings' love lives, making sure they all end up in committed relationships with their true loves.

When I enter, Calista is talking to LeeAnn at the reception desk. LeeAnn has a phone pressed to her ear and waves to me. She's been here for years and has seen Calista and I grow up.

I stand next to Calista and try some shallow breathing because her perfume drives me crazy. Actually, it's her body spray, the one she uses when she's going to work out. But she's used the same kind for as long as I've known her, and it spurs memories of us working out together or when I helped with her physical therapy when she was healing from her injury.

LeeAnn hangs up the phone. "Pete said he'll meet you in the lounge area. Says his apartment is a mess."

"Thanks." Calista leaves, not waiting for me, not bothering to spare me a glance.

"How are you, Rylan?" LeeAnn asks, giving me a pitying look I assume must be about my grandma.

"Good, thanks."

"Sorry about the playoffs." She cringes.

Ah, so that's what the look is about. I smack on a smile. "You and me both."

I hightail it out of there and join Calista in the lounge. A minute later, Alice and Jean join us.

Pete comes down a couple minutes later, pushing a cart. He's probably in his eighties, with thinning gray hair on top of his head, and wearing green sweatpants, a green sweatshirt that's a few shades lighter than the pants, and bright-yellow slippers.

He looks at us and frowns. "That old bat LeeAnn told me Calista Bailey was here." He smiles and shakes his head at Calista.

"That is Calista," Jean informs him.

"No, that's Aubrey. Right, Alice?"

I sit at the table. "I guess this explains the mix-up."

He turns to me. "Declan?"

I shake my head and try to refrain from laughing. They've either taken over for my grandma and her friends by setting us up or they put the one guy without a clue in charge of the slideshow.

"That's Rylan Greene," Jean says. "Ethel's grandson." She points at Calista. "Calista Bailey, Dori's great-granddaughter."

Our eyes meet briefly. It's rare we're called that nowadays, but I don't think we'll ever tire of it.

"Oh, then..." Pete looks at the slide machine the ladies brought in.

"Yeah, we're aware," Alice says.

"Huh." He frowns. "Then I have some bad news."

six

CALISTA

"What's the problem?" I ask Pete.

"I did the pictures of you two, which means..." He picks up a manila envelope that's labeled Calista and Rylan. "These are the right ones."

Jean sighs and sits down next to Rylan, who couldn't look more relaxed in his chair, slouched down with one leg resting on the other knee. He looks as though he finds this humorous.

"Well, how long will it take to make these into slides?" Alice asks, picking up the manila envelope.

"That's the problem. I only had so many of the slides left over from my company. I'm not sure I can get the stuff in time."

Even if he could get the supplies, I think we're dodging a bullet right now. Aubrey would die if I pulled out a slide machine. Plus, who is going to man it? And the pictures should be set to music.

"It's okay." I hold my hand out to Alice. "I can take care of this."

Rylan stands. "We can." He gives me a look that dares me to argue with him.

"I can." I give him a polite smile, so they don't think I'm steamrolling this venture.

"And me too." He arches an eyebrow.

For the love of God.

"Rylan, I have it. No worries. Thank you for all your work, Pete." I step forward and shake his hand.

"My mistake." He shakes his head. "Getting old sucks."

"It's fine really." I smile to make sure he knows it's better this way.

"Are you sure? Don't you have enough to do?" he asks.

I clutch the envelope of negatives to my chest. "I want to do this for Aubrey."

"Okay, then he helps you." Alice nudges Rylan to stand by me. "Best man isn't a title for someone standing around doing nothing."

"I said I would help. She's the one who said no." He huffs.

Alice blows out a frustrated breath. I've never seen this side of her. "Sometimes action is the best. Don't accept a no, you know?" Her blue eyes widen, and Rylan looks around as if he missed something. She quickly turns to me. "Thank you, darling. I'm so sorry about the mix-up." She shoots Pete a death glare and I'm about to ask him if he feels safe staying here tonight.

"It's okay. I'm happy to help. Honestly." I give Alice a small smile because now I'm a little afraid of her. I pack up to leave because even after two years, I feel like Great-Grandma Dori is going to come out of her apartment.

They say bye to us, and Rylan and I leave, giving LeeAnn a wave and walking to my SUV.

He slides into the passenger seat, and as soon as I'm inside, he says, "This is a setup. They've set us up."

I start the SUV and back out of the parking space. "Don't

worry, I don't need your help. You can go do what best men do."

"Best men plan the bachelor party and that's done already." He's quiet for a while and I hope that's the end of his argument. "We have to learn to be around one another. They're our best friends. They're going to have babies and we'll have to go to the baptisms and birthdays. They'll have anniversary parties and holiday parties."

The thought of him bringing some other woman to this long list of life events one day, his wife, the mother of his child... God, it crushes my heart.

My grip tightens around the steering wheel. "I'm being cordial, aren't I?"

"You're being immature."

I slam on the brakes at a red light and we both jolt forward.

"And now you're going to smash my head into the windshield. Jesus, can I drive please?"

I want to hit his smug face with my fist. If only I could give him a black eye. Maybe even two.

"First of all, yes, I don't want to spend the time with you, Rylan. That shouldn't be a surprise. Being cordial at Aubrey and Declan's future child's birthday party isn't the same as poring over pictures together. Pictures that are most likely full of memories from when we were a couple. I don't want to remember those moments because..."

The light turns green, and I press hard on the gas, his back flying into the seat. "Fuck, Calista!"

"It just wouldn't be good for us. I think you know that too. You're rarely home. Go spend time with your family."

"Is that some kind of dig?"

I pull onto the narrow roads that lead back to the cabin. "No, it's not. Don't let your guilt make you hear something I didn't say."

"I'm close with my family," he argues.

I shrug. "Of course you are."

"Not everyone can be attached at the hip all the time like the Baileys."

I shoot him a scathing look. "Loving and wanting to be with your family isn't a crime either."

A caustic laugh leaves him. "No, but it is if you're using it as an excuse not to fulfill your own dreams."

I round the bend and pull in the driveway right as another car circles the bend coming the opposite way. They honk and I flip them off. After I park, Rylan's staring at me with his eyebrows raised. Eyebrows he probably gets professionally waxed or plucked and threaded. I hope it hurts like hell.

"It's been so nice catching up. See you at the rehearsal." I take the keys out of the ignition and position them in my lap, waiting for him to get out.

"You're going to see me before then."

"Well then, see you when I have to." I shrug, feigning indifference.

"Fine, have it your damn way." He opens the door and slams it shut before getting into his rental.

I get out of my car, stomp my ass to the door, and disappear inside with a door slam that makes the whole cabin rattle. I sit on the couch, pulling my knees up to my chest and burying my face between them. How on earth can I still have feelings for that man?

It feels like forever before I hear his car start and he slowly drives down the driveway.

Good riddance.

I GENTLY SET the slide machine on the table, then drop the folder beside it, wondering how they got negatives of our photos. I'm going to need to get some pictures from Aubrey and Declan's families. I have some of my own I can use, but I need more than ones that involve us partying through our teens and twenties.

I open the envelope and see some pictures among the negatives. I can scan those and use them for the slideshow. I glance at the machine and huff, seeing the slideshow of Rylan's and my pictures. Those were hard to watch. And because I'm clearly a masochist, I turn the machine back on and flick through the pictures.

I click past the ones from when we were in our early teens, handing out water at a race in Sunrise Bay when Rylan's uncle was running for mayor. I went with my cousins Maverick and Jack, and I only agreed because I wanted to see Rylan. Since the double date that ended in us almost being arrested, I couldn't stop thinking of Rylan differently—the way my hand tingled in his as he helped me out of the windows, or the time he had to help hoist me down because I was scared. I knew something had shifted because of the way my body reacted.

By the time we were fifteen, I tried to hide my feelings, but when Great-Grandma Dori asked me to pretend to be dating him as part of a ploy she and Ethel had planned to get Rylan's brother, Xavier, with his best friend, I couldn't say no. I land on the picture of that day—the two of us eating ice cream, hand in hand. It was the first time Rylan showed me he was so much more than a soccer jock.

Rylan and I were already in the gazebo, pretending to be a couple as Xavier and his best friend, Clara, drove into Lake Starlight. Dori and Ethel were really pushing them together after their friendship had had a falling-out a few years before. At the time, I'd thought it was cute how these two grandmas meddled in the lives of their loved ones because they wanted them to find love and happiness.

After they suggested we get ice cream and hold hands, I suspected we might be a couple they were trying to get together as well. But we were so young. Surely they didn't want us to fall in love?

We were walking back to the gazebo when Rylan finally spoke his first word to me except for when he asked me what flavor ice cream I wanted.

"My dad is sick. Cancer," he said.

My stomach lurched and I glanced at him nonchalantly licking his cookie dough ice cream. "I'm sorry."

"Yeah, that's why Xavier's back in town. He hasn't been coming home during off seasons much since he and Clara had a falling-out, but he's helping my mom with my dad."

I had no idea what to say and he looked so sad. I couldn't imagine losing my dad. Even today, my dad and mom had gone away for the weekend and Great-Grandma Dori was watching us, but I knew they'd be home Sunday night.

"It's weird, you know. He was always so strong and healthy, and now I see him struggling to walk up the stairs to bed, or sometimes I find him on the couch in the morning. He's just not the dad I remember."

He waited for me to step into the gazebo first, and we sat next to one another.

All the words I wanted to say were locked in my throat. I didn't want to say the wrong thing. His free hand was on the wooden plank of the seat, and I covered his hand with mine and squeezed, causing him to look at me. "I'm here if you want to talk about it."

He nodded but said nothing.

"Did Aubrey tell you about her and Declan getting caught making out in his basement?" He changed the subject.

Although I wanted to help him talk through this stuff with his dad, he clearly didn't want to talk about it anymore.

I giggled. "Yeah, she told me."

I didn't mention that she'd also told me his hands were up Aubrey's shirt, although Declan had probably already told his best friend. He'd undone her bra and it was the first time they'd gone that far. I hadn't even had my first kiss yet, which felt embarrassing at fifteen.

I looked at Rylan and he smiled, biting into his cone.

"How many people have you kissed?" I blurted out the question.

The way his eyebrows shot up to his hairline when he looked at me, my cheeks heated and I wished I could take the question back. "Why?"

"I just wondered. I mean, Aubrey told me about how at your school, the girls really like you." I'm not sure why she always wanted to tell me that, it only made me depressed, but I still denied to anyone who asked that I felt anything other than hatred for Rylan Greene.

He shrugged. "Not many."

"So, like, under five?"

He turned in my direction. "Man, you really want details? Is this so you can call me a manwhore or something? Another arrow to draw at me?" The smile on his lips said he was teasing.

"Never mind. It's none of my business." I looked at my dad's restaurant, where Xavier and Clara were being set up by Dori and Ethel.

"How many have you?"

I didn't look back at him. "I asked you first."

He slid closer. "Do you want to kiss me, Calista?"

I turned my head to face him. My gaze landed on his lips where his tongue slid along his bottom lip.

My thighs quaked. "You're so full of yourself." I threw away my cone before I got to my favorite part—the pointy end of the sugar cone—just so I could get out of there. "I'm going to get my great-grandma now."

He grabbed my wrist. "Sit down."

"Don't boss me around."

He huffed. "Just sit. Please."

I did and tucked my hands between my legs, unsure what to do with them.

"I know you don't think so, but you can trust me." He slid his hand along my arm until he intertwined our fingers and, inch by inch, brought me closer. "Have you ever kissed someone, Calista?"

I shook my head and he smiled so brightly, it felt like the warmth on the sun on my face. "What's that look for?"

"Because I like that I'm going to be your first." His free hand weaved through my hair, clasping my head as he brought his face down on mine.

This is really happening. Rylan Greene is going to kiss me!

My heart thumped and blood rushed through my body until his lips touched mine, then like a light switch, my body instantly calmed. But the calmness only lasted a minute before he slid his tongue into my mouth and it glided along mine. I had no idea what to do. Did I let him lead? Did I kiss him back? I couldn't just sit there with my mouth open like a dead fish. He slid closer to me, squeezed my hand, and moaned in my mouth as he deepened the kiss.

The kiss was different than I'd thought it would be, but it was exciting, and when his tongue left mine and he pulled away, I whimpered from the loss of him.

We stared into one another's eyes for a beat. Did I thank him? No, that would be stupid. "Better than I thought," he said casually.

I never bothered asking Rylan again how many girls he'd kissed before me, because somehow, I didn't care. I'd remember our first kiss forever.

I touch my lips as if it happened yesterday. I still vividly remember the timidness of our first kiss. I ended up becoming so comfortable with those lips at one point... I wonder what it would be like if we kissed again.

seven

RYLAN

Jamison is going one-on-one against me to test my footwork. But all I've been doing since I got here an hour ago is asking him about Calista.

"I don't understand. She's not..." I want to say "my Calista," but she's not mine and she hasn't been for years. "Herself."

He sighs and nods. "I asked her to coach a girls' team and she refused. She says she's too busy." He kicks the ball out from under me and it flies back, so I jog back to get it. "Yer distracted." He shoots me a glare. "Are you sure something else isn't affecting your game? Mental is a big part."

"No."

Jamison kicks it out from under my feet again and I groan. He runs after it, then bends to pick it up, holding it to his hip. "Is it Calista?"

"We broke up a long time ago. I played a great season last year. Well, I played a great season until the playoffs."

He sits on the turf, and since it's a school day, it's just him and me here at the sports complex. Although I have a lot of older brothers, Jamison has always been a confidant I can trust when it comes to my career and life. I join him and stretch out my legs.

"But the wedding was fast approaching when you entered the playoffs."

I nod.

"So, you knew you'd see her soon. Have to spend time with her again."

I nod.

"I'm gonna be honest, you can only forget the people you leave behind for so long." He stares off at the open space and it's clear he's deciding how much to tell me about his past. I know part of it from looking him up. He made it to the big time before an injury, and he tried everything to get back in the game, losing his family in the process.

"I know I don't come home, but..."

He quirks his eyebrow.

I sigh. "It's hard to be here."

"Why?"

"Truth?" I look around the complex.

"If you want, but I'm not a therapist." He gives me a little smile to try to lighten the mood, I think.

It doesn't work. I swallow the lump in my throat. I can't have another playoff season like I did this year if I want to continue my career, so maybe talking to someone about what I'm feeling might help. "She's everywhere."

He smiles and slowly nods a few times. "Yeah."

I stand, needing to keep busy, I pace a straight line back and forth in front of my former coach. "Like here, there's a million memories from her damn pigtails to when we'd sneak in the basketball courts and kiss when they were empty."

Jamieson's eyes widen. "What? When did you do that?"

I wave him off. "Not until we were, like, seventeen. But

she's in my house, my basement." I close my eyes, remembering all the nights we fell asleep on the couch watching television after making out. "It feels like I can't breathe properly when I'm home. And knowing she's only a fifteen-minute car ride away... my body always feels overcharged with adrenaline, like it needs to go to her every damn time I'm home."

I won't mention last Christmas, when the last of my willpower waned and I ended up in Lake Starlight one afternoon. There are some memories I like to keep for myself.

I kick the ball into the net and of course it hits the metal frame and flies in the other direction. "Fuck, I suck."

I lie down on the turf and Jamison holds his legs up, wrapped in his arms.

"You don't suck. You're having a wee moment, but regardless, you've had a great career. One that people like me dream of, and I played professionally. But yer thirty, and I hope you have a long career but have you thought about what yer life looks like after soccer?"

My stomach sours with the thought of not playing. I shake my head. "Soccer is my life."

He raises his eyebrows.

"What?" My forehead wrinkles.

"Imagine having that taken away from you."

I blow out a breath, realizing we're circling back to Calista. "I was right by her side when her career ended. There are other avenues that would have made soccer a part of her life."

He laughs. "You make it sound so easy, but it's Calista we're talking about."

I bite my inner lip. When her soccer career was over, mine felt like it was rising. I'd just signed a huge contract and thought I'd be able to give her the life she deserved. That I could somehow replace the love she had for soccer.

When I look at him, he nods. "Believe me, I'm not one to

talk. I hit rock bottom before I figured out what was most important in my life. And it took even longer before I felt as if I could do anything about it. It's probably why I push Calista so hard to coach."

"So, since she's been back, nothing? No scrimmages, no women's league, no coaching?"

Jamison shakes his head. His concern for her is apparent. I thought maybe she was a shell of the person she once was because I was back and she was hiding from me. I guess I was wrong.

"She does the books, comes in here only when there are no other activities going on. She's pushed soccer out of her life since the day she returned to Lake Starlight."

"But..." She knows how shitty I did in the playoffs. I guess she could get wind of that from someone else. At the time, I assumed she watched my games. Wishful thinking, I suppose.

"Listen, I can't tell you what to do. You and Calista have a long history together, and I think a lot of people expected the two of you to be these soccer stars who would return home one day to get married and have kids. But you can't live your life on other people's terms. I just want to make sure you understand that one day, and no one can tell you when that is, someone is going to tell you that you can't play soccer professionally anymore. So what do you want yer life to look like when that happens?" He stands and grabs the soccer ball. "Now get your arse up and let's do some drills."

No professional athlete wants to think about retirement, but they know they can't play forever. One day, that moment in time is up—it's either an injury, your talent declines, or you get too fucking old and poof, the dream you've been living dies.

Yeah, the younger guys are a little faster than me these days, but I'm still the top player and I'm not going to hang up my cleats until I absolutely have to. But listening to Jamison, he has a point. If my soccer career ended today, what do I have?

Nothing. Absolutely nothing.

MY PHONE RINGS as I'm leaving the sports complex. My brother Jed's name flashes on the screen.

"Get your ass over to the park beside the high school. Your nephews are playing football."

"Jesus, you act like someone told me before right this second."

Jed's been giving me a lot of shit lately about not coming home for the holidays and I'm sure it has something to do with Mom. We all know how she loves to have us all home together.

"Just get your ass over here. Mom said she hasn't even seen you since you got back."

I saw her this morning, but I'm not going to argue with him. "I'm on my way."

I drive over to the field by the middle school that the football teams usually play on. As soon as I see the sidelines, I feel for my poor nephews. My entire family is lined up there, my mom pouring apple cider for anyone who wants it, and Xavier has the team huddled together.

Walking up to the field, I spot four jerseys with Greene on them and wonder how the hell people know exactly which player they're cheering for. My entire family is football. All my brothers played, including Xavier, who went pro. They were all quarterbacks. And then there's me and my love of soccer that none of them understood. They constantly said how boring my sport was, how it looked exhausting to run up and down that field and only score one goal a game.

"Rylan!" Xavier's wife, Clara, is the first to greet me, hugging me. "So happy you could come."

"Hey, Clara."

One by one, my sisters-in-law say hello. Presley comes over, then Molly.

"Who is the fourth?" I ask. If my math is correct—and it could be wrong, since I have twenty-two nieces and nephews—we only have three boys aged six and under that would be playing on this team.

"Peyton. She said there's no reason she can't play with the boys." Molly smiles. "She's number ten."

I smile. "Good for her.

I head over to the sidelines, and Jed puts me in a headlock. "Finally."

I escape his hands, and he winks at me.

My mom holds me as if she didn't just see me this morning, and my dad clasps me on the shoulder. They all act as though I've been gone for years. But the more I watch, it's obvious that this is a weekly thing. All the other parents are talking to my parents, and my brothers Cade and Xavier are coaching the boys.

"Do you want a chair?" my mom asks.

"No." I stuff my hands in my pockets.

One of the players runs down the field to score a touch-down. The crowd literally goes crazy.

"What age group is this?" I ask Presley, who's clapping next to me. She's not nearly as bad as Molly, who's whistling with her fingers.

Presley laughs. "Six." "I thought so."

"Kind of crazy, but you know your brothers. Their kids are gonna play football."

I nod, knowing none of them would consider soccer.

"So, how are you?" Presley is married to my brother Cade.

He and Jed are the oldest in our blended family, so I've known Presley since I was ten.

"I'm good."

"That's good." Then there it is, the frown and hand on my upper arm. "Sorry about playoffs. We had a big group turn out to watch at Truth and Dare."

I figured they'd get people together to watch at the brewery Cade and Jed own. "It's okay."

"I think I speak for all of us that we're happy to have you here for three weeks, even if you're here for Declan's wedding." Her smile is bright, but her tone says it all—I'm not here for them. Something catches her eye over my shoulder. "Oh, here come the older kids from school."

I glance over my shoulder. A huge group of my nieces and nephews are heading over to the field.

"They usually all stay after for clubs and stuff. Excuse me." Her hand brushes my upper arm again, and she goes to say hello to the older kids.

I follow Presley since we're in time-out for the fifth time since I arrived. I fist-bump my nieces and nephews, then overhear my niece Leighton tell Presley "not to worry about it" with some major attitude, so I turn her way.

"Hey, you can't talk to your mom like that."

"Oh, this is nothing, Ry. We're in the teenage years now," Presley says.

A few parents around her groan.

Since Cade is busy coaching, I pull Leighton aside. "I'm serious, Leighton, apologize to your mom."

She narrows her eyes at me. "Who are you? Oh yeah, our uncle. Everyone, y'all remember Uncle Rylan? You've probably mostly only seen him on television."

I'm taken aback by her anger. I was here less than a year ago for Christmas and I don't remember her being like this at all. We spent Christmas Eve playing cards, and I taught her and some of the older ones poker.

She walks away before I can think of a rebuttal.

"Just ignore her. She's in a mood." Presley looks at her daughter. "If I survive this, it'll be a miracle."

Presley's giggle suggests it's all fun and games, but I don't remember ever being that mean to my parents. My dad would never have tolerated it, that's for sure.

My thoughts are interrupted by cheers and Molly screaming for Peyton, who dekes out another player and hits the end zone. She spikes the ball and does a dance. All her teammates—a lot of whom are her cousins—run over to her until they're a pile on the ground.

My dad knocks his shoulder against mine. "Thanks for coming. It made your mom really happy." He nods in her direction, and it's clear from the way she's pointing at me that she's bragging to one of the moms. "She's your biggest fan."

This is my dad's MO—we act as if he's not my biggest fan along with her and he's not just as happy to have me home. Is this what Jamison meant? By the time my career is over, will it be too late for me to be really close with my family again?

My phone vibrates in my pocket, and I pull it out and see that it's my agent. "Excuse me," I say to my dad, who looks at the phone and frowns.

"Hey, Joran, what's up?" I walk away from the field to take the call, happy for the distraction from my guilt.

eight

CALISTA

My knee bounces, my heart races, and sweat pools along my hairline as I sit in Dough Me, a pizza place at the edge of Lake Starlight.

"This is completely unnecessary," I say to Aubrey, who sits across the booth from me.

"I know, this was Declan's idea and I hate to tell you this, but I kind of agree with him. It's just pizza." She's looking at her phone's camera and putting on lip gloss.

Meanwhile, I'm in jeans and a sweater that I've owned since college, my hair thrown up in a ponytail.

"You could've at least told me before I got here so I could've"—I run my hand down my ponytail—"looked decent."

"You look beautiful as always, and had I told you before, you wouldn't have come." She raises one perfectly shaped eyebrow and I roll my eyes because she's right.

I've already seen Rylan since he arrived in town, but I can't tell her because it's all wrapped up around this whole slideshow her grandma wants done, on top of the fact that I found out my great-grandma left me a cabin.

"Don't forget that I texted you the date for the final dress fitting." Her smile brightens. "I know. Can't wait to see you in your dress." Again... for the fourth time.

I love my best friend, but this whole process has been a reminder of everything I thought I'd be doing by the time I turned thirty. Although she and Declan have been together forever, everyone knows what happens. Soon married friends replace single friends. Sure, I'll get invites to the showers and the parties, and at first she'll try to set me up with some single, divorced dad.

When that doesn't pan out, we'll grow further and further apart. And for some reason, every time I see her in her wedding gown, a vision of me in a rocking chair with gray hair, all alone, comes to mind.

"And you're coming to the tasting next week for the meal with your dad?"

I plaster on a smile. "Wouldn't miss it for the world."

Rylan made out in this deal. Because while I've been a part of almost every major wedding decision, especially when Declan himself can't be there, he's escaped all responsibility. Which is why last night, when I was trying to put the pictures in chronological order, I wanted to drive over to his house and dump them in his lap. But a part of me worries he'd either pawn it off on his mom or wouldn't do it as perfectly as Aubrey would like, and I want this to be special for her.

The bell over the door dings. As usual, no one misses when Declan enters a room. He's boisterous with a confidence not too many have. Meanwhile, his sidekick, whose confidence should be overflowing, walks silently next to him, his head tilted down as though he doesn't want to be recognized.

"I see they're here," Aubrey says from the other side of the booth based on my reaction alone.

"Why do you say that?" I narrow my eyes in a playful way.

"Because all the color just drained from your face, except the tips of your ears. They're pink because it's Rylan and you may hate the man, but you lust for him all the same."

I flip her off and she giggles.

"What are you laughing at?" Declan slides into the booth and kisses her on the lips.

Aubrey shrugs. "Just girl talk."

Rylan stands on the outside of the booth and looks behind him, then slides in next to me.

I try to crowd into the wall, but his muscular thigh touches mine all the same. Our eyes catch briefly.

"Hey," he greets me first.

"Hi."

Aubrey and Declan watch us from across the table, probably wondering if their dire need to have their best friends stand beside them on one of the most important days of their lives was a bad decision.

"See, that's not so bad." Declan claps his hands. "I've been in court all day and I'm starving." He peeks out of the booth and holds his finger up to the server.

A teenage boy comes by, popping bubbles with his gum. "What can I get you?"

"We'll split a pitcher of beer and two pizzas. One large with green peppers and onions and another large with pepperoni and sausage." That was our usual order back in the day, the many times the four of us ate here.

"I'm not sure I can eat that. I plan on training when I get back home," Rylan says.

"Even in your off-season?" Aubrey asks.

He shrugs. "Wanna be the best you have to put in the

effort." He looks at the guy with a nametag that reads name NAMETAG instead of an actual name. "I'll have a salad with chopped chicken and light vinaigrette."

Declan stares at Rylan as though he doesn't recognize his best friend. Declan likes everything to stay the same. Doesn't do change well.

The kid doesn't write anything down but blows a bubble and pops it, so it explodes on his face. He uses his tongue to free it from his lips. "Cool. I'll be out with the beer."

"What the hell, Ry, a salad?" Declan wants to say much more, I can tell. I'm sure the phrase "chick food" would be what he would use except Aubrey would swat him on the back of his head.

"What? None of you have to be prepared in three months for a new season."

Aubrey's gaze falls to me, and I kick her under the table.

"I didn't mean..." Rylan whispers, and I feel his eyes on me.

I shake my head without looking at him.

Silence commences over the table until Declan can't stand it any longer.

"At least they can sit next to one another," Declan says to Aubrey.

Little does he know that every time Rylan opens his legs and our thighs brush, a shot of electricity hits me right between my legs. It feels as though the booth couldn't be any smaller, but I remember a time when we were younger and I felt as though we had too much room and wished Rylan would have to be pressed against me. But his shoulders are broader now, his thighs bigger and more muscular.

"Can we not?" Rylan shifts in his seat. "What?" Declan laughs.

"We're here." He looks at me for confirmation. I nod. "We'll do anything to make sure your day goes off without a hitch."

"I'm glad to hear you say that." Declan looks at Aubrey, who glances in my direction from the corner of her eye.

My stomach sinks.

"Why?" Rylan asks.

"My wife-to-be told me the other night how much she misses the four of us hanging out."

Oh god.

"And we're sick of this whole 'I'm on your side, she's on yours' thing. We all used to be best friends," he continues.

A strangled groan erupts out of me.

"So, we'd like it if for the next three weeks, we push all the shit between you two aside."

"We're fine." Rylan looks to me for confirmation.

"Yeah, we're… great." My voice is a little too upbeat, and if anyone knows I'm lying, it's the two people sitting across the table from us.

"Let's face facts here. We're gonna have a kid someday and guess who the godparents are going to be? You." He points at the two of us with the pinkie and pointer finger of his right hand. "Another event where you'll have to stand next to one another. This isn't the last time you'll be thrown together because of us." His hand disappears under the table, and I'd bet money it's on Aubrey's leg. Oh, how I miss the feel of Rylan's hand on my knee. "We can't all walk on fucking eggshells the whole time."

"So you're ambushing us?" I ask Aubrey more than Declan because it's not like her.

"We didn't ambush you, we just… we miss us and Declan's right, this isn't going to be the last time you guys are thrown together because of us. We thought it would be best to get it all out there."

Declan pushes a hand through his hair. "Aubrey's stressing

so much, she's up in the middle of the night because she can't sleep and she's skipping meals."

My gaze meets Aubrey's for clarification. She nods. My chest squeezes painfully.

"But we've been fine together," I say. I'm not exactly sure what they want from us.

"You tolerate one another," Declan says. "I don't want to argue about this. We want you both to be a part of this day, so we'd like you to attend the tasting for the meal as well as the cake, as well as picking out the songs for the DJ and any other stuff that comes up."

Rylan leans back in his booth. "You're kidding me. No other maid of honor and best man do that stuff, do they?"

God knows he's been a part of enough weddings with his nine siblings that he'd know.

"Some do," Aubrey says.

Rylan stares at her for a beat, then sets his gaze back on Declan. "Are you two trying to get us back together?" I'm glad he asked, because it was on the tip of my tongue. "Because I'm here to tell you that we're not not together for lack of trying."

Rylan putting a finality on our future coats me like a thick layer of paint. I know we want two very different things out of our lives, but I guess I never truly considered the door locked and bolted. It sounds like he has.

"Hell no." Declan puts his arm around Aubrey. "We would never want you together again. We just want you two to be able to coexist. One day you're each going to have your own partner, and if you guys are already friends again by then, it'll make it less weird when there's six of us hanging out."

I look toward the counter hopefully for that server and the pitcher of beer.

"I'm not trying to be an asshole here, Ry, but you haven't

really been involved in much as far as the wedding goes. C'mon, this is my big day."

Rylan sighs beside me. "I was playing, man."

"I know, but you had some days off, you could've flown home. We specifically scheduled the couple shower and engagement party around your schedule, and you missed them." Rylan opens his mouth to speak, but Declan puts his hand up to stop him. "I know you had an injury the team had to see to, and you couldn't leave Chicago. It's just... you're my best friend, and this is an important time in my life and I want you to be a part of it."

Rylan slouches in the booth, his head thrown back. Declan has a point. When Rylan's in season, the rest of his life is shut off. He has tunnel vision. I see the guilt Rylan's expression. He's always combative when he feels guilty. So I'm pretty sure he'll be anywhere they need him to be from this point forward.

"Fine," he says. "You have me whenever you want me."

"Man, imagine the ladies who would be jealous hearing you say that," Declan says.

Aubrey elbows him in the ribs. His gaze shoots to me. That comment would've been better if it had been just the two of them.

Luckily, the bubble-popping kid arrives with our pitcher of beer and four frosted mugs. Rylan pours Aubrey and me a drink, and before he can pour one for him or Declan, mine is halfway done. This is going to take every ounce of willpower I have—not just being around him, but being around him while doing wedding things, because I always thought it would be our wedding we'd be planning.

For the rest of the night, Declan has us in stitches about some case he just handled for a boy who wasn't properly trained on how to use a slingshot and his parents got fined.

Afterward, Declan and Rylan split the bill as they always

used to. I lay some money on the table for my portion and Rylan looks at me as if I've offended him.

"What? We're not a couple."

He slides the money my way. "I've got you."

I push it back toward him. "I don't want you to have me."

His eyes light up with mischief and his vision falls to my breasts for a minute.

"I mean, I don't want you to pay for me." I swallow hard.

He chuckles. Thankfully, Aubrey is in the bathroom and Declan is standing, talking to the people at another table, because the man knows everyone in our little cluster of small towns.

"Just keep it."

I huff, taking the money back and figuring I'll find a way to get it to him.

"Do you need my help with that slideshow?" he asks, irritating me. I already told him no.

"No. I had to reach out to Declan's mom for some pictures, but other than that, I'm good to go."

"Perfect." He smiles, but there's a condescending gleam to his eyes.

"Yep." I bump his hip. "Can I get out of the booth now?"

He swivels so his whole body is facing me. "I kind of like you caged in."

Again, his eyes fall to my lips, to my breasts, to the center of my thighs. My body feels as if it goes up in flames and I duck under the table to the other side of the booth, sliding out.

"Jesus, you don't have to go to crazy lengths to get away from me."

That's where he's wrong. I guess he doesn't realize that he affects me as much as he ever did. Time passes, but apparently I remain stuck in the same spot as I always was with Rylan Greene—wanting more.

nine

RYLAN

"Fuck, Calista, where did you learn that?" I'm panting with my fingers threaded through her long dark hair. Although whatever she's doing with her tongue feels fucking amazing, I'm pissed off that she learned it from some other asshole. Then she does it again and my mind blanks. "Come here."

Her body slides up mine, and the feel of her hardened nipples grazing my chest is everything I've missed. I can't wait to kiss her again. I'm not sure how we got to where we are right now, but I need her lips on mine. That's what I've missed the most—kissing her. The way her body curls into mine and the little moan that escapes her with the first swipe of my tongue.

"Come on, baby." What is taking her so long?

The top of her head comes out from under the sheet, her dark hair a mess from my hands, but I love it that way. I lick my lips in preparation for her lying on top of me, feeling her warm center along my thigh. The anticipation builds and I grab hold of her cheeks as she emerges all the way.

I'm about to kiss the living shit out of her when I blink and see Alice, Aubrey's grandmother. "I've missed this, Ry," she says in Calista's voice.

"What the fuck?" I scramble up my bed and a knock sounds on my bedroom door seconds before it opens.

"Rylan!" My mom stands there with her cell phone in her hand. "Why are you practically sitting on your headboard?"

I look down and my sheets are all askew. I'm sitting on my headboard, my hands still shaking. "I had a nightmare."

"Sorry to hear that, hun, but Declan's mom is on the phone for you. She called you first and when you didn't answer, she called me." She hands me the phone, then proceeds to open my drapes, mumbling to herself about what time it is before she collects my dirty clothes.

"Hello?" I answer.

My mom shoos me off the bed and I end up almost falling on the floor from her insistence.

"Hi, Rylan. How are you, sweetie? Listen, got a call last night from Calista looking for photos of Declan."

"Yeah, she's putting together a slideshow for the wedding."

"This late?" she asks. Declan's mom isn't really one who keeps her opinions to herself.

"Well, there was something already in the works, but it fell through and—"

She interrupts. "I gave the majority of pictures to Declan when we downsized, so my assumption is that they're in his storage locker. You'll handle this for me, won't you? I'm the mother of the groom, for Pete's sake, I have enough to worry about. We have family coming from out of town and I still have to get my dress fitted. There are a million things to do."

"Um…"

"You are back home, right?"

"Yeah." I watch my mom make my bed and try to really

soak it in since even my housekeeper back in Chicago can't get corners that tight. I miss them when I'm gone.

"Then it shouldn't be a problem. Thank you so much. See you in a few weeks, I'm sure."

The line dies and I sit on my desk chair, staring at the phone.

"What did she swindle you into doing?" Mom asks, straightening the comforter.

"Gathering pictures for a slideshow the grandmas put Calista in charge of." My mom sits on the edge of the bed.

"Calista?"

It's like every one of my family members turns into a German shepherd when I say the word Calista. They all sit at attention and drool for more information.

"I hope you're not going to make her do it all by herself. You are the best man, Ry."

I groan. I'm getting more guilt trips for my best man role than I get when I don't come home for the annual Greene family summer bash. I wave the phone. "No, Declan's mom doesn't have any pictures, so today I get to go on a scavenger hunt and get a breaking-and-entering charge in order to get them." I drop the phone on the bed and go over to my suitcase to pull out some clothes.

"Ry, this is a big deal to them. They're getting married. I know you…"

I turn, and she doesn't finish her sentence. Here we go again.

"Mom, it's not that I don't want to be with Calista. It's that there's no possible way for me to. I tried. We both tried. Long-distance relationships don't work. And as long as I'm playing, that's exactly what people here are going to get with me."

"I know it's hard with how much you travel and the late nights playing, but if you really love someone, it's worth it."

I laugh, but it's not genuine. My mom shoots me a warning glare, so I sober. "I tried with the person I loved most in the world, and we failed."

"Give it a second try. Sometimes the second time around—"

"And then the third is the magic?" I shake my head, wishing everyone would stop pushing. "If I fall in love someday down the road again, then I do, but right now, I have everything I need." Although the dream I just woke from would suggest I don't. Then again, what the hell does it mean that it was Alice's face and not Calista's?

My mom stands, her displeasure written in the sad frown lines on her face. "Well, it's your life. I always say I won't meddle like your grandmother, but I never thought I'd raise such a stubborn son."

"Mom," I groan, but she waves in frustration and leaves the room.

Fuck. This is why I don't come home. They want something very specific for me out of life and it's not something I can do right now.

I grab my clothes and head to the shower, hoping like hell I can rub one out without the haunting image of Aubrey's grandmother floating into my brain. Because if I'm about to put myself in the line of fire, I can't be aroused when seeing Calista.

THANKS to my morning wake-up call, I arrive at the cabin at ten in the morning with coffee and Danishes in hand, after knocking on her apartment and getting no answer. Calista's car is parked on the gravel driveway, so I knock softly on the door.

It's a small cabin, quaint and cozy and totally Calista's thing. A bunch of thoughts pop in my head, like whether she'll ever share this space with anyone else or will it be another secret we share? Will I come home years from today and find her here with another man? That thought shouldn't feel like a fireplace poker going through my chest, but it does anyway. I thought I'd moved on in the years since our breakup, but last Christmas really fucked me up.

There's no answer, so I walk to the window and see Calista asleep on the sofa with a blanket over her. Going back to the door, I turn the doorknob and it clicks open. Anger washes over me.

I walk in, shut the door, put the coffees and Danishes on the counter in the kitchen, and walk over to her. She's always been a deep sleeper. When we'd wake up spooning, I'd let my hands wander, but that was never enough to wake her. I pick up a pen from the coffee table and run it along her bare arm, but I'm not surprised she doesn't even stir. Her mouth is half ajar.

"Calista," I murmur, but I don't even get a groggy response.

Finally, I put the end of the pen to her nostril while she inhales. Her hand flies up, swats it out of my grip, and it flies across the room. She sits up and the blanket falls to her lap.

"What the hell?" Her eyes open and she blinks again. "Rylan?"

Damn, I should've never woken her. She's wearing the most threadbare shirt ever, her nipples poking out and saying good morning to me. I straighten and go back to the counter. I guess that whole session in the shower today was for nothing because I'm strung as tight as a guitar string again. I adjust myself on the way to the kitchen.

"What are you doing here?" She remains on the couch.

"Delivering coffee and Danishes. Do you know your door

was unlocked?" I set her coffee and the bag of croissants on the coffee table, then I sit in the chair adjacent to the couch.

She reaches forward and picks up the coffee, causing the blanket to slide off more and I see her cotton panties. There goes my dick twitching again. I glance at the floor. Sure enough, her jeans from last night are balled up on the hardwood. It seems odd to me since she always prides herself on being neat and tidy.

"Thanks." She takes the stopper out of her coffee cup and sips it. Her eyes close briefly and her body sinks into the couch. "So good."

"Still take it the same, huh?" We sit in silence, and I put my feet up on the table, crossing my ankles. "Once you're ready, let's get going?"

She looks down at herself and must notice her nipples peaked under the fabric. Her alarmed gaze meets mine and I nod, failing to hide my smirk.

"Don't be flattered, it's the same as morning wood," she says.

I hold up one hand and sip my coffee with the other.

"I'm serious, Rylan. It's not because of you."

I swallow, the heat of the liquid coating my throat. "Point is made. Literally."

She shifts forward but thinks better of it and makes sure the blanket covers her. I chuckle.

"Why are you laughing?" She snags the bag of Danishes and puts it in her lap.

"Because it's nothing I haven't seen. I know your body from head to toe."

She glares at me from the corner of her eyes. "Not anymore."

"Did you get a tattoo? Have a baby? Something that would change the body I memorized a decade ago?"

She inhales a deep breath, grabs a Danish, and bites off a huge chunk of it, allowing the crumbs to fall into her lap. I watch her with amusement. Does she think that somehow makes her unattractive to me? There's nothing she could do that would make me not want her.

"So, chop-chop." I nod at the food in her hand.

"Once again, why are you here?"

"To help with the pictures."

"I told you I had it handled." She takes another angry bite of the delicate pastry. The French would be offended.

"Turns out you don't, because I got a wake-up call from Declan's mommy."

Her face falls, and I can tell she's irritated his mom called me and not her. Her shoulders sink. "Where are we going?"

"Well, we have a busy day. First, we have to break into Declan's house, then I have to find his storage locker key and we'll break into there."

"Are you going to get me arrested again, Greene?" She finishes the Danish and sips her coffee before putting it on the table.

"Nah, I'm much smoother in my old age. But I'll definitely give your ass a boost like I did when we were fourteen." I smile and wink.

She blows out a breath, tears the blanket off of her, and prances into the next room.

Oh, she plays dirty.

The door shuts behind her, and I stare at my dick and shake my head. "She's off-limits, dude." As always, he never listens.

She comes out twenty minutes later, after I've played every game I have on my phone and was becoming bored. She's wearing a pair of black jeans and a plain black sweatshirt. Her hair is down, and all I want to do is wind the long dark strands in my fist while I fuck her.

I shake my head and stand. "Ready?"

She grabs her purse from the counter.

I wait by the front door. "Do you need lessons on how to use the lock when you're inside the cabin?"

"You think you're so fucking funny." She walks by me. "I'm driving!"

I shut the door. "You forgot to do something."

I stand by the door, and she turns from the driver's side door she was about to open. My smile widens. She stomps back to the front door.

"Has anyone told you how annoying you are?"

"Actually, you have. Numerous times."

She reluctantly and dramatically sits in the passenger seat, crossing her gorgeous legs.

"Ready to break some laws?" I wiggle my eyebrows before putting on my sunglasses. She says nothing. "I'll take that as a yes."

ten

CALISTA

Rylan parks down the block from Declan and Aubrey's house. It's a small house nestled into downtown Sunrise Bay, although once they're married, they're moving into a mini mansion in Winterberry Falls since it's a little closer to his office in Anchorage. Talk about happily ever after.

"Is this necessary?" I ask Rylan when he turns off the ignition and pulls his hood over his head.

"People recognize me here." He places his hand on the door handle, and I grab his other wrist before he climbs out.

"No, I mean, should we just ask Declan for the key? Breaking and entering seems serious."

He chuckles and smirks at me. "Where did my rebel girl go?"

"I don't even wanna know what that means." I push my door open and climb out of the confines of the car.

He keeps laughing, meeting me on the sidewalk. "Slow down," he says in that casual lilt that always pisses me off when I'm mad and he acts as though he's not responsible. "I just meant, you're all..."

"What?"

He motions with his hand, saying nothing.

"Spit it out!" I say impatiently.

"You've lost something."

I purse my lips, telling myself not to clock him. "Lost something?"

"That light in your eyes."

I put up my hand. "Just stop, Rylan. You're digging that hole deeper and deeper."

I move steadily toward Declan's house, thankful Aubrey's car isn't in the driveway. She's out of work more than she's working nowadays.

"Hold up." He grabs my wrist, his thumb running along the inner part, and I inhale a deep breath. "I didn't mean it like you think. And I shouldn't have said anything. I'm sure you're different around me than others."

I inwardly thank him for offering me the branch to swing away with lies. "Yes, you don't really bring the best out of me. Hence why I wanted to do the picture thing myself."

He studies me for a second and his mouth opens as if he wants to say something else, but he seems to think better of it. "Let's just get this over with."

I follow him as we peer around for neighbors. Rylan walks up to the front porch that resembles the latest Pinterest trends. I think of my bare-bones apartment and wonder what Aubrey thinks of my place. Surely after she marries and meets other married women, distance will grow between us.

He lifts the mat, and there's nothing but a stained piece of concrete showing the key had been there once upon a time.

"That's your bright idea, using the spare key?" I put my

hands on my hips, trying to hide myself in the corner of the porch so no passersby see me.

"How would I know he moved it?"

"Maybe you'd know if you spent any time here at all."

He glances at me with a death stare of his own. "I'm getting that enough from my mom and the rest of my family. I don't need it from an ex-girlfriend who doesn't want me around anyway."

Sometimes I'm amazed at what we can both convince ourselves of.

He searches every empty flowerpot and under the cushions of the furniture on the porch. "Man, Aubrey's really changed Declan."

"I'm going to the back door."

I look both ways off the porch and follow the concrete path around the back of the house. Thankfully, they back into a park that's empty right now. I twist the doorknob and find it locked.

"They aren't you," Rylan says behind me, and I swing an elbow behind me. "Shit. That's a rib." He coughs.

"Sorry, my hand slipped." I walk down the steps and search under every potted plant and lamp until I see the doggy door. "Here we go."

"Hate to break it to you, but neither of us will fit through there."

I scoff. "I can so fit through there. It's a large doggy door."

He raises his eyebrows in disbelief. Oh, game on. I'm going to prove it to him.

"When did they get a dog?" he asks as I lower onto all fours. "I always did enjoy you in this position."

I look over my shoulder. He's leaned back on the railing with his arms crossed, staring straight at my ass.

"Get a good look, because you'll never see me in this position again." I venture in, my shoulders giving me a little bit of trouble, but I shimmy one then the other through. "I'm inside!"

My voice garners their dog Bentley's attention. He barrels off the couch, limps over to me, and sniffs until he comes across my face, which he licks.

"No, Bentley." I move my head side to side until he stops and lies down, staring in the other direction.

It's then I realize my hips are caught. Fuck, all those brownies and sweets are the cause of this. But I will not allow Rylan to be right.

"Want me to push you through?" he asks, his voice muffled a bit since it's on the other side of the door.

"No." I wiggle and wiggle, getting half a hip through, but exhaustion makes me collapse to regain my breath. I shimmy and try every position, but I feel like a cork in a wine bottle. Someone has to either pull me or push me. "Damn it."

"Just say the word."

I can imagine his smug look behind me. "Rylan!"

"Yes?" he says innocently.

"One push, and don't you dare squeeze my ass cheeks."

"What do you say?"

I clench my teeth. "This was your bright idea."

"I just remembered I have to get back to my mom. She asked if I could help her with the Halloween decorations."

"Ry!"

He laughs. His hands land on my ass, and he pushes me through. Although I have some scrapes on my hips, it's worth it being free and in their kitchen.

"Still nice and firm," Rylan jokes.

I groan and unlock the door for him to come in.

Bentley barks, but he's facing the other direction. "So they really did get a dog?" Rylan asks.

"See what you miss when you don't come around?" I grab

a treat for Bentley and hold it out so he stops barking at Rylan, but he does the sniffing thing until he finds it in my hand.

We look around their immaculate house. I think I walked into a photo shoot for Pottery Barn. He keeps walking while Bentley keeps putting his nose between Rylan's legs.

Rylan rolls his eyes. "Is something off with him?"

"He's an elderly dog. They adopted him because he was going to be… you know."

He raises his eyebrows. "Be killed?"

I cover Bentley's ears and bring him closer to me. "Yes. He's blind and almost deaf. But his smell is as good as any, right, Bentley?" I run my hand over his light-brown fur.

"Where would the storage locker key be?" I ask, wanting to get this over with.

He scours the area for a moment. "In his office. If it's just his stuff in there, then I'm assuming that's where it would be."

We go to walk through the archway, but we can't fit down the hallway side by side, so he stops and motions for me to go first.

"Thank you." I nod.

"Uh-huh."

Declan's office is all mahogany, a drastic difference to how Aubrey decorated the rest of their home in light and airy colors. Rylan searches the desk drawers, and I sit on the leather sofa before I realize this is *the* leather sofa. I hurriedly stand and wipe my ass as though I sat in a garbage can.

The stories of the leather sofa accost my brain. Aubrey says Declan needs sex when he's stressed about a case. She comes in to check on him when it's late and they'll often do it on the leather sofa.

Rylan stops moving and looks at me. "What are you doing?" A smile creases his beautiful face as his eyes take in the leather sofa. He and Declan must've had the same conversation. "Now you have to shower."

"I see they're both oversharers." I help him search, but there's no strategy on my end. I'm just looking aimlessly through the office.

Then Rylan opens a drawer and finds an envelope from the storage place with the number of the unit written on the outside. "Got it."

Rylan beams and starts to walk out of the office when the sound of the garage door opening makes him stop. He looks at me. Oh shit. I run to the window and see Aubrey's car outside by the mailbox. She pulls into the driveway, and we have no choice but to tiptoe to the back of the house. Bentley is unable to keep up with our scent, so he's walking around in circles.

Rylan leaves first, and I lock the bottom lock of the back door and slowly shut it behind me. Then we run along the backyards until we cut through a side yard close to where Rylan's rental car is parked. Thank God we brought his car because she would've recognized mine.

Once we're inside the car, we recline our chairs so no one can see us and we're both struggling to breathe while laughing. I can't even remember the last time I felt this exhilarated. Even though I doubt Aubrey would've had us arrested had she caught us, it would've ruined the slideshow surprise. I can't deny that breaking and entering and the accompanying adrenaline rush was fun—just like when we were fourteen.

Our eyes meet as our laughter fades. Rylan's gaze drops to my lips, and that charged electricity I always feel around him grows stronger.

One kiss. No one would have to know.

Rylan peeks up and raises his seat, freeing us from making a mistake. "We're good. Let's get over to the storage center."

I move my seat up and buckle in. "I feel like she's going to smell us or something. Like I'm gonna get a call from her asking why I was there." I check my earrings and jewelry to make sure I didn't lose anything.

"The only one smelling us is Bentley." He turns the corner away from Aubrey and Declan's and another laugh bubbles out of me.

Rylan glances at me. "That's what I'm talking about."

"What?"

"There's the Calista I fell in love with."

I suck in a breath and face forward. He cannot say things like that without me thinking that somewhere inside him there's still some love for me and that maybe we do still have a chance.

Hope is a bastard. What no one ever tells you is that you can't tell when what you're feeling is false hope, and by the time you figure it out, it's too late.

eleven

RYLAN

We arrive at the storage locker, and of course there's only one entrance and an exit door out back. I don't trust that our keys will work out back though, it's probably just there as a fire exit. I look through the window and see Troy West behind the counter. He knows I'm not Declan.

"I always thought they had their own entrances into specific parts of the building," I say.

"This is Sunrise Bay, not Chicago." She moves to climb out, but I grab her wrist.

"We have to come up with a plan. I know that guy from high school." I point at Troy.

"I could act like Aubrey."

"Their wedding is everywhere and you're the complete opposite of Aubrey."

Her nostrils flare and the corners of her lips turn down.

I roll my eyes. "Seriously? You're hotter than Aubrey. Does that appease you?"

"Well, I mean. Aubrey's hot."

My hands clench. "What do you want me to say here without going over the line?" She would not be pleased if I told her exactly what I think and how much I crave her.

She smiles. "Okay, topic closed. Are you telling me we have to sneak in again?"

"You had fun the first time."

"That's because there was no real threat. Aubrey and Declan wouldn't have pressed charges. This is real." She points at the building.

"I don't think I can convince Troy to let us in. His girlfriend dumped him because she liked me back in high school so…" I shrug.

Calista rolls her eyes. "Of course, she did. What if we just walked in like we have a unit there. I mean, we have the key for Declan's unit. Maybe he won't question us."

I shake my head. "It's a small town. I'll bet Troy knows each and every person who has a unit here."

Calista's shoulders sag. "Yeah, true. Well, we have to get the pictures." She sighs. "We have no choice, so let's go."

I smile, happy she's going to go along with this because so far, today has been the most fun I've had with her in years. A small part of me doesn't want it to end.

"How about you go in there and act like you're interested in getting a unit? Have him show you one, and I'll sneak in."

Her forehead wrinkles. "And what about me?"

"Ask to go to the bathroom at some point. Meet me at the locker."

She nods. "Doesn't exactly seem foolproof, but okay."

"Don't worry, Troy will be distracted by you. But I gotta park down the street."

I park in a nearby industrial lot, alongside the cars of the employees. We walk along the sidewalk, then I wait on the side of the storage building while Calista takes a deep breath and steps inside.

I watch through a sliver of the window on the side of the building. Troy takes his ponytail out and throws his long brown hair back in the elastic band. Calista puts her hand in her back pockets, thrusting out her breasts, and Troy takes the bait, staring more at her tits than her face. I swallow my annoyance because that was all part of my brilliant plan of sending Calista in there. He passes her a brochure, and she picks it up, her hand grazing his. Red curtains my vision, every muscle in my body taut.

Troy takes out his ponytail again and slicks it back again. It must be something he does when he's nervous. I'm not sure what Calista asks, but Troy digs into the drawer and pulls out a set of keys. He puts a sign on the desk that says he'll be right back. Seriously, how many hundreds of people's stuff is in the back, and he leaves a sign?

Once they disappear through the door to the units, I go through the main door. Going to the door behind the desk, I look both ways, not seeing Calista or Troy. I glance at the envelope to check the unit number. I couldn't be any luckier because as I walk the hallways, I realize Declan's unit is in the back on the second floor. The farthest point from Troy once he returns to his desk.

I just barely hear Troy say she looks familiar, but he can't place her. He smoked way too much pot to remember her from when she was my date at our prom.

"I'm just moving into town. Not enough room in my apartment for all my stuff," Calista says.

"Are you sure you're not from around here?" he asks for the fifth time.

"Positive."

"Well, this is our smallest, and they go up from here. Have a look and see what you like."

I open the door to the second floor, and it's really fucking hard to be quiet when you're surrounded by cement and steel.

How did I get myself into this position? I should be in my condo or at a pub in Chicago, wallowing with my teammates. Then again, most of them are on vacation either with their families or for a bachelor trip.

Finding Declan's locker, I open the lock and slowly slide the door open, hoping the distance from the first floor to the second muffles the noise a bit. It opens and I laugh at all the half-packed boxes. Totally Declan.

"What the hell is that?" Calista's voice behind me has all the air leaving my lungs in a rush.

I spin around to face her. "How did you get up here?"

"He left me to go answer a phone call, and when I went out to check, he was smoking a bowl in his car. So I figure he'll just assume I left." She shrugs and enters the storage locker. "So, this is where Declan stashed all his bachelor things..." She picks up the half-inflated blow- up doll. "I feel bad for her. Maybe I should inflate her so she doesn't lose her dignity."

I have no idea where he got the blow-up doll, but probably from a bachelor party if I had to guess.

Calista inspects boxes while I'm still standing in the door-way. Is this what happens when you decide to marry someone? You store away all remnants of your previous life?

"You know, I feel guilty. What if we find some dirty secret Declan wouldn't want us to know?" She cringes.

I step inside and start on the opposite side of the unit as her. For the next hour, all I find is tax stuff, his old high school awards and trophies, and some clothes from when he was a baby.

For a moment, we thought we hit the jackpot when we

opened a box full of Christmas ornaments he made when younger, but there were no flash drives or photo albums in there.

Surprisingly, Troy never comes up. Then again, I'm not sure he's employee of the month material.

"I'm starving," Calista says. "I should've brought those other Danishes."

I glance at my phone and see that it's after four now. "Maybe we should come back tomorrow. I'll take you to dinner."

"No!" she yelps, then leans in closer. "I mean, we're here and I don't want to break in again."

This slideshow better be a showstopper with all the effort we're putting in.

We continue on. By the time our stomachs are growling and we're both annoyed with one another, we stare at one last box.

"It all comes down to this," Calista says.

"Yep." I pick it up and put it on the chair she was sitting on before opening it.

My head falls back in relief when I see picture frames, a few picture albums, and office stuff in there. I pick up a Ziploc bag filled with flash drives.

"Thank God, I'm about to pass out." Calista snags them and heads to the door.

I figure we don't have to put things back the way they were, since I'll tell Declan after his wedding about the pain in the ass his slideshow was.

We're about to shut the locker when we hear Troy call, "If anyone's here, you're mine for the night!"

Calista looks at me, eyes wide.

Troy maniacally laughs as if he's in some horror movie and Calista steps closer to me. Then all the lights turn off, and we hear the door he goes through shut and a lock click into place. "Oh my god! No, no, no. You're kidding me, right?" Calista steps out into the hallway, but it's completely dark except for the small light emanating from our storage locker and the exit signs lining the hallways. "Are we locked in here?"

"I think so." I glance at my watch. Five o'clock on the dot. "I thought these places stayed open all night?"

Calista rolls her eyes. "It's Sunrise Bay, Ry, so no."

"Gotta love a small town."

She throws herself in the chair and shuts her eyes. "You don't need to say it. Everyone knows how much you hate small towns."

Her tone has an edge as if I've been throwing that in her face all day. If we were in Chicago, we'd be leaving right now to go get something to eat, but I'm not throwing that in her "I love small-town life" face.

I prop myself on a plastic container. "We have no choice but to wait it out."

She pulls out her phone. "We need to order a pizza or something."

"What don't you get about we're locked in here?"

She drops her phone on her chest and groans, her feet flailing up and down like a toddler.

"Back in the day, we'd spend the time wisely." She rolls her eyes, and my joke dies. "I was kidding."

"Well, since your friend has a blow-up doll, have at it." She gestures weakly toward the plastic princess.

"He's your friend too."

She doesn't say anything, and strained silence settles over us.

I'm not going to spend the entire night locked in a storage room fighting with her. So I dig into a box I remember seeing some flashlights in and hold one out for her.

She looks at it then at me. "What?"

"Let's explore." I shine it under my chin to produce a spooky face. "Like you said, it's Sunrise Bay. I bet some people don't have locks on their lockers."

"More breaking and entering? I should've known at fourteen that you were a delinquent." She swivels her legs down and stands, turning her flashlight on and following me.

The whole complex is in a square shape, and there are only two floors. I shine the flashlight back and forth as we walk down the hallway, but most people do, in fact, have locks on their lockers.

"Voilà," I say, finding one with a lock that's hanging open.

"I don't know. We're violating someone's privacy."

"Are you hungry? Maybe we'll find some food."

Her stomach growls, and I open the locker, which is smaller than Declan's. It's wall to wall boxes and everything has been labeled with a label maker.

"Man, I need this person to come to my house and organize," Calista says.

I shut the door because nothing seems to have a label that would indicate there's any food. We walk down the hallway, Calista's hands entwined in the back of my shirt. I kind of like it, so I don't razz her about it.

We find another one that's unlocked, and it's the biggest unit. With our flashlights, I can see boxes spread out, a few small pieces of furniture, and a lamp. I turn on the light.

Calista gasps. "And you thought Declan was bad?"

One of the boxes is open and overflowing with fuzzy handcuffs and nipple clamps, dildos and vibrators galore.

"Someone kinky lives around here," I say.

She peers over my shoulder into the box, and I wonder if she's remembering that time I found her vibrator. I refrain from making the joke because she's definitely not going to be okay with it.

A loud bang sounds and I pull her into my body.

"What was that?" she whispers.

I'd like to think it's a box that fell somewhere, but it definitely came from the outside docking area. I quickly turn off the light in the unit and shut the locker door, standing on the one side. Fuck, Declan's is still open.

"Oh my god, Ry!" Her body shakes in my arms.

"It's going to be okay," I promise her.

But that was before the loud sound of breaking glass and a door being pushed open rings out. So much for no crime in small towns.

twelve

CALISTA

Rylan whispers for me to stay calm, but I can't stop shaking. I feel as if I'm back in Chicago when that crowd bombarded us leaving the stadium after Rylan's team won. Everyone wanted a piece of Rylan and he tried to keep me safe next to him, but it was no use; eventually I slipped out of his grasp.

We hear people cutting off locks and pushing doors open. From the sounds of it, there are only two of them. Men talking to one another.

Rylan steps out of my grip, and rummages for something from the sounds of it. He returns and hands me something long. "We need some sort of protection. You also have your flashlight."

The men's voices are growing closer, and my heart is about to burst out of my chest.

"It's okay, I've got this." He's trying to reassure me. I know Rylan is strong, but these men could be three hundred pounds and what if they have a gun?

My stomach contracts painfully, and the air is ripped from

my lungs. Oh god. I hold whatever he gave me tighter, ready to beat the living shit out of whoever these men are if they try to hurt us.

If this slideshow for Aubrey and Declan doesn't turn out to be fucking magical and something they watch every year on their anniversary, I'm gonna lose my shit.

"This one doesn't even have a lock," the guy says.

The door of the unit we're in springs open. I hide behind Rylan, but he uses his flashlight to hit the guy over the head.

"What the fuck?" The guy circles around. Rylan continues hitting him over and over.

"Big Joe?" the other guy calls, but all Big Joe can do is give a strangled cry.

Before I know it, Rylan turns on the light and he's got Big Joe—which must be an oxymoron nickname for the thinnest man I've ever seen—in his grip. "Handcuff him." Rylan nods toward a pair of the fuzzy handcuffs.

"Seriously?"

"Is she gonna give me a lap dance?"

The excitement in Big Joe's voice makes me cough up bile. Rylan bashes a fist across his face and the man spits blood millimeters from my feet. My shaking hands secure the man's wrists, and we lower him to sit on the floor.

"Skinny Rick! We've got company!" Big Joe shouts.

Obviously we're not used to this whole thing, otherwise we would've put something in his mouth to shut him up.

I grab a piece of fabric from the box which turns out to be a pair of panties. "Open wide."

"I hope they're your—"

I shove them in his mouth.

"Motherfucker, you better stop talking to her like that." Rylan's fist rains down on Big Joe again.

Skinny Rick comes around the corner and once again, he's

not what I expected. Rick must weigh about four hundred pounds.

"Ry!" I scream when Skinny Rick comes up behind him. Rylan hits him with the flashlight, but the man only blinks.

"That's the best you got?" he says, giving a come-hither motion with his hands.

He could break Rylan in two. At first Rylan is fighting back, circling him as though they're in a boxing ring, but Skinny Rick throws a fist and gets Rylan across the cheekbone. I see red and jump on the guy's back, hitting him with my flashlight and whatever Rylan gave me.

Smack. Smack. Smack.

"You'll have to do more than that, little girl," he says, spinning as if I'll lose my balance.

I clench my thighs tighter along his rolls of fat and the thing in my left hand starts buzzing. He stops and I stop, and we both stare at it.

"You gave me a vibrator?" I look at Rylan over Skinny Rick's shoulder.

He gets a hit in on Skinny Rick because we're both confused. Rick swears and his hands reach back to get me off him, but those short arms can't manage it.

We continue this way for what feels like another few minutes, but what might only be another thirty seconds and I don't see how this is going to end. Then the vibrator buzzing in my hand gives me an idea.

I scratch Skinny Rick across the face, and he howls in pain, so I use the opening to shove the vibrator in his mouth. He chokes, and I use all my strength to keep his hands behind his back while he's trying in vain to spit the vibrator out of his mouth. "Get me something to tie him up with."

Big Joe is mumbling around the panties I put in his mouth. Skinny Rick is wiggling to free himself and biting the vibrator. "Oh, that's not nice. I bet you don't like to be bitten," I say.

Rylan glances back at me as he digs into a box.

"He's like a dog with a chew toy. Get me something to put in his mouth too."

Rylan runs over. We can't get Rick secured with handcuffs, so we use some rope to tie his hands together. We push him on the floor away from Big Joe. I lift what Rylan gave me and look over my shoulder. He shrugs.

"Sorry, big guy." I secure the ball gag across Rick's face. "Breathe through your nose." I tap his nose and stand.

"Shit, I didn't think you had it in you." Rylan laughs.

"Now what do we do?"

"I'm gonna call my brother." He digs his cell phone out of his pocket. Hopefully, he'll keep it quiet as to why we're here or we'll have to say we were outside and saw them break in, then came in after. "Do me a favor and lock Declan's unit upstairs?"

"You want me to go up there by myself?"

He laughs and runs his hand down my arm. "Never mind, I don't want you out of my sight anyway."

I choose to ignore the way his words send a warm sensation through my chest.

He dials up his brother and walks into the hallway.

"And you're going to jail." I point at Skinny Rick. "And you're going to jail." I point at Big Joe.

Then I realize I still have the vibrator in my hand, and I toss it back in the box. I'm not eating anything until I get some hand sanitizer.

FISHER GREENE IS nothing like Rylan. He's grumpy and stern and always oh so serious. But like all the Greene men, he's gotten even hotter with his salt-and-pepper hair.

He came in and took Rylan to the side while his deputies, Mato and Peterson, replaced the fuzzy handcuffs and rope with real handcuffs and escorted both men to their police vehicles. Mato returns, but Peterson doesn't.

"So is this your storage unit?" Mato asks.

"I have a representative from the storage locker company coming down. They'll have to board up the outside exit," Fisher says, coming around the corner.

"No, it's not ours," I answer, unsure what story Rylan used.

"They were just passing by and saw the crime in progress." Fisher turns to his little brother. "Next time, call the police first. Don't play at being the hero. Lucky for you, they were a couple of thugs more interested in vandalizing than stealing."

Rylan comes next to me. "Yeah, we will."

Mato looks from Rylan to me and studies me for a second. "Funny you two are together again—when a B and E is happening, at that."

"We didn't commit a crime," Rylan says rather convincingly.

"Hmm?" Mato raises his dark eyebrows and pushes himself off the wall. "This is one kinky fucker, whoever's locker this is."

We all look in the box.

Fisher shakes his head and goes to meet the owner of the building outside while Rylan takes the time to run upstairs and lock up Declan's unit.

Fisher says we can leave, and we walk down the street to Rylan's rental car. I'm fairly sure Fisher didn't believe us, but he said he's been looking for Big and Skinny since they graffitied a big boulder by the bay last month.

Once we're secure in the car, I let out a relieved breath, thankful nothing more happened.

"Now I'm going to feed you," Rylan says, starting the ignition.

"You don't have to. Just take me back to the cabin."

"There's no food there. I'll grab a pizza."

My head suddenly becomes heavy, and I lay it on the headrest, staring out the window as the darkness of Alaska blurs past. At some point, my eyelids feel as if they weigh a thousand pounds. As hard as I struggle to keep them open, I lose the battle as Rylan's scent surrounds me and I drift off thinking of when we finally made things official.

We were seventeen at the drive-in movie with Declan and Aubrey. Rylan had borrowed one of his brother's trucks, so we were in the bed while Declan and Aubrey were in Declan's parents' SUV.

Since we'd been thrown together so often because our best friends were dating, our hatred had waned into a mutual appreciation that at least we had a lot in common.

A group of girls from Sunrise Bay walked by the tailgate, all lifting a hand to wave at Rylan. "Hi, Ry!" they said in unison.

I bit down my jealousy. He wasn't mine.

"Hey," he said back and spread out a blanket for us, then reached inside the cab and pulled out some pillows too.

"You really came prepared." I positioned my pillow against the cab of the truck and slid back to rest my back against it.

"It's not my first time." He smiled.

I was still getting used to seeing his smile pointed in my direction, but it lit something inside me that I loved. He settled in next to me, and I liked the heat wafting off of him because the night was a little chilly. I looked at Aubrey and Declan in the back of the SUV next to us, but they were already making out and the movie hadn't even started yet.

I put the popcorn bucket between us and handed him his drink.

"Thanks."

The group of girls walked by again, waving at him.

This time, anger got the best of me. "How do they know you're not with me?"

Rylan's eyebrows shot up and his usual smirk appeared. "But you're not."

I gestured in the direction they'd headed. "They don't know that."

"They're just girls from school."

"Girls who want to date you." Even I'd admit that my tone had a jealous lilt to it. Damn it.

He stared at me until I fidgeted. "Do you want to date me?"

"Ugh. No." I did. I totally did, and I was pretty sure we both knew that.

But I felt him getting closer to me too. Our relationship was transforming again. The texts came with more emojis and were way more frequent. He'd always pick me up if we were expected at the gym at the same time rather than just seeing me there.

"You sure about that?" He was still staring at the side of my face, but I wouldn't give him the satisfaction of seeing that I was lying. Plus, there was no way I would tell him first that I liked him.

He leaned closer, whispering, "Positive?"

The big screen flickered to life, and the lights dimmed around us, surrounding us with darkness except for the light coming from the screen.

"Movie time!" I said too enthusiastically.

He laughed, moving away from me. He stuffed his hand in the popcorn and ate it next to me while we watched the previews. A lot of kids were still milling around, and I swore I heard those girls laughing nearby. It grated on my nerves.

Rylan must've noticed because he held out the popcorn for me. "Hungry?"

I dug my hand in and came out with a huge handful, using my other hand to pick up the kernels that had dropped in my lap and toss them in my mouth.

When the movie started, Rylan slid a little closer to me. My pulse picked up and my throat went dry, unsure of what to do. I felt as though I'd been ready for the past three weeks for him to make a move. I put the popcorn back between our thighs and he sighed, moving away from me.

"What?"

He shook his head. "Nothing."

"Fine." I grabbed more popcorn and ate three or more pieces at a time, still unsure why I was so mad.

"Calista?"

I turned to him, and his face was so close. "What?"

Of course, the girls picked that moment to walk in front of us for the third time, but Rylan's gaze didn't stray. Actually, he moved the bowl of popcorn and shifted his weight to be closer to me. I had no idea what to do, so I sat there like an idiot, making him break the entire distance. His hand went along my cheek and his fingers pushed into my hair. His palm was so warm as he tilted my head and lowered his lips to mine.

At first he brushed them softly with his, but I still felt heat and arousal deep in my core. A girl groaned and scoffed, but once his tongue slid along my lips, I opened for him and forgot everyone around us.

The kiss didn't last for nearly as long as I would've liked, but after he closed it, he remained only millimeters away. "Will you be my girlfriend?"

I nodded, losing all pretense. "Yes."

And that was it. There was a lot more kissing, and I didn't remember either of the double feature movies. All I remembered was the way Rylan's hands felt as he skimmed them up under the hem of my sweatshirt and how soft his lips were. I think I knew then that I was in trouble.

thirteen

RYLAN

I park in the driveway of the cabin. Calista's head still leans against the seat, as it did most of the drive, her soft breaths making her chest rise and fall. I don't move because I don't want to. I soak in the scene in front of me. The girl who stole my heart when we were so young is sitting next to me after our roller coaster of a relationship and there's nothing I can do to make her mine again.

Today was so fun, and I saw a glimpse of the Calista before her injury. Before the dream she spent her entire life trying to accomplish died, life spitting her out without giving her a second glance. Witnessing her despair was devastating and frightening for an athlete who was just as dedicated as her. One play in one game when you're riding high can take you out.

I smile, remembering her on Skinny Rick's back, sticking a vibrator in his mouth. If only things were different... but they aren't. The reasons we broke up are still there. Nothing has changed, so it's wrong of me to want her.

I climb out of my car as quietly as I can and walk to her side of the car. I unbuckle her and slowly bring the belt back before rummaging in her purse for the key to the cabin. Then I pick her up bride style, securing her in my hold as I shut the passenger door. She feels too light, and concern for her gnaws at my guts.

Using the key and holding her, I manage to open the door, then I place her on the couch once I'm inside.

As I round the old coffee table to set her down on the couch, I catch the corner with my foot and end up just kind of dumping her onto the couch.

"Ry?"

Her voice is sleepy, and memories flood me from late games when I'd return to the condo. She always insisted I wake her up when I got in to let her know I'd returned. We had some incredible sex on those nights—some that lasted until morning.

"Get some sleep." My hand reaches for her face, but I retract it before my knuckles brush across her cheek.

"Stay?"

She can't be serious. I'm barely holding on right now. All I want to do is pick her up and take her to the bedroom. But I know my answer before I even say it.

"Sure. Until you fall asleep again." I lower myself into the chair adjacent to the couch.

Instead of falling back asleep, she sits up, the blanket falling to her lap. "I'm hungry. You?"

I chuckle and she laughs because I am.

"What's funny?" she asks.

"That you were dead to the world two minutes ago and now you want to eat."

She shrugs. "Wok For U?"

"Orange chicken?"

She nods. "And egg rolls."

"I'll go pick it up." I didn't bother stopping for pizza on the way home because she was sleeping, and I didn't want to wake her.

"I'll go with you." She stands.

"All right, but don't be surprised if we're in Buzz Wheel tomorrow."

Lake Starlight's gossip blog that reports all the happenings of the townspeople went twenty-first century and is now an app. An app where people can vote on how they feel about whatever the gossip of the day is and where they can anonymously pass along pictures or tips. No one knows who's behind it, or if they do, they aren't talking.

"It's late enough now. And everyone knows we're in the wedding party and have been thrown together to do wedding tasks."

We leave her cabin and I stop outside the door as she walks to my car. I clear my throat and her boots crunch the gravel as she turns. I shift my vision to the door.

"It's Lake Starlight," she says, stomping over to lock the door.

"And earlier tonight was Sunrise Bay. Practically identical small towns."

She locks the door and doesn't say I have a point, because getting a compliment from Calista is rare, but she doesn't argue, so it's pretty much the same thing as a compliment.

When we arrive in downtown Lake Starlight, I see that Calista is right. The town is void of people, but Li, the owner of Wok For U, is still working alongside his son, David, who I assume will take over the restaurant one day.

Calista and I walk in, and Li's face lights up. I knew this was a bad idea. He rounds the counter and hugs her tightly. Li goes way back with the Baileys and is always razzing Calista's dad, Rome, about who is the better chef.

"Rylan." He shakes my hand. "Nice to see you two... again."

I'm sure there's more he wants to say but doesn't.

"We wanted to get some takeout. We're working on a big project for Aubrey and Declan's wedding since I'm the maid of honor and Rylan is the best man." She smiles so wide someone might think she's lying.

Although the story is true, she's laying it on kind of thick. The way Li's eyes shift between the two of us says he thinks so too.

Dave comes out wiping his hands, then gives Calista a hug and me a handshake. "I heard on the scanner that you two were at a storage locker earlier."

My stomach drops. "You did?"

"Yeah, I listen to it at night sometimes. Sunrise Bay is going downhill." Dave laughs and I shake my head at his humor.

"Pretty soon we'll lose our number one small-town Alaska credentials. Then maybe Lake Starlight will finally have a chance." I wink at David.

He nods in acceptance of our banter. "At least Wok For U will always be the best Chinese restaurant in the three counties."

"You got us there. I only eat here." Which hasn't been for a while, so I cannot wait until we get some orange chicken.

David goes back in the kitchen and comes out ten minutes later with our take-out bag. "Enjoy, you two. Good luck on that big project you're working on." David winks at me.

I might as well put the damn article up on the Buzz Wheel app myself.

We say goodbye and climb back in my car.

"They're going to report us to Buzz Wheel," I say, turning the keys in the ignition.

"No, they won't."

I look around. Although I don't see anyone lurking,

someone else probably saw us. But there's nothing I can do about it, and I would never give up my day with Calista.

"I'M STARVING." Calista tears open the bag, tossing aside the sweet and sour and soy sauce packets.

The fortune cookies get tossed too and I pick them up. I make sure none of them are broken. "Let's take care of the fortunes."

"I forgot you're such a believer," she says, opening the carton of orange chicken and sticking her face in to inhale the scent. "So good."

Well, I guess my suspicion that she isn't eating was wrong, but that means she has lost a lot of muscle. Back in the day, she was never hard for me to carry, but she definitely weighed more. And it's not that I care whether she has the muscle or not. It's just a reminder of how much she's changed, no longer doing the things she used to love.

"I don't even know if there's silverware or plates here." She goes to the kitchen and opens some drawers. "There is, but..." She lifts a very tarnished silver plate.

"David gave us plastic cutlery," I say. She comes back to the couch, and we eat in silence since there's not even a television here. "What are you gonna do with this place?"

Her gaze shifts around the room, and she shrugs. "I have no idea. I mean, I don't want to replace anything because I don't want to lose Great-Grandma Dori. But I'm not going to eat off of silver either."

"Are you gonna tell people about it?" I eat a piece of orange chicken. "Would your cousins be jealous?"

None of this is my business. Calista isn't my business. But if I know her, she feels guilty that she was left this cabin.

"I don't know. Great-Grandma kept it a secret, but I'll feel selfish if I do that. I'm sure all my cousins want a part of her too." She sits down on the couch, crossing her legs and opening up chopsticks. She grabs a piece of orange chicken and falls back to the couch. "So good."

I take another piece and hold it up on my fork. "Amazing that even Chicago doesn't have a Chinese restaurant that compares to Wok For U."

She points her chopsticks at me. "You're finally admitting it?"

There's humor in her tone rather than the anger there usually is whenever we compare our small hometowns to Chicago. In fact, last time we talked about this, she dumped an entire carton of orange chicken in the trash saying it was disgusting.

"I did, didn't I?"

She narrows her eyes playfully. "I kind of want to hear you say it again."

I lean in close to her, reaching forward to grab an egg roll. "Wok For U has better food than any restaurant in Chicago," I repeat, and a smile transforms her face. "Happy?"

"Very." Her eyes sparkle.

Jesus, it means everything to see that spark back in her eyes, especially knowing I'm the one who put it there.

I sit back in the chair and eat my egg roll. I want to ask her a bunch of questions, but I'm mindful that she hasn't asked me once about my life back in Chicago. Maybe that's the way we should keep it. If we cross the line into some new type of friendship, the line will undoubtedly get blurry.

"I'll come over tomorrow to work on the pictures, but I'm training with Jamison first thing in the morning. I could bring lunch."

She shakes her head. "That's okay. I got this, Rylan.

Concentrate on yourself and spend some time with your family."

I knew she'd say that, and I have no plans to do what she says. "My siblings work, and my nieces and nephews have school. I can spare a few hours to help you. Do you really think I almost got pummeled by Skinny Rick to not get credit for the slideshow?"

"Well, don't feel obligated." She shoves another piece of chicken in her mouth.

"Why don't you come to the gym with me? It'll be like old times." I try to keep my voice light and airy.

She laughs and almost chokes on her chicken but manages to swallow it. "And make a fool of myself? No thanks."

"You used to help me all the time."

She looks at her knee and back at me. "That was before."

I lightly tap her knee with my foot. "You're healthy now."

"Rylan…"

She doesn't want me to fight her, and I guess it isn't my job to fight her anymore. Although I loved seeing the Calista I fell in love with several times tonight, the contagious smile and laugh that makes my life brighter, she's going to do what she wants. She's as stubborn as they come and that's saying some-thing coming from me.

I hold up my hands. "Okay. Let me know if you change your mind."

She says nothing and places the chopsticks in the container, standing. She grabs her laptop, puts in one of the flash drives we got from Declan's storage unit, and the first picture that comes up is him and Aubrey at prom our senior year. They're at my parents' house, in the front where my mom plants flowers every year.

"Prom," she says, glancing at me behind her.

I shift over to sit on the couch as she sits on the floor. She clicks a few times and I wonder if it's to see a picture of us or if she just wants to see how many she has to choose from.

"They really have known one another most of their lives," I say.

"We have them beat by a few years." She smiles up at me with that cocky, competitive smile of hers.

She puts the pictures on slideshow mode so she can continue to eat. I lean on the couch and watch a montage of our best friends dating, but I really want to see Calista and me instead. I deny myself the urge to kiss her and tell her how much we're meant for each other, that there's a solution to what's keeping us apart.

Instead, we continue watching, as if the fact that this wedding could've easily been ours isn't on either of our minds.

fourteen

CALISTA

I wake up on the couch and immediately think that tonight I'll go back to my apartment because my back feels as if I slept on a slab of concrete. I briefly tried the bed last night but the mattress was so old I couldn't sleep from the metal coils poking up into my back, not to mention the insane amount of squeaking every time I'd so much as move a muscle on that thing.

Fumbling for my phone to check the time, I see a text from Rylan.

Attached is a screenshot from the Buzz Wheel app. I really wish I knew who was behind this thing.

From the angle of the picture of us leaving Wok For U, it wasn't taken by David or Li.

Then there're a ton of comments on the post under the question, "Are they or aren't they?"

Some people say I'm holding out; others say he's chasing

me again. Everyone thinks they know something about us and our breakup, writing things they have no idea about. Someone even says that he came home to have me lick his wounds and give him an ego boost, to which someone responded, "Get a fucking life." I smile, knowing it's Rylan. He never could keep himself from commenting.

All they know is that we ate Chinese together.

Let's hope they didn't follow us. If you want to keep that cabin a secret, watch your rearview mirror.

Always so paranoid.

Have you ever come home to find some girl half-naked in your condo?

My fingers move to respond. Come on, Calista, think of something sharp-witted. But all I can imagine is what Rylan might have done with her. When I don't respond, he comes back with another message, knowing me well.

I kicked her out. Jeez, Calista when will you ever give me the benefit of the doubt?

I pinch the bridge of my nose. It only took a string of four texts before we're arguing again.

Another picture comes through. It's Rylan in his shin guards and shorts, showing all the defined muscles in his thighs.

Last chance

I have better things to do, like take a shower.
Heading to my apartment, so whenever you're
heading over just text me.

Sure

The four-letter word says more to me than it's supposed to, I'm sure. Why does he want me to go to the gym with him? He's a professional soccer player.

I gather the garbage and take inventory of what I'll need when I'm here before packing my bag and heading to my apartment.

Downtown Lake Starlight is a buzz of activity for the fall fair. How did I forget this was coming up? I park along Main Street and walk up to my apartment that was once Aunt Juno and Uncle Kingston's. Thankfully, Uncle Kingston kept it as an investment, so he gave me a great deal on the rent. Plus, it helps that my cousin Brinley moved in after her world was torn apart. We're a great duo—a barrel of laughs, let me tell you.

I open the door and find Brinley on the couch, eating her oatmeal with fruit. She's been away for a couple days for work, so it's good to see her. She's a creature of habit and so much like her mom, my aunt Savannah, that you'd think she was a clone. She's watching the morning show, the steals and deals. Her habitual shopping trips have become more frequent as of late.

"Come! Check out these scarves. Cashmere." She pats the spot beside her on the couch. I drop my bag on the kitchen table and join her on the couch.

She pulls her phone out of her back pocket. "I'm going to order us some. Should we get some for all the aunts? For Christmas?"

I must have a look on my face like she's crazy.

"Yeah, we don't exchange gifts like that. I just love them

and they're so cheap." She waves me off. "Whatever, we only live once, right?" Her thumbs move across the screen, and she smiles when she's done, stuffing her phone in the back pocket of her jeans.

I stand to go to the kitchen to get a cup of coffee.

"So... Buzz Wheel had some interesting news to report." She follows me, rinses her bowl, and puts it in the dishwasher. She's ten times the roommate Dion was.

I roll my eyes and walk past her.

"Hey! Cousin here." She points at herself with her manicured nails. I examine mine. Shit, another thing to add to the list. "I deserve the details other people don't get."

I go to my bedroom, but she follows me again and lies down on my bed.

"We have to do this surprise slideshow for Aubrey and Declan's wedding. Alice from Northern Lights asked me, and I couldn't say no."

Brinley's eyes widen. "Do you think Great-Grandma gave them those directions?"

"What?" My forehead wrinkles.

"Come on. Great-Grandma was always messing with people's relationships." She picks up a pillow and positions it on her lap.

"I don't know how Great-Grandma Dori could do that from the grave, Brin."

She throws the pillow at me. "No, I mean, like, maybe she left directions. You know what she told me when Sawyer and I got married?"

"What?" I sit on the edge of my bed because any time Sawyer's name comes up, I give Brinley one hundred percent of my attention.

"If she'd known I was going to settle down earlier, she would have put me first, but she figured it would be you and

Rylan. I didn't really know what she meant at the time, but now maybe I do."

I sit there. What she's suggesting is ridiculous.

"Did you sleep with him?"

"No!" I screech. "I have some self-control."

"Really? Because I happen to remember a few times..."

I throw the pillow back at her and she laughs, hugging it to herself. "Where were you then?"

Shit. I never thought about having to explain to Brinley about where I've been spending the night since she wasn't around but this is Lake Starlight, of course she knows I wasn't here. "My parents. I needed to borrow my mom's computer. Something is wonky with mine."

Please forgive me for lying, I say to myself, hoping the heavens will hear me.

"Oh." She frowns as though she's disappointed I wasn't boning Rylan.

"Yeah, I'll be back and forth between our place and there until I'm done with the slideshow."

"Let me help you guys. I have nothing better to do."

"You really want to look at Aubrey and Declan's life through the years, Brin?" It probably comes out harsher than I intend, but I know it won't be good for her.

Her smile dims, and she stands. "How am I ever supposed to get over him if everyone handles me with kid gloves?"

I follow her into her room. "You know what? That was stupid of me. Come, we'll make it a girls' night. Wine and desserts."

"No. You're right. I'm already worried about their wedding."

Guilt makes my stomach turn because Brinley is the one who could use that cabin, not me. Twenty-four and a widow.

She needs the solitude to grieve her husband's unexpected death.

"Want to go get lunch though?" she asks.

"With you, always. Let me just shower."

She smiles. I figure my showering and getting myself together will give her some time to have a good cry in private, since I know our conversation has probably led her in that direction.

After Sawyer died, she tried to live in their house, but ultimately moved back in with her parents before she ended up here.

WITH DOWNTOWN PACKED, we end up grabbing food from Lard Have Mercy and sitting in the square to eat it. It's chilly, but not too bad.

"Did you know that my dad proposed to my mom during Art in the Park?" Brinley says. My gaze strays to the artists' area of the fall fair.

"I didn't. How romantic."

"It's crazy how romantic he is with my mom. Was Rylan like that with you?"

God, I don't really want to go there. The memories are accompanied by a feeling of loss, but if this is the conversation she needs to have right now, I'll have it.

"Yeah, he would always make a big deal of my birthday. He'd decorate the entire condo and make me breakfast. Reserve a table at some fancy restaurant and send me flowers, then he'd always buy me two gifts, one lingerie set he always said was more for him than me and something I'd asked for."

We didn't break up because he wasn't a good boyfriend or because he was a cheat, even if that's what gossip blogs reported. I always trusted him when he went out without me or when he traveled for games.

She chews a bite of her tuna sandwich. "I miss Sawyer every minute of every day. Sometimes I don't understand you, Calista." Her eyes soak in all the families walking around the square.

"What do you mean?"

"I'd leave my life if it meant I could be with Sawyer again. I'd leave here."

I bite my pickle and set the rest of it on the wax paper from my sandwich, then I bring my legs up to my chest. "You say that now because you lost him."

"You lost Rylan," she retorts.

I nod. "I know."

"You might think you're fooling everyone, but I see it. Maybe you're transparent to me because I feel it too."

"What do you see?"

"The yearning. In that picture from last night." She pulls her phone out and shows it to me.

I push it away. "I've seen it."

She holds it in front of my face. "Look at your smile."

"I smile, thank you."

"Not like that. Not like when you're with him." She puts her phone away. "I'm surprised your face doesn't hurt from using all those muscles it hasn't in years."

"I could say the same thing about you!" I screech and look around to make sure no one hears me.

"There's a difference."

"Like?"

"The one who makes you smile still has a beating heart and a warm body."

My stomach sinks to my toes. How do I even respond to that?

"Yeah." She crumples up her bag. "I know how to kill a mood. Sorry." She stands and tosses the bag in a nearby litter can.

My phone buzzes and I pull it out of my jacket pocket. It's a text from Rylan.

> Just finished in the shower, I'm on my way to the cabin.

> I'm in the square with Brinley. Give me twenty.

"Who's that?" She peeks, and I bring my phone closer to my chest. "Rylan," she says in a syrupy sweet voice like a lovesick teenage girl.

> Sure, I'm gonna grab a new flash drive anyway for the final copy on my way there.

> Thanks.

> Don't thank me. I selfishly want Declan to be indebted to me when my wedding rolls around. Although he'll be doing a helluva lot more than a slideshow.

I suck in a breath at the thought of Rylan marrying some other girl. It literally makes me feel as if I'm going to throw up.

> Aubrey texted me earlier to remind me that we have the menu tasting tomorrow at three.

> Can't wait.

"What does Rylan Greene want?" Brinley asks.

"Nothing, he's just going to help with the pictures."

"Oh. That's nice, but I bet he's really trying to get in your pants."

"Brinley!" I throw my trash at her and she laughs.

"What? You're hot. He knows what he lost. Pull down the shirt a little, maybe take the bra off."

"I'm not trying to sleep with him," I say.

"Why not? You said he was the best you've ever had." "I didn't have a ton to compare him to."

"I bet he has a lot to compare you to now."

I stand. "We don't know that. The gossip blogs lie."

Although they report that Rylan gets around, that he has a woman in every city, I don't believe it. Even if that makes me naive.

"He did always have eyes for you." She hits my shoulder with hers.

We reach our building on Main Street and she's headed for the door while I'm going to my car.

"What will you do today?" I ask.

She stops and gives me that expression I read as "I'm not your responsibility."

"I guess it's Uncle Denver and Aunt Cleo's turn to keep me occupied because I'm going over to teach the twins how to braid hair. Cleo's idea." She rolls her eyes. "One day, someone will forget their turn in the rotation of 'let's keep Brinley occupied.' It's like everyone thinks that one day, Sawyer will just leave my mind like he never existed."

I hug her. "We're all just trying to help."

She nods, but I hear the shudder in her breath from stopping herself from crying. "I know. Now go play, and if you're not getting anything out of the deal, at least get sex."

We laugh, and I walk to my car as she goes through the door.

I start the car and send Rylan a text message.

I'll be there in fifteen.

I'm already here.

Damn, he's fast.

I find myself in the cabin's driveway in ten minutes. He climbs out of his car, smirk in place.

I should've made him wait thirty.

My eyes need a break after staring at these pictures for hours. Thankfully, we're almost done. I stand and stretch. Calista looks up and inhales deeply. I look down and see my shirt has risen, showing off my happy trail disappearing into my jeans.

I hold out my hand, and she stares at it. "Let's go explore."

"Explore what?" Her eyebrows rise.

I shake my head. "Dirty mind." I put my hand out closer to her.

She finally accepts it and I help her up from the floor.

"We deserve a break." I guide her toward the backyard that I figure has to have a path down to the lake.

She slides on her shoes and grabs a sweatshirt. We walk out the door onto a wooden deck that needs to be redone. Some boards are missing, some eroded into the ground, and the trees are way overgrown. But if Dori was set on keeping this place secret, she wouldn't have had anyone come to take care of it.

I gesture for her to step off the deck into the forest.

"It's all wooded and I do not want to encounter a bear or a moose," she says.

I lift an eyebrow in challenge. She huffs and rolls her eyes, but she walks toward the edge of the yard. I catch up, and soon I hear water from the lake lapping at the shore.

"I knew it," I say, walking faster.

"Knew what?"

The brush is thick, and I open it up as wide as I can so no stray branches scratch Calista behind me.

"Thanks." She walks through, and I follow her. "Oh my god!"

I step next to her, and sure enough, there's the lake. There's no dock here, but based on the water level, there could be. Scanning the area, we seem to be in an alcove of some sort.

"It's so beautiful and peaceful." She hugs herself.

"It is. Even more so once you clear it all out." I turn around. All you can see is thick brush, not the cabin.

"Do you think I should? I mean, people will be more likely to find this place."

I stuff my hands in my pockets. "Do you really want to just stay inside the whole time when you could see all this?" I wave my hands in front of me.

Her gaze tracks the movement of my arms. "I don't know. I do know I wouldn't want interruptions."

"What is it you're planning on doing here?"

She pokes me in the chest. "Now who's thinking dirty?"

"I fully admit to having a dirty mind when it comes to you." I wink.

She huffs in irritation. "You have to stop doing that."

Before I can soak in more of the breathtaking view, she's back on the path, returning to the cabin.

"I'm sorry, doing what?"

"Saying all that innuendo." Her footsteps increase in speed, and so does mine.

"We've always played like that with one another."

"We did. But there is no us anymore, Rylan." She opens the back door, slips out of her shoes, and takes off her sweatshirt, leaving her in a crop top long-sleeve shirt that hangs just below her tits, giving me a glorious view of her abdomen before her leggings' waistband.

"I know that."

"Do you? Because..." She shakes her head and goes to the fridge, grabbing a bottle of water.

"You have water?"

"Yeah... I thought you bought it and snuck in here to make a point about me leaving the door unlocked, I just wasn't giving you the satisfaction of mentioning it." She downs half the bottle.

"I swear, I didn't."

"Who did then?"

We both look at the front door. Could the grandmas have brought us water?

"There's fruit and other snacks in there. It has that jerky you like so much, so I thought for sure you brought all of it."

I shake my head.

She huffs. "Does that mean the grandma gang is coming in here?"

I grab a bottle of water for myself as she disappears into the bedroom.

"OH MY GOD!" she screams.

I rush in there, abandoning my water bottle on the counter. "What?"

She holds up a box of condoms. "This was in the nightstand, along with this." She tosses a Kama Sutra book onto the bed. "And this." A bottle of massage oil comes next. "And I think that's it. Except for a Bible." She shakes her head.

I sit on the bed. It creaks and I sink toward the middle. "At least they got the size right." I point at the XL on the condom box.

She blows out a breath, her hair moving out of her eyes, and storms out of the room.

"What? You know they didn't tell my sister Posey that the nightgown they gave her was a fertility gown until after she wore it to bed with Gavin. I think we got off easy." I go back to my water and pour it down my throat.

"Why would four senior citizens who aren't related to us want us together?"

"This is what Dori and Ethel did. They fixed people up. My assumption is that Dori told Alice what to do. I mean, the woman knows us."

"She knows what size condom you wear?" She crosses her arms. Damn, I still love the way it pushes up her tits.

The plastic of my water bottle crinkles when I squeeze it a little tighter. "Can you please not do that?"

"What?"

I eye her top.

"You're kidding me, right? Control yourself, Rylan, you're thirty years old."

I swallow the last of the water and smash the bottle between my hands so it's half the size. I toss it in the black trash can that's seen better days. Walking over to her, I invade her space and she lowers her arms.

"Do you have any idea how hard this is for me?" I whisper.

She looks up. "And it's not for me?"

"I've loved you since I was God knows how old. Definitely seventeen," I seethe, wanting to put her over my shoulder and take her to the bedroom, shut the door, and remind her over and over how good we are with one another.

"Me too. God, I still..." She slowly shuts down. "It was mutual. Our breakup."

I stare at her for a long time. "Was it really?"

Her eyes challenge mine. "Yes."

I nod and grab my keys off the counter. "Keep telling yourself that, Calista. Maybe one day you'll believe it." I slam the cabin door behind me.

I waste no time putting the key in the ignition and racing out of the driveway. Damn it, why does it always escalate so fast between us?

On my way to my parents' "Stay" by Rihanna comes on and I'm transported to my parents' basement when we were seventeen.

She writhed under me, widening her legs for me to slide between them.

"Are you sure?" I'd asked her a million times already. It was the first time for both of us, but I thought part of Calista didn't believe me when I told her I was a virgin. Well, if she didn't believe me, she must have after I broke the third condom trying to put one on myself.

There was no one I would've shared my first experience with besides Calista.

I lowered myself on her, kissing her, hoping it would relax both of us, but I could tell she was anxious. I wanted it over with, and I wanted to experience what Declan had told me was the best feeling he'd ever had.

My parents were out for the night, and we came home after practice, sneaking down to the basement where we would usually hang out. Except that night she'd told her parents she was staying at Aubrey's.

Being the youngest after my parents had raised nine children had its benefits. One was that they were older, and the other was that as long as the police weren't called, they let me do pretty much what I wanted. They had no idea that Calista was over, and I intended to get her out before they woke up the next day.

"Rylan, just do it. There's no way I'm going to enjoy this."

I stared at her and wondered how much I'd be hurting her. How would I continue when I hit the resistance of her hymen? Declan had even admitted it was excruciating listening to Aubrey whimper as she clung to his shoulder blades.

"Okay. Okay." I was convincing myself as much as I was Calista. I ran my knuckle down her face. "I'll be as gentle as possible."

"Thanks." She looked as if I was about to give her a cortisone shot.

I guided the tip of my dick to her opening and slid partially in. Holy shit, nothing had ever felt so tight.

"Damn, Calista," I said. "Are you okay?"

She nodded. "Just do it. Like a Band-Aid. Get it over with."

I kissed her again, trying to keep my mouth on hers as I used everything in me and slammed into her. She cried into my mouth and her legs tensed as her arms wrapped around my neck. I was desperate to move, but if it was gonna cause her pain, we could chill like this.

"Okay?" I asked again.

She nodded. "You can move."

So I did. I slid out and slid back in, and her eyes fluttered closed. I hoped it was feeling good to her and not that she was counting the seconds until this was over.

"You feel good," I said. "So warm and wet."

She looked up at me, her eyes filled with tears.

"Shit, Calista. No. Forget this."

Before I could pull out of her, her hands clung to my upper arms. "No. I want to get to the point where we enjoy this. I want to feel close to you, and I do right now. It'll just be this time and then we'll be good, and we can…" She smiled. "You know."

She meant all the things Declan and Aubrey were doing now. They kept bragging about the different positions they were trying and what felt good. And I was glad I wasn't the only one of us who wanted that too. I loved Calista, and I only wanted those feelings to grow.

I'd gotten into Stanford to play soccer and Calista was waiting for her letter to arrive any day now. We'd go to the same college, both play soccer like we'd dreamed, and play the professional leagues afterward. It would be hard, but it would work for us. We were different than other couples.

"Come on, Ry." She raised her hips off the couch, and I moved again.

The more I circled my hips, moved in and out, the better it felt. I wanted to last as long as I could and hoped that Calista would come.

My lips traveled along her neck while I whispered to her how much I loved her. My hands grasped her breasts, and I thumbed her nipples like she liked. Usually she'd moan and convey how much she loved that, but this time I got no reaction.

She smiled at me as though she could read my mind. "It's okay. You come."

She felt good, and I had to think of other things to stop myself from coming too quickly, so when she gave me the okay, I plunged into her one more time and my body jerked forward a few more times before I finished.

I stared at her naked under me, and I couldn't wait until I could make her enjoy the two of us being together as much as I had. Although the juvenile hornball I was wanted to do it all over again right away.

"I love you," I said, slowly withdrawing.

"I love you too," she said.

The best part of the night—other than the sex—was after we cleaned up, we laid on the couch watching television and I held her for the entire night. In that moment, I knew there was no one else out there for me. Calista Bailey was mine, and that was never going to change.

sixteen

CALISTA

"I'm so happy you came. You've been MIA lately." Aubrey looks at me with those inquisitive eyes. "And I saw Buzz Wheel... you guys were at Wok For U."

"We're not getting back together," I say, walking farther into my dad's restaurant. I spent the night at my apartment, so I walked over.

"I know that. Of course I do."

She doesn't. She and Declan have wished for Rylan and me to rekindle our relationship since the day we broke up. They don't understand our breakup, and as much as I've been trying to lately, maybe I don't either. I mean, the reasons we split still hold up—my future is in Lake Starlight, and Rylan's is his soccer career in Chicago. He has no interest in ever returning to a small town, wanting to raise his kids in a big city where everyone isn't a part of everyone's business and doesn't know who you are when you walk down the street.

"Hey, Dad." I kiss his cheek as he's preparing things for the taste test.

Aubrey and Declan hired my dad as their caterer, and

121

although he rarely does things like this, he's doing it because they're my best friends and he loves Aubrey like a daughter.

"Heard you made Buzz Wheel?" The corner of his mouth inches up.

"Who told you?"

My dad doesn't read it. Said he doesn't want to find out what his kids are doing before they're ready to tell him.

He shrugs. "Dion."

"Figures."

"Your brother is such a snitch." Aubrey snags a carrot. "Thanks, Mr. B, I haven't eaten anything all day. We're in diet crisis mode." She looks down at her nonexistent stomach.

My dad and I share a look and shake our heads.

"Well, where's the groom? I'm almost ready. I know you have a cake, but wondered if you wanted some small desserts as well? I have a new pastry chef who's amazing."

"Sure. That's a great idea." Aubrey smiles at him.

"Great. I had her whip some samples up yesterday. Go sit at the table we put together.

Olive will be here shortly so she can discuss pastries with you."

"I miss Nori," I say.

My dad's pastry chef for over twenty years recently went back to New York to open a bakery and take care of her elderly parents. Nori was originally from New York and met a local, Owen, when she moved here with her daughter to start working for my dad.

"Well, I'm sure New York City is culture shock to Owen." My dad chuckles and continues to chop spices.

Aubrey and I go into the dining room of my dad's restaurant. I'm tempted to eat outside, but the cold is setting in and Aubrey is always cold anyway, so I sit at the table.

Declan and Rylan walk in a few minutes later talking about

the fact that Nashville is the leader in the playoffs so far. Declan wraps his arms around Aubrey's waist and tugs her to him, kissing her.

"Well, hello to you too," she says, a pink flush to her cheeks.

"Hey," Rylan says and sits down next to me.

"Hi."

"What happened? What's this?" Declan looks at us. "You were just getting orange chicken together. I thought for sure you guys would be cordial."

"We said hello," Rylan says with wide eyes.

"Yeah, you said hello like you hope one of you gets a razor blade in their meal." He pulls out a chair, takes off his suit jacket, and hangs it on the back of the chair. "What happened?"

"Nothing. It's fine. Let's just do this taste test." Rylan stands and tucks his chair under the table.

"You're leaving?" I say louder than necessary.

"I'm going to say hello to your dad. I'm not the complete loser you think I am."

The napkin twists in my hands.

"What is wrong with you two?" Declan says, following Rylan.

My dad asks Rylan how he's doing, how's Chicago, if he still goes to the restaurants he recommends. Rylan mentions one chef friend of my dad's who was happy to have him and his friends as guests one night and said to say hello.

"Probably some girl," I mumble.

Aubrey leans over the table. "Are you okay?" Her gaze flicks behind me. "It's just hard. I thought I could do this."

Her smile turns down. "Then don't. You can go. We don't need you for the tasting. This is all Declan's idea. I told him it wasn't going to work, that there's hurt deep down between the two of you. Seriously, Calista, go."

She's giving me the opening I want, and still my ass is planted on the chair.

What is my problem with Rylan? We had a rocky start when he got to town a few days ago because it was uncomfortable, but I've never hated him, not even when I walked out of his condo with my suitcase in tow. But last night, he pissed me off. I'm frustrated too. And I want to sleep with him. But I'm not going to because we can't cross that line. It only ends in disaster. Basically, my head and my heart are all kinds of fucked up when it comes to the man talking to my dad right now.

"I'm good, but thanks for the offer."

She straightens and positions her napkin on her lap. "You just tell me if it changes, okay?"

I nod.

The men return, and Rylan sits in his chair before positioning his napkin on his lap. "Everything looks great. I'm not sure how you'll choose."

"I love your dad," Declan tells me.

The two of them like my dad because he used to be a juvenile delinquent like they were. My dad thought the arrest after the Netflix break-ins was funny. Mom did not. And my dad still loves Rylan as much as he did when we were together. Traitor.

"Okay, guys, we're doing soup first because it has to be hot to enjoy." My dad brings out a tray and places a bowl of soup in front of each of us. "This is my lobster bisque."

He heads back into the kitchen.

This goes on for the next hour. Dad does family style when it comes to main entrées, and while Aubrey and Declan are arguing about the soup, a beautiful woman comes into the room with a tray of small desserts.

"Hi, I'm Olive, the pastry chef for Terra & Mare." She looks around the table and stops, her eyes landing on Rylan. He's not so good-looking that you lose your train of thought. "Rylan Greene?"

"One of your conquests?" I ask under my breath.

He narrows his eyes at me, then smiles at the woman, putting out his hand. "Yes."

She sets down the tray. "I'm from Chicago, so I'm used to seeing your face on the billboards and stuff. Plus, I baked for you once." She blushes. "I was just starting and I'm sure you don't remember. You were in a private room and the chef threw me a bone."

"Where was it?"

I have no idea why my body is so jittery with irritation right now.

"Rebels. It was an almond cake, dipped in whipped cream and topped with a chocolate dome."

Rylan's eyes light up. "Oh, I remember that dessert. I don't usually eat them, but we were celebrating."

"Yeah, it was…" Her gaze drifts to Aubrey and me. "Well, anyway. Nice to meet you." Her eyes go to Aubrey and Declan, who have moved on to the salad for arguing purposes. "For the bride and groom, I have a variety of small desserts, from cream puffs to éclairs to small cakes. I can make some replicas of your actual wedding cake if you know what it'll look like. But these are a huge hit in Chicago right now."

Rylan excuses himself to answer his phone when it rings.

"Thank you. They're beautiful, aren't they, Calista?" Aubrey kicks me under the table.

I quickly unfold my arms and straighten up. "They are. Hi. I'm Calista, Rome's eldest daughter." I hold out my hand and Olive shakes it.

"Sorry, I should've introduced myself to you personally.

Especially before you saw me gush over Rylan Greene. I had no idea he was from around here."

"He's actually from Sunrise Bay, a few towns west of here, but yeah."

She stares at his empty seat. "Is he your…"

"Used to be. Those two have been hot and heavy for the majority of their lives," Declan says, inspecting a cream puff with a raspberry on top of it.

"Oh, you don't think I was…" Her eyes widen and she looks worried.

"No. I'm used to it. I lived in Chicago with him for a few years."

"Yeah, cause I kind of have a… or at least I'm interested in…" She laughs. "I can't label it, but safe to say I have no interest in him."

I laugh. "Relax, Olive. It's okay." I suddenly feel bad for being a sour bitch while she was talking to Rylan.

"Okay, well, let me know what you think." She walks away.

Rylan returns but doesn't slide his chair out to sit. Instead he stands next to me, peering down at me. I ignore him and bite into an éclair, telling Aubrey how good it tastes.

She stares at Rylan, then me.

I follow her vision since he's being a spectacle. "What?"

"Let's go."

"We're taste testing," I say as if he's an idiot.

"They don't need us. Right, guys?" His eyes never leave mine to grant them even a glance.

"No. Go." Declan waves.

I wipe my mouth with my napkin and rise from the table, Rylan putting his hand on my lower back to make it all the more urgent for me to leave.

"Hold on, bucko," I say, grabbing my jacket and purse from the nearby table. "I have to say goodbye to my dad."

Ignoring Rylan's exasperated expression, I go say goodbye to my dad and Olive. Rylan does too, and we both compliment the food. My dad's eyes are on us the entire way out of the restaurant. Even as Rylan opens the door of the restaurant for me and his hand falls to the small of my back to guide me out.

Once we're out on the sidewalk, I circle out of his hand touching me. "What is your problem?"

"We're going somewhere."

I mockingly laugh then sober. "No." I cross my arms.

"I have no idea why you're giving me so much attitude because I find you incredibly attractive and it's hard not to think about fucking you every minute I'm with you, but whatever. Keep acting like this." He tries to undo my arms.

I'm sure we look like two siblings fighting in the street.

"What are you talking about?" I allow my arms to drop.

"The reason you got mad at me last night. Because I told you not to push up your tits."

I huff and look around the area for eavesdroppers. A few people across the street are pretending to have a conversation, but they're looking at us.

"Fine. But it better not be a hotel."

"Oh, you caught me, I booked us a by-the-hour room."

We reach his car, and he opens up the passenger door and I slide in, securing my seat belt. He rounds the front of the car and slides in next to me. I spot my dad's face in the window as he wipes his hands on his apron, watching us. I might as well prepare for a phone call from him in the next twenty-four hours.

"Tell me where we're going," I say.

"You'll find out, but first I want to know why we went from starting a pretty good friendship again to this."

"What's this?"

"You treating me like I cheated on you. Asking if I slept

with that Olive girl. Fuck, Calista." His foot slams on the gas and he turns the corner at a speed that makes me grab the holy-shit handle.

"Stop driving like an asshole."

"You'll never be happy. You don't want me, you do want me, which is it? Because acting jealous over a pastry chef that baked me a dessert at a restaurant one time is just fucking ludacris."

"Let me out!" My hand hovers over the handle.

He pulls over to the side of the road, slams the car in park, and locks the doors. Then he grabs my face and guides me to him, and his lips are on mine.

All my willpower dissolves in an instant and my tongue thrusts into his mouth. The kiss is rabid and uncontrolled. He undoes my seat belt, pushes back his seat, and grabs my hips, pulling me over the center console onto him.

"Fuck," he says, his thumb running over the front of my neck. "You taste so damn good."

His lips travel up my neck to my jaw and cover my lips again, his teeth biting my bottom lip. My hands run down his firm chest, his muscles bulging, and I have to see him without a shirt, let my hands explore. I have two buttons freed when blue and red lights flash behind us.

"Mr. Rylan Greene! I think you're due at Black Moose Community Park," Fisher announces over the speaker of his police vehicle. "Please tell your passenger to get off your lap and secure herself in her own seat. Drive over there doing the speed limit and keep your hands to yourself for the duration of the ride." Then he hits the siren.

"Jesus," Rylan mumbles.

Talk about embarrassing. I slide off his lap and back into my seat, putting my seat belt back on, my face flushed.

"What? We decide to make out on the one day he has to be

in Lake Starlight for something?" Rylan shakes his head and starts the car. He looks at me. "We'll continue that later. And damn it, you still taste amazing."

My cheeks grow even hotter. I have no idea what I'm doing, but that felt really good. Too good to push it away, that's for sure. Damn the consequences.

seventeen

RYLAN

I park my car in the lot above the field and the good ol' Sunrise Bay Sheriff parks next to us. I look over and he's got a smug expression. Asshole.

"What are we doing here?" Calista asks.

I'm hoping that after our kiss, her attitude with me has evaporated. Although I do want to revisit that when I take her home.

I bite my lip. "My niece's soccer game."

She blows out a huge breath. "Rylan… and your entire family is here, aren't they?"

"Not all of them, no."

"Fisher is." She waves to where he's knocking on the glass.

"Listen, we don't have to stay the whole game. Just until halftime. But they're up my ass about not spending time with them while I'm home, and Declan's up my ass about not doing enough for the wedding. And at least it's not football."

She smiles and opens the door. "Fine. I'm stranded anyway. But next time, don't trick me into this. Got it?" She steps out and shuts the door. "Fisher."

I try not to smile at her implication that there will be a next time.

"Nice seeing you again," Fisher says. "For a couple who isn't together, you sure are together a lot."

"Your brother can't take no for an answer."

She walks up the hill with him as I trail behind.

"So, I wanted to thank you two... we just ordered twenty ball gags for the department."

Calista laughs and I smile at being able to unapologetically watch her. I love her laugh.

It's as if someone injected a needle filled with happiness into my heart every time I hear it. "How can you say that with a straight face?" she asks.

Fisher shrugs. He's by far my grumpiest brother.

We reach the field and my niece, Maisie, is on the bench, her feet kicking back and forth. As usual, the coach is only playing her best players. During our weekly phone calls, my mom told me this has been going on.

"Look who I found." Fisher thumbs toward Calista and thankfully, for once, doesn't out me for making out with her.

I'd hate to give my family false hope that I'll be returning home more than I do. Still, they swarm her as though she's a long-lost relative no one has heard from in years. She smiles and accepts their hugs and well-wishes, and she compliments my parents on how wonderful they look, tells my sisters how beautiful their hair is or how she likes their lip gloss or outfit, and hammers out comebacks to my brothers when they give her shit for being with me.

Soon though, Mandi stands next to her, and I come up along Calista's other side.

"That's my daughter, Maisie. She's nine." Mandi points across the field.

"Well, her red hair doesn't give it away. Then again, I guess she could be Posey's, but she looks tall for her age." Calista looks around for Mandi's husband, Noah, who is, like, six-five or six-six or something crazy like that.

"Noah's running late from a photo shoot, but he'll be here by the half and he's going to go berserk if Maisie isn't on the field."

The stress of kids' sports seems unreal from a parent perspective. I don't think I really realized it when I was young. I wonder what kind of dad I'll be. If I'll even have kids by the time I retire from soccer.

Calista watches the girls and I do too. Yeah, some of them are good, but there's no reason Maisie shouldn't be out there.

"Does she like it?" Calista asks Mandi.

"She did before the season started, but when it got to games and she just sat on the bench except for a minute here or there, she lost interest."

"Can I say something please?" I ask Mandi.

Calista's hand lands on my forearm. "Give it a bit."

The other team scores two goals on the goalie who's busy staring at her shirt and shoes and doesn't even realize that the ball flew past her.

"This is ridiculous." I cup my hands. "GOALIE!" The girl looks behind her, then at me.

"BLOCK." I show her with my feet and hands. "YOU'VE GOT THE GLOVES!"

"Rylan," Mandi seethes.

"Oh, Mandi!" A woman with long blonde hair approaches. Her makeup is flawless, and although she's wearing boots, they're the fashion ones that will do her no good in Alaska.

"Who's this?" I ask Mandi, thumbing toward the blonde.

"I'm the goalie's mom." She puts her hands on her hips. "Mandi, so great that Maisie always has the most fans on the sideline. I told my husband the other day that those Greenes sure have time on their hands. Especially since Maisie doesn't see the field too much."

"What do you want, Kara?" Mandi asks, and the bite in her tone says she is not a fan of Kara. And Mandi doesn't hate anyone.

"I just wanted to remind some of your members..." Kara eyes me and Calista laughs.

Kara's vision shifts to Calista and she looks her up and down. "That we have to allow the coach to coach. I get that you"—she wiggles her finger at me—"are some sort of soccer player, but you don't understand girls' soccer."

I cross my arms and stare at her. "And the difference is?" I can't wait for this woman to tell me.

Calista puts out her hand. "Hi, Kara, I'm Calista Bailey."

The woman shakes her hand. "Bailey as in from Lake Starlight?"

She nods. "Yep."

"Which one are you from? My husband went to school with Phoenix and Sedona."

"I'm Rome's daughter, the other set of twins, but I did play soccer from the time I was six until I was twenty-six. And that coach isn't teaching them what they need to know in order to play, and the fundamentals are the same whether it's girls or boys."

She huffs and looks at Mandi. "Did you bring them here to, like, butter up Coach Baxter because your daughter rides the bench?"

I step a little closer to Kara, and Calista stands shoulder to shoulder with me as though we're protecting Mandi.

"There's no reason a nine-year-old should be on the bench. And maybe if your daughter was on the bench, she'd try a little harder as a goalie," Calista says.

"Mandi, I'm sorry, but I'm going to have to talk to the

director of the park district about how many family members can come to a game. It's just too much for the kids." Kara turns around and goes over to the other moms with jackets that would never keep them warm and their Starbucks cups.

"Man, she's something," Calista says.

"She's a bitch," I add.

The refs blow the whistle for halftime.

"Sorry, Mandi, but I'm going to intervene." I walk across the field toward the coach.

"No, Rylan!" Mandi calls.

I don't make it a quarter of the way across before Calista is at my side.

She puts her hand on my arm to stop me. "I have a better plan."

"What?"

"How about we work with Maisie?" She blows out a breath. "Enough so she knows the rules. She can handle the ball with her feet, bounce it off her head. Then when she's put in for a few minutes, she has a real chance to show why she deserves to have a spot. If you go over there like some half-cocked uncle, they'll brush you off or make things even harder for Maisie."

Calista isn't wrong. Although we both dominated at Maisie's age, we've had challenging times in our careers where we were riding the bench until we pushed ourselves that much harder.

"You're willing to do that?" I want to rub at the warm sensation in my chest but refrain. "Because when I asked you to come to Jamison's...?"

"For that little girl who looks like she's about to break out in tears, hell yes. For you who doesn't need me at all, no." She puts her arm through mine and forces me to turn back the way we came, escorting me across the field.

"Good decision, uncle," Kara says to me, and I flip her off by rubbing my middle finger along the bridge of my nose.

Childish? Yes. Deserving? Absolutely.

Do not fuck with my nieces or nephews.

"I'm offended, by the way," I whisper in Calista's ear. "You always gave me the best workouts."

She shakes her head and doesn't knee me in the nuts, so I'm going to assume our make- out session did something to soften her to me.

We finish watching the game, and when Noah shows up and sees Maisie on the bench by herself again, I tell him our game plan. After the game is over, all the players get their snacks, and we say goodbye to my family, who tell Maisie she did a good job even though she didn't play a minute of the game. Gotta love family.

"Maisie!" Mandi calls her over. "Do you remember Calista? When we went to Chicago when you were younger to see Uncle Rylan play, she was hanging out with us while we visited?"

She shakes her head but doesn't shy away from me.

Calista puts out her hand. "I'm a friend of your uncle Rylan's. I've known you since you were a baby, but I haven't seen you in a few years."

"Nice to meet you." Her voice is low, and I hate that I don't hear the confidence we should.

Calista gets down on her knees and asks, "Do you like soccer?"

"I did, but I can't really play. I'm not that good." Maisie frowns and brushes her red hair from her face.

Calista's head falls back. "Oh, I bet that's not true. When I was your age, I had to go against your uncle Rylan, so I under-stand feeling like you're not as good. But the harder I worked, the better I got. And don't tell anyone, but I beat him a few times."

Maisie's eyes widen.

"A few, and I was probably sick with the flu when it happened," I say.

Noah laughs.

"Do you want me to show you a few things?" Calista asks. "And if you don't, that's fine too, but sometimes you have to take advantage of your connections."

"Connections?"

Calista takes Maisie's hands. "Maisie, your uncle is one of the best professional soccer players in the league."

"I am the best," I argue.

Calista shakes her head. "And his ego is as big as his paycheck," she tells my niece with a saccharine smile. "Which brings up confidence. The more confident you are, the better you play," I say.

"Yes, but first let's teach you how to control the ball with your feet." Calista stands, and Mandi tosses her Maisie's soccer ball. "You up for that?"

Maisie nods.

"Okay, so I had a coach who used to tie my hands behind my back, but I trust you. Let's stick them in your pockets."

Maisie does as asked and Calista kicks the ball onto the now-deserted field. Maisie follows her. I don't interrupt, allowing Calista to teach my niece how to be the best soccer player she can be.

Mandi comes along next to me. "She's something else, huh?"

"Yeah." I put my arm around my sister's shoulders. "She's going to be great. And she's going to prove herself to that idiot coach and those bitchy moms."

"I meant Calista, you idiot." Mandi shakes her head.

"You've been home for a short time and already you two were reported on Buzz Wheel. Couldn't stay away, huh?"

In truth, I can't. "It's Declan's wedding. We're thrown together because of our roles.

Once that's over, I'll be back in the city, and she'll be here. It'll go back to how it was."

"One day, Ryguy. One day." She kisses my cheek and ruffles my hair like she used to when I was younger.

"What?"

"One day, you'll open your eyes and figure it out for yourself." She jogs out onto the field and claps for Maisie.

Calista teaches Maisie not to let the ball get too far away, and a little footwork on how to control the ball as she's moving it up the field. Calista secures her dark hair into a ponytail, watching Maisie kick the ball down the field.

"Kick it into the net!" I scream.

After she kicks it in the net, I can't stand on the sidelines any longer. I run out there and pick her up, swinging her around. Calista, Mandi, and Noah all meet us and high-five Maisie.

I mouth a thank-you to Calista and she shoots me a smile that says it all. She may have lost some of the twinkle in her eye, but she's still got that heart of gold.

CALISTA

After Rylan drops me off at the cabin because I declined dinner with his family, I sit on the couch and decide to torture myself by plugging in the old slide machine and watching pictures of us flicker across the wall.

Our kiss in the car was awesome. If it hadn't been for Fisher, I probably would have begged Rylan to take me right there on the side of the road. What does that say about me?

It's like the sexual spark between us cannot die even if we've ended our relationship. I have to keep reminding myself that after this wedding is over, he'll be returning to Chicago and I'll stay here. Nothing has really changed.

I go through all the pictures, but I still think we need more so I pull out my laptop and go to my pictures. Specifically, my sophomore year at UCLA.

After high school, Rylan and I decided to end our relation-ship because I didn't get a scholarship to Stanford. We knew the distance would be too hard, and we didn't want one of us to ruin what had been a good relationship by being tempted to do something stupid, or for neglecting the other while we were both pursuing our dreams. Even though we broke up, I think we thought we might find our way back into each other's lives whenever life allowed.

So after the summer of senior year, we went our separate ways. Unfortunately, soccer kept us so busy, I didn't see Rylan again in person until my sophomore year of college.

I was in the Laundromat, washing my clothes and studying at the same time, when a loud group of guys came in with a huge bag of clothes. Some of them lifted the lids of the washers while three went to the machine that sold detergent and one went to Polly, the attendant, and asked to change in cash for quarters. I glanced up but quickly went back to my studies.

Until a guy came and sat next to me at the table. I didn't glance in his direction, keeping my eyes trained on my textbook.

"Hey, I'm Josh."

His voice was so close, I glanced up and nodded. "That's nice."

"Okay." He leaned back and stretched out his legs.

That was when I caught sight of the indent on his shins from shin pads. My eyes traveled along the floor, and sure enough, all of them had indents on their shins from shin pads. They all wore red shorts and my stomach dropped. Out of all the Laundromats in this city, he picked this one?

I slammed my book and tucked it in my backpack, which made me look at the guy who was smiling at me.

"You look familiar," Josh said.

Not sure why. I doubted the guy went to the women's soccer games when we played Stanford.

On the days when Rylan was playing down here, I steered clear of the stadium, but today I'd gone to the game, blending in with the student body just to see him as up close as I could get. Sure, I watched his games if they were televised, but I wanted to see his messy brown hair and those hazel eyes that pierced my soul.

"I don't know from what. We're from Stanford. Hate to break it to you, but we gave your boys a beating today." Josh leaned back in his chair with his arms across his chest.

Then I felt his eyes on me. I slowly turned and he was paused, putting quarters into the machine. He dropped them and some other guy complained but picked them up and started the washer.

Never breaking our eye contact, Rylan walked my way. "Oh my god, Calista!"

Josh snaps his fingers. "That's where I know you. From Ry."

"What?"

Rylan shook his head. "Josh has a habit of breaking into people's phones and looking at photos."

My heart flipped over the fact that he still had pictures of me on his phone. I bit my bottom lip and Rylan's eyes dipped to watch me release it. "Oh."

"This is crazy." Josh sat up. "What are the chances, right?"

We nodded.

"Want to go get coffee?" Rylan asked.

I stood. "Yes."

He stepped aside to allow me past, and I told Polly I'd be back in case my clothes were finished before I returned.

Once we had gotten our coffees and sat down at a table outside, Rylan kept looking at me as though he couldn't believe I was there in front of him. "You look great."

"Thanks." And he did too. The boy I'd said goodbye to my senior year had turned into a man. I saw it on the field today, live and in person. His muscles were bigger and more prominent, his features transformed into a strong and defined jaw. "Why are you guys here?"

"It's Coach's thing. He makes us do our uniforms when we're out of town."

"You guys won. You deserved the win today."

One side of his lips quirked up and I realized I'd given away that I had watched.

"What did you think of that goal in the third?" he asked.

No sense pretending I didn't know what he was talking about.

"It was a good move."

"Number three had no idea, and the goalie was caught completely off guard."

He laughed. "I've been working on my footwork this entire season."

"Congratulations." I think I always knew Rylan had the dedication, love, and most of all the talent to make it far in this sport.

"Thanks."

As happy as I was to see him, this wasn't us. All formal compliments and thank-yous.

Before, we'd always make fun of one another and give each other a hard time. But it had been so long since I sat across from him. Now that he was here in front of me, I realized how much I'd really missed him.

I hadn't dated anyone seriously since I started college, whereas he was Stanford's rising star, always somewhere and usually with a girl on his arm from what I heard. Not that I could complain. We weren't a couple.

"Do you live nearby?" he asked.

Finally, it felt as if we were on the same page. It had been a long time for me, and being with someone who knew my body, had taken his time to become its master... damn, it was too tempting to resist.

"When are you leaving?" I asked.

"Our bus is out of commission, so they put us up at the hotel. But we're under a strict curfew of nine."

I glanced at my phone. It was only six.

He smiled, and I shook my head. "Let me grab my clothes."

"I'll tell the guys I'm helping you."

We walked into the Laundromat. All the guys knew what was going on but were gentlemen enough to play along with our ruse.

We weren't in my apartment more than half a minute before Rylan's lips were on mine.

"Fuck, I couldn't look at you and not have my hands on you." He pulled my shirt over my head and unclasped my bra.

"Down the hall. I don't know if and when Maverick will be home." Thank God it didn't seem like my cousin was home right now. I stripped his shirt off of him and my mouth fell open at how defined his lean muscles were now.

"Keep looking at me like that and we're not gonna make it to the bedroom." His voice had that scratchy edge it always did when he was turned on.

"God, can I touch?" I ran my fingers down the ripples in his lower abdomen.

"Your touch still makes me hard." He picked me up and walked down the hall.

"This is me," I murmured along his lips when we reached my room.

He went inside my room and closed the door with his foot before he lowered me to the bed. I watched as he kicked off his shoes and pulled down his shorts. Since he was commando, his dick sprang up and my mouth watered.

I'd had sex in college, but I hadn't climaxed with any of my other partners. My vibrators were doing the job, but I knew that after Rylan was done with me, I'd be limp, sore, and in a state of bliss.

I got up on my knees, my hand sliding between our bodies to cradle his length. He pushed my hair off my shoulders and stared at me for so long I grew uncomfortable. I broke the distance and kissed his collarbone while I fisted his dick and pumped him.

"Shit, don't stop."

One advantage to being with the person you lost your virginity to is that afterward, you discover what you like with each other. I knew exactly what got Rylan hot because we'd experimented together. Not to brag or anything, but I could get him to blow his load in less than two minutes with my hand or my mouth if I wanted, and it was no different when he got his hands on me. I moved my fist faster, twisting at the tip just the way he liked, and his eyes drifted closed.

When I thought he might come, he put his hand over mine. "If we have time later, I'll take you up on that, but I don't want to leave here without being inside you."

I had condoms, but I'd gone on the pill at my mom's insistence when I started college. I'd never not used a condom, but something inside me wanted to feel Rylan so badly.

"I'm on the pill," I whispered as he lowered my shorts and panties.

He paused and looked at me, a question in his eyes. "I—"

"Ry, it's been years and I haven't slept with anyone without one, but I don't want anything between us."

He blew out a breath. "I've never not used one." His gaze fell down my body and he put one knee on the bed, lowering himself over me. "I've really missed you. I'm not sure I knew how much until I saw you."

I knew exactly what he meant. It was easy to push aside thoughts of him with how busy college was, between sports and studies. There was always a distraction.

The tip of him pushed past my opening, and his lips went to my neck as he slowly plunged inside me with a groan. My hands clung to his biceps. He felt so good, and we got into the rhythm we'd mastered during those months after we'd first had sex, both of us remembering what made the other person feel the best. My legs wound around his waist, and he got up on his elbows, his eyes piercing into mine as he thrust in and out, drawing pleasure to the surface. It felt so good, I wanted to scream from the agony that after today, I may never get this again.

I reached back to grab the headboard, and Rylan's hands slid up my arms and clasped our hands together.

"Come for me," he whispered. "Say my name. Tell me how good I make you feel. That no one else does what I do to you."

"Only you, Ry, only you." My orgasm peaked and overflowed. I praised him over and over as I came down from one of the best orgasms of my life.

"Fuck, watching you come on my dick makes me crazy."

He picked up one of my legs and held it straight up against his chest and drilled deep inside me. It felt so good I didn't want him to stop. Ever. Thrust after thrust hit me in different places, then he groaned and slowed, pumping inside me.

"Shit, I was gonna pull out."

If he was concerned, he didn't show it. He just lowered his body over mine, not pulling out of me, and kissed me until he grew hard again.

I took him to his hotel at nine on the dot and he kissed me goodbye in the car. Neither of us made any promises, but I cherished our short time together.

The next week, he was tagged in a picture on Instagram, and sure enough, he was with some girl. He had his tongue down her throat.

After that, my life just spiraled out of control.

I shook my head to clear my thoughts. Yeah, I cannot allow myself to get stuck on this ride again.

nineteen

RYLAN

I wake in my childhood bed, my mom picking up my dirty clothes and putting them in a laundry basket.

"Mom, I can do that."

"You can?" She bends down and gets a sock from behind my chair.

"Well, who do you think does it in Chicago?"

She laughs. "A service? Your assistant?"

She has a point. I do have a service that does my laundry. I travel a lot. "Well, thanks." "I feel bad for your housekeeper." She touches my leg over my comforter. "Everything okay with you and Calista?"

"We're not together, Mom." I sit up in bed, not wanting to do this twenty questions thing. Thank God Fisher kept our making out to himself or this interrogation would be ten times worse.

"It's sweet what she's doing for Maisie."

"It is."

She stares at me for a moment, and I look away. She wants

me to crack and blab everything going on inside me, but I'm not there. I don't even understand half of it myself.

"You could have shown Maisie too?"

"I could've, but I'll be going home soon, and this way, Maisie will have Calista around. Plus, Calista needs soccer back in her life. It's a win-win.

Her eyes zero in on the laundry and sadness washes over her. "That's always hard to hear." She collects a sweatshirt off the chair.

"What?"

"That you consider Chicago your home." She looks around my room and smiles softly. "You're my only child who is hell-bent on living far away. Did I suffocate you? I know it was different for you because most of your siblings were out of the house by the time you arrived. Your dad and I were older when we raised you."

"Shit, Mom, no. But I can't play professional soccer here."

She nods, tears building in her eyes. "I know, but when that career ends, you're not coming home, right? That's what the breakup was about between the two of you all those years ago."

I run my hand through my hair. "I don't know. I mean, yeah it was, but..." I cannot give my mom false hope. "I wish it was different, but it's not."

She nods. "I know. Thanks for coming to dinner last night. Everyone was very happy to spend the time with you."

"Really? It didn't seem like it. All I got was grief about how my nieces and nephews don't know me and how I can't buy their love at Christmas."

My mom shrugs. "You can't have everything in life, Ry. I wish you could, but you can't. It's a hard pill for your siblings to swallow that they're at the bottom of your list of priorities, and they express that. But it doesn't mean they don't love the time they do get to spend with you."

I sit there quietly, not sure what to say.

"One more thing, and I know it's none of my business. I'll say this and then leave."

I groan. "What?"

"Since you came back, you've spent a lot of time with Calista. And it's so clear to everyone in both of your families that you two still love one another. I can't imagine how unimportant she must've felt all those years ago in order to leave you. Sometimes I curse that I ever put you in soccer, but your dad tells me how wrong that is because of your love for the game. But a sport doesn't love you back. It doesn't take care of you when you're sick or listen to you when you need someone to vent to or tell you everything will be okay when you're overwhelmed. You won't grow old with soccer, Rylan, and that's just the facts. All this to say that I hope you know what you're doing, and if you don't, you should really consider stopping before you hurt Calista again. I know the man I raised, and he wouldn't want to hurt the woman he still loves."

She shuts the door behind her, and I look out my window at the perfect view of the bay in the distance. I sit there contemplating my mom's words for a few minutes before my phone dings with a text from Calista.

> Great news! I finished the slides. We're all set, so go enjoy the rest of your vacation with your family.

> Also, our fight made Buzz Wheel. *eye roll emoji*

I pull up the Buzz Wheel app and find a picture of us outside Terra & Mare with a caption, "Trouble in paradise so quickly?" I read through the comments and there are numerous theories as to what we were arguing about. Most are absurd.

> I still want to see you.

> I'm going to meet Mandi and Maisie at the gym today if you want to join us. 4 pm when she's done at school.

I toss my phone on my bed and run my hands through my hair, tipping my head down. This is why I rarely come home. It's so much easier living in complete denial of my feelings for Calista and pretending like she doesn't exist.

SINCE I STILL WANT TO TALK TO Calista about what happened last night—and preferably not in front of my sister and niece—I drive over to the cabin, hoping she's there. Thankfully, her car is in the driveway when I pull in.

I knock even though the door is probably unlocked knowing Calista.

I hear movement, then she opens the door. "I told you it's all done."

"Yeah, but I want to see the finished project." The lie slips easily off my tongue. We both know Calista would be ten times more anal than I would about the slideshow, but if I tell her I'm here to have a meaningful conversation with her, she'll probably shut the door in my face.

"Oh, okay. Have a seat at the kitchen table and I'll boot it up on my laptop." She looks tired with dark bags under her eyes. I wonder how late she stayed up last night so she could be done with this project, so she'd have a legit reason to kick me out of her life again.

Not a good sign.

I sit down and she leans over me to put the flash drive in the laptop and start the slideshow. She even put the montage of pictures to music.

"I was torn between two songs or three. Three seems long for people to sit through. I mean, Aubrey and Declan will love it, but I'm not sure about their guests." She sits in the chair next to me.

When it's finished, I shut the computer screen. "It's great. Perfectly them."

"So, I have your seal of approval?"

"Would it matter?"

Her eyebrows rise. "Maybe you should tell me the real reason you're here."

I inhale a deep breath. "Our kiss." My fingers tap on my legs. Suddenly, an antsy feeling comes over me, and I can barely stay seated.

She nods, mouth pressed in a line. "Yeah."

"I really liked it."

"Do you want a water?" She gets up off the chair.

"Please stop trying to avoid the conversation we should have had by now. Just tell me why you stayed up all night to finish the slideshow. Was it to limit your time with me?"

Her forehead wrinkles as she reaches into the fridge. "What? No, I just couldn't sleep, and it's been hanging over our heads. This way you have time to spend with your family and stuff." She brings me a water anyway and sits back in the chair at my side.

"You're acting like I don't know you." I open the bottle and swallow a big gulp.

Her eyes widen. "Then you should trust that what I'm telling you is true."

"The kiss freaked you out. Just say it."

She paces in front of the couch. "Fine. I got home last night and started thinking... remembering... and our past doesn't allow for us to be so careless and stupid, Rylan. There will always be that spark of electricity between us that barely takes a flick of flint to ignite, but I can't ride the roller coaster anymore. I crave the merry-go-round—stable and consistent."

I huff.

She looks at me and comes back and sits down. "Do you remember when we ran into each other at UCLA?"

"Jesus, Calista, I told you that girl was no one. Just someone to go to a stupid event with."

"But you never called me after that. And I know—"

"It's what we decided," I interrupt, my hands fisting on the table.

"And where will this go now if we continue down this road? If I had invited you in last night and we'd fucked on every surface in this place, where would that leave us after the wedding when you go back to Chicago?"

"I don't know," I answer softly.

"Exactly. God, Ry, I loved being in your arms again and feeling your lips on mine, but every time we allow ourselves that high, I crumble into the depths of depression afterward. I used to convince myself that it was okay, that I could separate the physical us from the emotional us, but I suck at it. You're in Chicago, living it up, and I'm here surrounded with memories of us."

"But you chose that!" My voice is loud with frustration. "I wanted you with me!"

She puts up her hand. "Just please accept this. I'm not saying this to hurt you, and know that I'm hurting myself too...

but we have no future, Rylan. We want two different things. It's time for us to finally move on from each other. Let's tear down the roller coaster and get off the ride." Tears build in her eyes.

"Fine." I stand abruptly and the chair scrapes across the floor in the quiet of the cabin. "I'll keep my hands to myself from now on."

"Thank you." She follows me to the door. "It's only two more weeks. Surely we can handle being around one another for that long."

I nod, my eyes burning, and walk out. "See you at the sports complex later."

"Great. I'm sure Maisie will enjoy having her uncle show her some of his moves."

I turn and she smiles as though she's not as affected by this conversation as I am, but then again, she's never denied me before. I always thought the sexual tension was too great for one of us to put the other in time-out.

I leave her house hurt and pissed off, but I understand what she's saying—I am leaving soon.

I climb in my rental and drive around for hours, not wanting to come into contact with anyone. One of the many great things about Chicago is that not everyone knows you. Sure, some people recognize me, but a lot don't. It's easy to hide in a city of millions and I miss that anonymity right now.

My phone rings and Joran's name flashes across the screen. I park along the edge of the road and answer it.

"Hey, Joran."

"Finally! Sometimes I go forever not able to get through to you up there. Are you sure you're not staying in an igloo?" He laughs at his joke, but I don't bother. I've heard the same shit about being from Alaska my entire life.

"What's up?" I ask.

"Your off-season is booking up with endorsement deals, my friend. I mean, your contract is the bread and butter, but endorsements are where the gravy is, am I right?"

I always wonder how many espressos Joran consumes in a day. Having to be peppy and treat athletes with kid gloves all the time has to grow annoying.

"What companies?"

"You've got a razor, deodorant, and energy drink offer. It's the trifecta of athletic endorsements. And I'm working on some underwear too. So once you're done up there, we've got a few busy months ahead of us. The razor brand said they need you on set the day after that wedding. Everyone else I've spaced out a bit more. Just shoot the commercial, do some voice- over ads for radio, and let the money roll in."

I don't say anything because for a moment after I left Calista's, I thought maybe I could stay in Alaska longer than I'd planned. Maybe we could figure something out. Not a ton of athletes are successful at it, but Calista and I could give a long-distance relationship our best shot. But how can I make that promise when I'm doing endorsements and other shit like that during the off-season? I only have so many years to set myself up for life and I have to take advantage while I can.

"Fine, book me as much as you can." It'll be good to keep busy once I leave here.

"That's my guy! You got it."

I hang up and pull back onto the road. When I reach Lake Starlight, I pull up near the side of the lake and climb out of my truck, then I sit on the hood and stare at the lake.

Everything today, from my mom to Calista, runs on repeat in my head. I never thought I was selfish. It's so rare that anyone gets the opportunities I've had. And I fucking hated being a Greene in our town. All the shit I got about my grandma choosing between two brothers, a story so old it didn't even matter anymore. And then my mom ended up with my dad after she got divorced from his cousin. It left a lot of room for ribbing growing up. Not to mention how much everyone was always up in our business because we were Greenes. All of it is bullshit. But that's what you get in a small town.

Could I ever willingly choose to come back to that life? I don't think so. I wouldn't be happy, and in turn, I wouldn't be the guy who could make Calista happy. The same would be true if Calista moved to Chicago to be with me.

The wind whips my hair, and I climb back in my car to head toward the sports complex.

If I'm early, I'll get some practice in.

I turn on the radio during my drive, trying to distract myself from my thoughts, but a song comes on that I remember playing at Calista's great-grandma's ninetieth birthday and I'm sucked back into the past.

RYLAN

t twenty-one, I came home for the weekend, and my mom didn't tell me that Grandma Ethel was picking me up until I was already at baggage claim. When I came out, she and her little gang of geriatrics were waiting for me in the retirement home van, complete with a narcoleptic driver.

But the worst part was that Calista and her brother were getting picked up too, which meant all three of us were traveling back together. Calista had been giving me the cold shoulder after we'd run into each other at UCLA.

She climbed on the bus, and Dion, her brother, snapped a picture just as she saw me. He laughed and said he was reporting it to Buzz Wheel. She sat in the seat across from me and damn, she looked so good. I wasn't sure if it was because she was in season, and I wanted to ask her why she wasn't playing today, but she'd made it clear that she wanted nothing to do with me. I knew her schedule by heart and caught any game I could, but they didn't air a lot of women's games.

Then my grandma asked, "Ry, sweetie, tell Dori about your girl."

Calista looked over from the corner of her eye, and I didn't have it in me to be the bigger person. Truth was, I kind of liked her jealous, as fucked up as that was.

I stared at her when I replied, "She's nice."

Dori said nice was boring, and the conversation shifted to Dion thankfully. But my lie tasted bitter, and I couldn't stop thinking about it the entire ride to Lake Starlight. Calista stayed in her own little world, granting me none of her attention.

We pulled into Lake Starlight, and I told my grandma that I'd grab an Uber back to Sunrise Bay, but before I could, I was thrown when I saw Calista crying in her dad's arms.

Fuck.

When Dori's party rolled around, I didn't have to beg my grandma to let me take her. I had my suspicions she liked the idea of Calista and me being a couple, and this was my chance to set it straight.

Walking into Glacier Point banquet center with Grandma Ethel on my arm, I gave my head a shake when I saw all the Baileys dressed alike. I scanned the crowd, eager to spot one specific person.

She stood with a group of her younger cousins, a sea of little girls in white dresses surrounding her as though she was their queen. She sneaked them each a cake pop from the table displaying a white-and-pink tiered cake with flowers cascading down to the base and a single pink candle on top. I guessed they'd opted not to have the big 9-0 on top of her cake.

"There're my friends." Grandma patted my hand. "You're good, right?"

"I'll be great. Have a good time."

She'd already slid her arm out of mine before I even answered. It was sad that my grandma had more friends at a party than I did. Then again, it was a party for a ninety-year-old.

"Rylan!" Jamison patted me on the back, putting out his hand for a shake. "I didn't know you were coming."

His little son, Conor, stood at his side, dressed like a miniature version of him. I'd known the kid since he was in his mom's belly. I held out my fist and Conor bumped it with a smile before sneaking behind his dad's legs. He'd always been shy.

"Grandma wanted me to drive her." I smile.

Jamison matched my smile with a knowing look of his own. "We've all been there."

His little girl, Isla, ran over and he swept her up. I fist-bumped her and she bumped me back harder than her brother had.

"Hey, Rylan!" Isla yelled.

"Can't say I'm upset about the way it all turned out though." Jamison kissed his daughter's cheek, and she squirmed to get free.

"Come on, Conor!" She grabbed her brother's hand and dragged him away.

Another kid in the same gold shirt and black all the Bailey boys were wearing joined them, and they headed to the bar.

"So, how's Stanford? What are your plans for after graduation?" Jamison asked.

That was the question of the fucking year. My dad was on me, my brothers were asking, even my grandma had inquired. My older brother Xavier tried to be a guiding force since he'd been down this route with football. Soccer was a different beast than football though, especially in the States. Since I'd started playing in college, my body had never been so beat up. I couldn't imagine what going pro would be like, but what else was I gonna do? Sit behind a desk and put my degree in business to use? That sounded like a jail sentence.

"I'm not sure," I answered as honestly as I could.

Jamison had never pushed me. He'd sat me down my freshman year in high school and talked to me about my options and where I wanted to go with the game. As cocky as it sounded, I knew I would have options after college because I was a skilled player.

"Well, don't rush into anything. That's all I'll say." He patted me on the back. "Want to get a drink? You're legal now, right?"

I nod. "Sure."

We headed to the bar, passed a few Baileys, and shook hands and exchanged hellos. It wasn't until after I was holding a beer that I remembered I shouldn't be. We were at the tail end of the season with a bye week, but I still had to stay sharp.

Someone bumped into me, and I almost spilled my beer all over the front of my suit.

Calista walked by with her cousin, Jamison's oldest, Palmer. She didn't smile, but I saw her lips quirk, betraying her. "Oh, sorry."

"No problem."

They disappeared into the hall by the bathrooms. Maybe it was because I was the youngest in my family, but I loved how Calista was always with her cousins and paying attention to them even though they were younger.

I stepped away from the bar and glanced out into the hall. Calista was hugging her cousin while Palmer cried. Calista's hands ran up and down the length of Palmer's back.

"Shit, is that Rylan Greene? Tell me my sister hasn't seen you yet."

I turned to find Dion behind me.

"Damn it. Can you believe this shit show?" he asked.

We looked around at all the lookalikes. I lifted my wrist to check how long before Dori was supposed to make her "surprise" entrance.

"My grandma is her best friend. I can believe it." I rocked back on my heels. "Plus, I had to slip the DJ the music she wants played when she arrives."

He ran his hand down his face.

"Do I even want to ask?"

"'Raise your Glass' by Pink." I choked on my beer from the laugh sputtering up my throat. "I thought for sure it was going to be Dean Martin or something."

"Did you really?" Dion asked with no surprise on his face.

"Nah. I half expected 'Gin & Juice' by Snoop Dogg."

Dion spit his drink all over the floor, laughing. "I can actually imagine her doing that." He imitated Snoop Dogg with his hand in the air, moving his body to the beat of the music.

"What's so funny?" Calista joined us and crossed her arms, apparently unimpressed.

"Rylan is. Who knew he was so funny!" Dion smacked me on the back and grabbed a waitress, telling her about the spill on the carpet.

"Dion!" Jamison's son Callum ran up and pulled his cousin away to discuss video games.

I turned to Calista. "I guess that leaves us."

"I need a drink."

As she turned, a squeal erupted through the speaker and I looked toward the front of the room, where my grandma had the microphone. She tapped it as if she was a comedian or some pop star everyone had been waiting to hear from. "She's pulling in now. Everyone hide!"

The lights went out before I could find a place to go, and the only source of light was the candles floating in the bowls on each table.

"Is this really necessary?" Calista said in a low voice.

My body buzzed at having her so near in the dark. I stepped closer to her when I knew I shouldn't. My hand fell to her hip as though I had no control of my appendages. She stiffened for a moment, and I held my breath until she sank into my hold. Her back fell to my chest, her head on my shoulder. One thing I'd always liked about Calista was her height—I didn't have to bend down to kiss her.

"What are you doing?" she whispered. Her minty breath fanned across my cheek.

"I have no idea."

I allowed my lips to fall on hers, knowing the consequences. She hated me, but she couldn't deny me. Which would probably only make her hate me more.

I slid my tongue along the seam of her lips and she opened, her tongue sliding into my mouth and meeting mine. She swiveled in my hold, her arms moving around my neck, and my hands slid down her back. The kiss wasn't nearly as powerful as that first one years ago—more like a homecoming—but the longer it lasted, the more I wanted to push her under the table so that when the lights popped on, we'd still be in a bubble where no one knew anything.

But sadly, we were warned before the lights popped back on.

My grandma's whisper into the microphone was an ice bucket over my arousal. "She's here! Shhh. One. Two."

At three, I ended the kiss and stepped back right when the lights turned on. I blinked and took a slug from my beer as if nothing was new.

Everyone screamed surprise, and Pink's voice sounded from the speakers. Dori pretended to be surprised, and her small great-grandchildren rushed to her as if she'd had the entire thing choreographed.

I side-eyed Calista. Her hands were over the back of a chair, gripping it so hard her knuckles were white. Her back rose and fell with her deep breaths. Our eyes caught for a moment, and I knew she felt what I was. She wanted to leave this party and be alone with me.

"I should go say happy birthday." She walked away before I could protest.

I headed to the bar to get a water because I still had to drive tonight. Calista's dad, Rome, sidled up next to me, ordering two drinks.

"Hey, Rylan," he said.

Anxiety ratcheted up my spine over the fact that two minutes after I'd made out with his daughter in the dark, he was approaching me. It was as though he could sniff out my desire for his eldest daughter. "Hi, Mr. Bailey."

He waved me off. "Rome is fine."

"Okay." I cracked open my bottle of water and gulped half of it down as if maybe he could somehow smell his daughter's minty breath on my mouth.

"I'm gonna get to the point. Are you the reason my daughter had tears in her eyes when she got off that van?"

I thought back to days earlier when I'd seen Calista with her dad. "No." I shook my head.

"You sure?"

Because I was so zeroed in on him, I didn't see Calista approach from behind her dad.

"It wasn't him. I got kicked off the team," she said.

It was like the air all rushed from my lungs.

Well, fuck. How could such a skilled player like Calista get kicked off one of the best women's teams in collegiate soccer?

I shouldn't have cared about the answer. I shouldn't have kissed her. Hell, I shouldn't have even been there. But regardless, none of it felt wrong. Maybe it was time I confessed what I'd been feeling since I saw her last and finally see where we'd land.

Her dad swiftly moved her out of the room, and she glanced at me over her shoulder. To hell with the water, I ordered another beer.

A half hour later, she returned and told me that she'd recently fallen into a slump and missed too many classes, causing her grades to slip. Her coach was trying to work with her and her professors. I realized I couldn't throw my feelings on her plate when she had so much piled on already, so I made the most of my evening. Although we flirted and danced, I didn't venture over the line again. She needed to concentrate on herself, so she'd reach her dreams. And because I cared about her, that night, I kept us over that friend line because she needed a friend a lot more than she needed another round of sex.

twenty-one

CALISTA

That Saturday, Aubrey and Declan were adamant that the four of us go see the band they had hired to play at their wedding.

So now I'm in the bathroom, reapplying my lipstick and wishing I would've chosen a dress that wasn't so short.

"I don't get it. You guys kissed and then you cut him off?" Aubrey puckers her lips in the mirror.

"We kissed, his brother stopped us, and when he came over to obviously get what he wanted, I turned him down."

Aubrey leans her shoulder on the wall. She's in black leather pants that show off her legs and a formfitting shirt. "But you wanted to?"

"Of course I wanted to. That's the problem though. We do this whole roller-coaster thing where the anticipation on the ride up is wonderful and when we reach the peak, it's exhilarating and fun, but I can't handle the lows anymore. And there's always a low after the high with us, because we don't share the same vision for our lives."

"Oh."

I slide my arm through my best friend's. "I know you and Declan want us back together. It would make everything easier, but I'm sorry, nothing's changed. His life is in Chicago and my life is here."

"I don't want you guys together."

I stop her in the hallway. "What? I thought you did?"

"Not if it's going to be like all the other times. You guys were fighting so bad at the end. I could tell you two hated each other when Declan and I came to visit. I never want to see you like that again. We just want you to get along."

"Oh." I don't know why there's a flutter of disappointment in my stomach. It had felt good thinking we had someone rooting for us.

"Have you ever considered friends with benefits?"

My mouth falls open. "It's like you didn't hear anything I just said."

Was she right though? Maybe if I loosened the reins on my expectations, he wouldn't consume me like he always does.

She grabs my hand. "Come on, the guys are waiting."

Rylan looks good tonight. He's wearing a V-neck T-shirt that's snug to his body, showing off how muscular he is. His hair is gelled, which looks good, but I never preferred it because I liked to run my fingers through his hair.

When we reach the standing table, he hands me a drink— raspberry vodka with lemon- lime soda.

"Thanks," I say.

He nods in response.

Things are awkward between us now. They were later that day after our conversation too, when I saw him at the sports complex with Maisie.

I dig into my purse and slide out a twenty. "For my drink," I say loudly enough for him to hear me over the music.

He looks at the money as if it's an insult. I half expect him to slide it back, but he leaves it on the table and turns his attention to Declan and Aubrey. The three of them talk about the songs and what a great cover band they are.

I take out my phone and scroll through social media, unsure why when I should be dancing and having fun with Aubrey. I tug at the hem of my dress, wishing I had opted for pants like her.

I feel Rylan's eyes on me, and I look up. He stares at me for a beat before taking his drink and moving closer to the band. They announce that they're taking fifteen, and Declan quickly joins Rylan, leaving Aubrey and me at the table. I'm not really interested in her advice at this point, but she does deserve my attention, so I put my phone back in my purse.

"They're going to talk to the band. Rylan has some songs he wants to know if they can play." She shrugs.

"Want to do a shot?" I ask, because I can't be sober and get through tonight.

She grins. "When do I ever say no?"

I flag down the waitress and ask for two shots, bartender's choice, and hand her the twenty Rylan left on the table.

She returns with two shots for us each. "Those guys over there bought the other ones."

I glance over my shoulder, then look back at Aubrey. The guys are attractive and technically I'm single, so I can accept on our behalf.

"Tell them I'm sorry, but I'm getting married next week."

"I'll take it. I'm single as a free bird." I down my first shot. The burn makes me cough.

"You didn't even cheers." Aubrey holds up her shot glass.

"Sorry." I raise the second one. "Cheers to you being a beautiful bride." I clink my glass to hers and we down them.

Rylan walks over and looks at the empty shot glasses. "So, this is our night? Me playing babysitter to you?"

I point at him with the shot in my hand. "You don't have to do anything because I'm not yours."

"Those guys over there sent them to us." Aubrey points at the table of guys.

His nostrils flare as I down my third shot. The two of us are in a stare down before I place the empty glass on the table and raise my hand for the waitress.

"Another round," I say, my eyes not leaving Rylan's.

"Hold up." Rylan digs money out of his pocket. "Let's send some shots back to the douches, shall we?"

"Such a nice gesture." I look at Aubrey, who looks at Declan. "See, we can play nice."

"Okaaayyy," the waitress says before she disappears to fill our order.

"What am I missing?" Declan looks between us.

"Oh, you didn't hear? These two made out in a car, Fisher found them, and now Calista has informed Rylan that they won't be sleeping together this time around and that has pissed Rylan off. And probably left him sexually frustrated."

A part of me wants to laugh at the sheer glee in Aubrey's eyes at getting to fill in Declan in front of Rylan.

"I'm not pissed," Rylan says before sipping his beer.

"Well, we're back to them hating each other again," Aubrey informs her fiancé.

The waitress returns.

"Yay! Thank you." I pick up the shot as soon as she has it down on the table.

Looking over at my new friends, I hold it up in the air. Then I down it and they down theirs. One guy winks at me.

"Good now?" Rylan asks, voice seething.

"Yeah, but that's four and my tolerance is a little low." I grab Aubrey's shoulders. "Let's dance!"

The song "i hate u, i love u," by gnash (feat. olivia o'brien) plays, and I point at Rylan.

"This is, like, our song!" I shout over the music and smile.

He doesn't. "Then we should be the ones who dance to it."

He takes my hand and leads me to the dance floor. Thankfully, it's the club version of the song, so I wiggle my ass into him and wrap my arms around his neck.

"Let's be clear on something," he leans in to whisper into my ear. His knuckles glide down the sides of my body until his hands mold to my hips and his fingers dig into my flesh. "You are mine." I try to turn around, but he holds me in place, circling his lower half into my ass. "And I'm yours. No matter what you might think, there is no one besides you."

I close my eyes, his breath sending goose bumps up my neck. "Ry—"

"No. I accept your decision, but don't you ever think that I used you for sex. It's so hard having my hands on you knowing I can't do everything I want to do. And that's not because of how good we fuck, Calista. It's because when I'm with you, all my other problems vanish. We have two weeks left and I was going to try to stay away, but if you think I'm gonna sit back and watch you flirt with other men, you're so fucking wrong."

The song ends and he leaves me alone on the dance floor while I try to make sense of his words and the feelings they brought up.

The band comes back on stage and announces that it's their final set. Aubrey joins me as the shots really take effect. "Feel It Still" by Portugal. The Man plays, and we scream since we love this song. Our hips move and we circle around, dancing only with each other. We clap our hands along with everyone else on the dance floor. The girl singer does a fabulous job of making the song uniquely hers.

I close my eyes and feel the beat, moving to the music as though it's running through my veins. Another song comes on, then another, and Aubrey and I don't leave the dance floor. Rylan and Declan stand at the table, sipping their drinks and watching us until "Cupid Shuffle" by Cupid comes on. When he hears the song, Declan practically jumps over people to get to the dance floor. In fact, everyone in the whole place is racing to the dance floor.

One of the guys who bought me a shot comes to my side, smiling at me. I figure he can dance next to me, but seconds later, Rylan stands between him and me. I don't care though. I just want to dance and keep feeling as free as I do in this moment.

The four of us are laughing as Declan exaggerates every dance movement. I accidentally run into Rylan and my hand lands on his chest. He catches me, and our eyes don't stray from one another's. We go through the dance steps with me in front of him, his footwork as flawless as it is on the soccer field. I wrap my arms around his neck and his hands are on my hips, directing me.

Who am I kidding thinking that he could be this close and I'd be able to not sleep with him?

"Shit!" Declan screams.

We turn to see Aubrey helping him up from the dance floor. He limps to the table. Rylan leaves me to go tend to Declan, but he waves Rylan off as he approaches. Aubrey gets him on a stool.

"Keep having fun, everyone. I'm fine." Declan cringes when he tries to move.

"What is it?" Aubrey asks, concern all over her face.

"My groin."

"Your groin!" Aubrey screeches. "We're going to be married in less than two weeks. We have to consummate the marriage."

Rylan and I laugh.

"I'll be able to fuck, baby," Declan says. He motions toward the dance floor. "Go!"

Rylan takes my hand and leans close. "Dance with me?"

I look up at him and nod.

"Always Remember Us This Way" by Lady Gaga plays, and Rylan gives a nod of thanks to the band, who smiles back.

He takes my hand and entwines our fingers, tucking them between our bodies as his free hand presses at the small of my back to bring me as close to him as I can. We move around the dance floor, and I lay my head on his chest, closing my eyes. His scent is intoxicating.

Will I ever feel as safe as I do when his arms are wrapped around me?

He kisses the top of my head as the song ends, and I look up at him.

"I wish things were different." His gaze is so intense I can't look away.

I nod. "Me too."

We stand on the dance floor, staring at one another. I'm unsure where this leaves us. His thumb and forefinger lightly touch my chin, drawing my face up.

He bends and presses his lips to mine. "I'll always love you."

I nod, tears welling in my eyes.

"I'm really sorry, guys," Aubrey says beside us, startling me, "but Declan needs to go to the hospital."

I look over at Declan, and he has an entire bottle of Jack Daniels in his hand. We all rush back over to him.

"They're going to give you pain pills." I rip the bottle away from him.

Rylan helps him up and holds the majority of his weight with Aubrey on the other side. I have our purses and the keys to open Declan's fancy SUV. After he's in the back of the car, Rylan asks for the keys.

"We'll talk later," he says, and I nod, handing him the keys.

Aubrey is all, "sweetie, baby, it will be okay," while Declan howls in pain. She loses her patience when we're about ten minutes away from the hospital.

"This wouldn't have happened if you didn't try to show off," she snipes.

Rylan and I look at one another from the corner of our eyes. We've seen them get like this when a situation is out of their control. I'm sure the pressure of the wedding doesn't help.

"I was dancing and having fun with our friends."

"You always want the laugh. Well, look, now we can't consummate the marriage."

I bite my lip to keep from laughing.

"I promise I'll fuck you, and it's not like we're some mob couple where we have to show the sheets the next morning. I've been fucking you for over a decade."

She huffs. "Declan, this is our wedding night we're talking about. I've dreamed of being carried over the threshold, you undressing me. If you saw the lingerie I got for you, you'd be in agreement."

Rylan clears his throat.

"I'm sure it will all be okay." I try to ease the tension, but when Aubrey gets going, there's no stopping her until she runs out of steam.

"When do I come first, huh? Always wanting to show off to everyone and I'm the one lately who gets the hungover Declan, the 'I'm too tired' Declan, and now the 'I can't fuck you' Declan. Well, I've had about enough—"

"We're here!" Rylan announces and stops outside the emergency entrance.

I open my door and go in to grab a wheelchair. Rylan gets

Declan seated in it, but not without a bunch of wincing and cursing.

"I'm going to park the car with Rylan. You okay?" I say to Aubrey, dipping to get in her line of vision.

"Yeah. Go." She waves me off.

I climb into the passenger seat. We wait for Aubrey to get Declan through the sliding doors, then Rylan goes around and parks in the designated area.

He turns off the car and looks at me. He opens his mouth, but before he can say a word, I cross over the console and smash my lips to his.

twenty-two

RYLAN

fter Dori's birthday party, I'd check on Calista from time to time to make sure she was doing okay. She managed to get her grades up and was put back on the team.

Two years had passed since then, and we'd both been making sure our soccer careers took off. I ended up graduating before her and was drafted to Chicago. She sent me a nice text message offering her congratulations and saying how she always knew I'd be the number one pick someday.

And then came her turn. She got drafted to Chicago, too, and from what I gathered from her social media, she lived with a group of girls in Chicago. It really was ridiculous how little the female players were paid versus the men. But in every picture, she was happy and smiling.

I sat at a restaurant table with my date, Candice. She was a nurse in the children's wing of one of the hospitals in Chicago, and we'd met when I was doing a celebrity visit last week. When she left the table to go to the bathroom, I pulled out my phone to pass the time. The first thing I saw on Instagram was a picture of Calista wearing a very short dress with three of her fellow players.

I couldn't resist any longer and sent her a DM.

Hey. When do I get to take you out for congratulations?

A message popped up almost immediately.

Did Rylan Greene just slide into my DMs? If only the girls knew.

Remember, that's not all I've slid into when it comes to you.

Dirty. Keep talking. ;)

I looked up and there was still no sign of Candice. It felt wrong doing this while I was on a date with another woman. It was an asshole move to be sure, but when it came to Calista, I'd never had any control over myself.

Drop your friends and meet me at my place.

Oh, Mr. Greene, you think I'm that easy?

I'll make it worth it. And I've never thought you were easy. I just thought I was your soft spot.

You're my kryptonite. All my walls crumble with you.

The feeling was mutual. I had wanted to give her time, let her secure her future on the team before I actively went after her. I told myself just last week to give her more time—the first year in the league would be hard and I didn't want my presence in her life to add to that stress. But her dress... fuck me. I hammered another message.

> Tell me where you're going.

> Find me and you can have me.

She snapped an obscure picture that made it hard to tell her location, but there was a line outside, so I knew it was a club.

> Okay Red Riding Hood, the Wolf is on the hunt.

"Sorry, I got a call from my mom, and she didn't understand what I meant when I said I was on a date. It's been that long." Candice laughed and sat down.

How had I completely forgotten about her? I was such an asshole.

"That's okay, I have to call it a night anyway." I raised my hand to the passing waiter for the check.

"Oh." She frowned.

"Yeah, a friend just called and said she's in town." I scrambled with my phone and forwarded the picture to my buddy Rolando, who'd grown up here and might know where Calista was.

"She?" Candace's face turned sour, and I couldn't blame her. I was an ass for leaving her.

I signed my name on the slip and pushed the bill to the side. "I think you're great, Candice, but did you ever have that one person in your life? The one who wanders in and out? Where it's the right person but the timing is never right?"

She scoffed. "No."

"Well, I do, and this is her. I'm sorry to be so abrupt about it, but I promised her a drink. I'd bring you, but—"

"That's quite all right." She stood and stomped away from the table.

Rolando called me as I made my way across the restaurant. "I thought you were on a date?"

I watched Candice flag down a taxi. "Not anymore. I need to get to wherever that place is right now."

"This is intriguing. You drop one date to follow some chick that's sending you on a goose chase."

I bit my cheek. "It's Calista."

"Ah."

He was the only one I had told about her, and mostly because he always wondered why I barely dated. Candice was my first date in a long time and that was only because she felt small-town to me. She was a nurse at the kids' cancer unit.

I flagged down the next taxi that came my way. "Come on, do you know where that picture was taken?"

"I think I want to meet this Calista. Pick me up."

I groaned, and got in the taxi that was waiting for me.

Twenty minutes later, Rolando and I were outside a club that looked as if it could be the one in Calista's picture. Kaleidoscope was the name, and it was popular. I had just been last week.

"Let's try it," I said, and I paid the cab driver before filing out.

I showed the picture to the bouncer, and he shrugged. "You know how many girls look like that in there?"

Annoyed, I stuffed my phone in my back pocket, handed the guy a hundred, and he released the rope.

I looked at Rolando as we walked into the main room. "It's packed."

He shrugged. "It's Saturday."

He ventured to the right, and I went to the dance floor to see if I could spot her. Calista loved to dance, and I figured if she was anywhere, it would be there.

My phone vibrated in my hand, and I looked down to see a message and another picture from her.

Bouncers were assholes, maybe you can use all that clout you have and get us in the next place.

"Rolo!" I shouted.

He was already cuddled up with some girl, but he came over and I showed him the picture.

"That place I know," he said.

We left the club and slid into another taxi.

The next club was called Mystic, and a blue neon line ran the perimeter of the building. The line wasn't as long as the other club, but there was no sign of Calista or her friends.

I was talking to the bouncers when another message came through.

Hurry wolf, Red Riding Hood is getting tired.

I handed another hundred to the bouncer and we made our way inside.

It was just as packed as Kaleidoscope. Except this time, when I went to the edge of the dance floor, my dick twitched as though it was a divining rod and could sense that she was near.

"Can you get me a VIP?" I asked Rolando.

"Can I get you a VIP? Give me a damn break." He ventured off.

Calista came into view. My jaw was clenched as I snapped a picture of her ass grinding into some asshole and sent it to her.

I believe that's mine.

I watched her pull out her phone and laugh at my message. She looked around. Because of my height, it didn't take her long to find me. Our eyes caught, and she sauntered over in her fuck-me heels, wrapped her arms around my neck, and leaned in.

"All yours," she said, and I pressed my lips to hers.

"How much have you drank?" I asked. I didn't want her regretting anything we did tonight.

"Only a few. I probably danced them off."

"Good." I slid my hand down to hers and tugged her off the dance floor.

"I have to tell my friends." Calista looked over her shoulder at the dance floor.

Just then, Rolando came over and nodded toward where he'd gotten VIP space. "So, this is the Calista?" Rolando's gaze fell down her body.

"Don't make me poke your eyes out."

Calista looked up from her phone and giggled. "That's me."

"Calista, this is my teammate Rolando. Rolando, Calista." I reached into my pocket and handed him the rest of the cash I had. "Listen. Take care of her two friends. Get them to VIP, drinks on me for the night. Do. Not. Leave. Them. And don't fuck them either."

Rolando laughed and held up his hands. "They're safe in these hands."

He winked at Calista, and she pointed out her two friends on the dance floor. Once we knew Rolando was with them, I led her outside.

"Jeez, Mr. Wolf, you're awfully bossy. Is this the professional soccer player Rylan Greene side? Where is that shy boy who broke three condoms?" she whispered outside the taxi.

"He grew up." I opened the door to the taxi, ushered her in, and took her to my condo.

She didn't leave for three years.

Well, she left, but it was a waste of rent at her place with her friends. After her first year, she moved in with me. Although we were busy traveling, we had a lot of phone sex, and it was all worth it when we were home together. I went to her games, and she came to mine. I thought we were there, living out our happily ever after.

"ARE YOU SURE? You can't take this back," I say. Calista's practically in my lap and the last thing I want is to deny her, but I don't want her to fall into a depression again.

"I'm sure. I was stupid to think I could stay away. I'll be okay, Rylan. I know what this is."

I push back the seat of Declan's SUV and she climbs into my lap, her fingers attacking the buttons on my shirt. She spreads the shirt open and gazes down at my bare chest. "I can't wait to lick them."

"My abs?"

She nods. "Yes. I missed all of you."

Her dress sits at her waist, giving me a peek at her black panties.

"You know I love black." My hand falls between her legs and I tease her with my thumb over her soaked panties, massaging her clit.

"Oh god." She rocks her hips on my lap. "I really need you."

She falls forward on top of me, and I move her hair off her shoulder, kissing the skin there.

"Baby, we're in a hospital parking lot."

"I don't care. It's the middle of the night and I'm aching for you."

My fingers fiddle with the zipper on the back of her dress and I lower it, the sound magnified in the enclosed space. She sits up, and I help her free the dress from her arms and watch as the fabric falls to her stomach. Her tits are bare for me, and I glance up at her eyes.

"You just gonna look?" She takes each breast in her hands and tweaks her nipples.

My dick twitches in my jeans. "Hell no. God, Declan's

gonna have my ass." I motion with my head toward the back seat. "Get in the back."

She slides through the opening between the two front seats, shimmies out of her dress, and takes off her panties. I'm too big, so I get out using the door and into the back seat.

She sticks her panties in my pocket. "For you."

Damn, I don't remember Calista ever being this kinky, but I'm enjoying the hell outta this.

When I don't say anything, she takes the panties out of my pocket and dangles them off one finger in front of my face. "Unless you don't want them."

I grab them and shove them back in my pocket before I undo my belt and zipper and push my pants and boxer briefs down to my ankles. "Ride me."

She straddles me, and I run my dick along her wet slit. Her arms come around my neck as I tease her. "God, Ry. Fuck me."

I guide my cock inside her and she sinks down until I'm fully seated. She moans and closes her eyes. "Nothing has ever felt so good."

Unable to hold back, I bring her face to mine, capturing her lips until she moves.

"Oh, baby, I missed you. I missed this. Missed us," I whisper in her ear.

Once she's got a good rhythm, I tease her tits, grabbing them and pinching her nipples. Something I know she's always loved.

"I'm not going to last long," she pants.

"Me either. You're way too wet... too warm... too tight."

Our mouths are frantic and searching, needing to know we're in this together. That whatever lives between us is alive and we can't kill it no matter how hard we try.

"Oh god!" she shouts, and I thrust my hips, getting as deep as I can.

Sweat coats our bodies, which only makes it easier to slide together.

"I love—"

She puts her finger over my lips. "No. Don't say it."

"I can't say I love your tits?" I play it off as though I wasn't about to tell her how much I love her—because I do. No matter if I ever spend the rest of my life with her, she'll always be my number one. No one will ever compare to her.

She smirks. "You can say that." Her breathing is labored as she moves over me. "Good, because I love your tits." I pinch one of her nipples between my teeth. "I love your ass." I grip it in my hands and squeeze. She moans. "And I love this fucking pussy."

"I'm coming." She rocks her hips, dragging her clit over my pelvic bone. I only know this because of the first time she discovered it. It was so hot watching her take what she wanted, use my body for her pleasure.

"Take it all," I tell her.

She slows, her speed faltering as jolts of pleasure hit her. She falls on my chest when she's done and lays her hand over my heart. Her eyes open slowly after the orgasm recedes. "How do you want me?"

"Do you have the energy?" If we were in a bed, I'd flip her over and give her a break, but we're in a car and I'm not a small guy, so this is the best position for us.

"Always." She gets up and lifts off my dick, slamming back down.

Her tits bounce in my face, and I capture a nipple in my mouth as her hips circle. She increases the pace slowly and I take her hips in my hands, pulling her off and on my dick, wet sounds filling the car. I can't get enough. Soon my fingers dig into her hips and I still, slowly pumping everything I have inside her.

"You're on the pill, right?" I ask way too late.

She nods and falls on me, my dick still inside her. I run my fingers down her spine, and she curls into me farther.

"Are you okay?"

She looks up at me and her hand runs down my face. "I'm perfect."

I kiss her forehead. "Me too."

Our phones buzz.

Calista grabs hers, laughs, and shows me her text from Aubrey.

> You better not be fucking in Declan's new car.
> Especially since according to these doctors,
> I'm not fucking ever again.

I roll my eyes. "She's exaggerating."

"I know, but we should get in there."

We dress and find some napkins in the glove box to clean up with, but I'm fairly certain we smell like sex. I take her hand as we walk across the parking lot, but as the doors of the emergency department slide open, she slides her hand out of mine.

I pause, taken by surprise. I guess she did figure out a way to separate her feelings from sex.

twenty-three

CALISTA

I'm getting used to this whole friends with benefits and pushing all my feelings aside thing with Rylan. The sex is beyond amazing, and we don't discuss his inevitable departure, so it's all working out. I do feel guilty about the time I'm taking away from his family though. It's been about a week since the hospital parking lot hookup and Declan is fine now, though he swears he can barely walk. My guess is that he enjoys giving Aubrey a heart attack every day.

We've done cake tasting and talked to the photographer. There's only one more major task and it's the final dress fitting. Aubrey picks me up at my apartment, and we drive over to the store in Winterberry Falls.

As we climb out of her car, the Northern Lights Retirement Center shuttle pulls up. Alice and her sidekick, Jean, get off, both clapping and smiling when they see us. "You invited them?" I whisper.

"They insisted. My mom isn't coming." She walks toward Alice. "Hi, Grandma."

"Big day is almost here." Alice beams. "Hello, Calista."

"Hi." I wave with the hopes that will stop the hugs, but no, they each put their arms around me.

"I don't know what it is about weddings. They get me all giddy." Alice puts her arm through Aubrey's, and they walk into the bridal store together.

I wait for Jean to go in front of me, and I follow, ready for anything they try to pull today.

Ashlyn, the owner, is waiting for us. "Welcome!" Her hands motion in front of her. "Coats. Everyone give me coats."

Each of us removes our coat and hands them over to her.

"There are fresh bagels, donuts, and coffee in the refreshment room. Although I doubt you'll be here too long. All the changes have been made and the dresses should be a perfect fit. Let me make sure everything is ready to go. Be right back." She heads toward the changing rooms while I glance around the sea of white.

Jean stands next to me and signals to the dresses. "Have you ever gotten married?"

I shake my head.

"Come close?"

"I've never been proposed to, so that's a no."

"Nonsense, we all know Rylan was going to ask you," Aubrey says, checking out some of the other dresses.

"Let's do the maid of honor first," Ashlyn says and waves me over to the fitting room.

I give Aubrey a dirty look as I depart. Rylan was years away from asking me to marry him, but it doesn't mean we weren't deeply in love and committed to each other. He was never a commitment-phobic person or gave me reason to think he'd cheat on me. Sure, he wasn't an over-the-top romantic guy, but he showed me he loved me in other ways.

Like the time I said, no one ever makes signs for the women's soccer league like they do for the guys. The next game he showed up, he held a white cardboard sign with "#24 Owns My Heart" written on it. Or the times I missed home and he'd fly out my mom or Dion or Brinley to visit me at away games. He'd always act interested when my dad told him to visit one of his friends' restaurants in the city, even if they weren't his thing. The baths he'd draw for me after a game, the ones he'd join me in after the horrible losses. I could go on and on about how Rylan showed me how much he loved me.

"There you go." Ashlyn's voice pulls me back to reality as she hangs my dress on the hook in the fitting room. A phone sounds somewhere in the bridal shop and she looks between me and the direction of the phone.

"Go answer it, I'll manage." I wave her off.

My fingers slide over the satin of the burgundy dress. I take off my jeans and sweatshirt, kick off my shoes, and slide into the dress. One shoulder is bare, and there's a strap on the other shoulder. It's formfitting and has a slit that goes to midthigh. Aubrey picked it because she said it looked good with my skin and hair color. She truly is the best friend a girl could have. Especially since Alice was here that day and she wanted me to wear a hideous pink tulle dress.

I hold the dress in the back and look into the mirror—and that's when I see it.

"Oh shit," I murmur, stepping closer to the mirror. There's a bite mark on my collarbone.

"Come on, Calista, I have a lot on my list today." Aubrey knocks on the changing room

door. "And I can only hold off on those donuts for so long."

I go to my purse on the bench and dig for concealer, but my makeup bag isn't in there. "I'm coming!"

Aubrey's going to have a fit even though I can definitely cover it with makeup.

I open the door and turn so she can zip the dress up for me.

Then I turn back around and she steps away, eyes wide. "You're gorgeous. Damn, you're gonna upstage me."

The fact her eyes didn't go to the spot right away has me hoping she might miss it completely. It should heal in time for the wedding, but I'll have to tell Rylan to control himself.

"Come. Stand on the pedestal." Ashlyn waves me into the bigger room.

"Oh, it's a perfect fit. Like a glove. Aubrey can go," I say.

Ashlyn shakes her head. "Nonsense, get over here, Calista Bailey."

I nod and walk over to her, Aubrey following. "Your ass looks amazing in it. I should've put you in the pink tulle number."

"Told you!" Alice says to her granddaughter. "You're the bride. Everyone else has to resort to looking crappy on the day of the wedding." She sits down.

Meanwhile, Jean is flitting around everywhere.

I step onto the pedestal and Ashlyn zips me up, tugging and running her hand along the dress. She walks around me, inspecting as she goes, and Aubrey smiles at me through the mirror. Ashlyn lifts the hem and lets it float back into place.

She stands in front of me and takes off her glasses, biting the end, her head shifting from side to side. "It's perfect."

I move to step off the pedestal, but her hand on my stomach stops me.

"Oh." She points at the spot on my collarbone with her glasses. "What's that?"

"What?" I play dumb because Aubrey's ears just went up like a German shepherd's.

"What?" Aubrey walks toward me.

"She has a blemish." Ashlyn puts her fingers over it and scratches it. "It's a…" She leans in so close she's millimeters from my skin. "Bite mark?" She rears back. "Were you bitten by a dog?"

Aubrey comes up, and since she's not as tall as me, she has to step on the stool beside the mirror. "Calista doesn't have a dog." She looks at the spot and her mouth forms a thin line. "I'm gonna kill him."

"It'll be gone by the wedding," I say.

"I don't understand," Alice says. "A dog bit your collarbone? But it's so little."

She puts on her glasses to get a look. Now I have three women hovering over my boobs. Fantastic.

I might just kill Rylan myself.

"Concealer will do the trick," I say. "It's not a big deal."

"But it's noticeable." Aubrey shakes her head. "The two of you have the worst timing ever. I'm going to try on my dress."

Ashlyn's hands slide down my body. "Everything else looks good." She waves to the side for me to exit.

I hurry and change so that I can go to Aubrey's changing room without the grandmas listening in. I knock on the door, and she opens it.

"I can't zip it up. Ashlyn said she'd be right back but my grandma called her over and who knows how long that will take." She's tugging, and I stop her before she does any damage.

"Here, let me." I'm able to slowly get the zipper up. I look at her reflection and smile wide. She's an effortlessly beautiful bride. "You look phenomenal. And I'm sorry. I promise it'll be gone by the wedding, or I'll cover it with makeup."

She nods and a tear slips down her cheek. "Hey," I say. "What's the matter?"

She shakes her head. "I'm just scared for you."

"I'm good. Don't worry about me. This is your day."

She turns around. "I told Declan last night that if Rylan

hurts you, if when he leaves, you turn into that shell of a person you were when you first came home from Chicago, it's all our fault because we threw you two together."

"No." I shake my head. "Not this time, Aubrey. It's not gonna happen. I am the queen of compartmentalization now."

Her perfectly plucked eyebrows arch, and I wipe a tear off her cheek with the sleeve of my sweatshirt.

"I'm serious. I'm gonna be fine." I'm fairly sure I'm convincing her as much as myself. "Now, this is your day." I wipe the rest of her tears. "Let's have fun, okay?"

I open the door and wait for her to leave the changing room.

"You're just stunning, sweetie." Alice's hands go to her mouth.

Jean comes around a line of dresses and her mouth opens with an O when she spots Aubrey. I sit on a chair and watch Ashlyn appraise Aubrey like she did me.

"Don't worry, I don't have any bite marks." Aubrey smiles at me through the mirror and I'm thankful we can joke about it so soon.

"You know what?" Alice looks at Jean and then at me. "You should try on a wedding dress."

I laugh. "Um... no."

"Come on." Alice takes my hand. "You don't mind, do you, Ashlyn? In fact, Jean never got married. You too. Both of you try on dresses."

"Oh, uh..." Ashlyn's shoulders slump because she won't tell Alice no.

"It's fine. I have no idea what style I would even go with," I say.

"Mermaid," Aubrey and Ashlyn say at the same time.

"Okay, don't think too hard about it." I can't help but chuckle.

Something comes over Ashlyn. "Actually, I've got just the one. I've been dying to see it on someone, and your body shape is perfect. Would you mind?" She clutches her hands under her chin.

This is hitting a little close to home, but I have always wondered... "Sure. I can do that for you." At least this way I don't seem pathetic.

"And this is a good one for Jean." Alice thrusts a bagged dress into Jean's chest.

Jean whispers something to Alice, but Alice shoos her to a changing room.

"I'm going to get out of this before something happens to it!" Aubrey shouts since I'm on the other side of the store with Ashlyn now.

She sorts through a few dresses and then hands one to me. "Here you go."

"Are you sure?" I ask because she didn't seem too keen on the idea at first.

"Absolutely. Would you mind if I took a picture or two?"

"As long as they stay right here."

She laughs. "Of course they will."

I take the dress and change.

When I'm done, Aubrey zips me up. "It looks gorgeous on you." Her gaze washes over my body. "Seriously, Calista, it's like it was made for you."

My hands run down the satin mermaid-style dress that barely puffs out at the bottom. The simplicity suits me. No beads or stones, just fabric tucked and stitched, accentuating my curves. "It's a beautiful dress."

"You can't keep her all to yourself. Come on out," Alice shouts to us.

Aubrey opens the door and I step out, walking down the

hallway. I step up on the pedestal, and Jean walks out at the same time.

"Seriously, Alice?" Jean holds her arms out to the side.

Her dress is like one big puff. Puffy skirt, puffy arms. The frail older woman looks as if she's playing dress-up.

"This is ridiculous!" She stomps away and slams the door of the fitting room.

"Grandma, you better make that right," Aubrey says.

Alice stomps down the hallway, and I hear heavy whispering.

Ashlyn appears with a veil and a camera. She holds up the veil. "Do you mind?"

Aubrey snags it from her. "She doesn't."

"Why do I feel like a dress-up doll?" I ask, staring at myself in the three-way mirror.

Aubrey steps on the stool next to me and clasps the veil in place, after which Ashlyn takes a couple pictures from different angles.

"I would've done my makeup a lot nicer today had I known." I smile at Ashlyn.

The door dings that someone has come into the shop and Ashlyn calls, "I'll be right with you." She continues to snap pictures.

"I'm here to make sure it's safe for Decl—" Rylan appears through the maze of white dresses. Our eyes catch in the mirror and whatever he is saying dies on his lips.

His gaze coasts over my body and my nipples pebble under his attention. His tongue slides out of his mouth, and he licks his bottom lip, his eyes never leaving mine.

"What is it?" Aubrey asks, but Rylan doesn't bother answering. He steps forward but stops again. Aubrey waves her hand in front of his face. "Earth to Rylan."

"Is this the biter?" Ashlyn asks.

"In the flesh, but usually he talks." Aubrey continues to wave her hand.

He blinks and comes out of his trance. "Did I miss something?" Rylan asks, a wry smile on his face.

"No," I answer. "I was just trying this on as a favor for Ashlyn."

"Oh." He finally looks at where Aubrey stands in front of him. "Declan's outside."

"I should change."

I lift the bottom of the dress and walk to the changing room, feeling Rylan's eyes on me the entire time. He'll probably hightail it back to Chicago on the redeye tonight.

"Here's your bride," Alice announces Jean as I walk by.

"You look beautiful." I place my hand on her arm. This time Jean is in an elegant lace dress that suits her perfectly.

All I can think of is Rylan's eyes as I change out of the dress. How many times did I imagine how he would look at me as I walked down the aisle toward him? Now I have my answer. But I think I was better off imagining it, because I'll never forget those hazel eyes for the rest of my life. And I know that if any other set of eyes is waiting for me at the end of the aisle, it just won't feel right.

twenty-four

RYLAN

With three minutes left in Calista's game, my heart was beating out of my chest. Not because the game was close. Calista had scored two of the three goals and the other team hadn't made one. Everyone knew the game was over, but still her coach kept his starting lineup on the field. Their season was close to ending and he probably felt like he couldn't chance a loss, although it would've taken a miracle for the other team to come back.

I put my hand in my pocket for the millionth time since I'd arrived, making sure there wasn't a hole in my pants and the ring hadn't slid out. Everything was planned for that night after her game. The fact that the game had gone so well for her made it even more perfect for a proposal.

I watched her run down the field, and her footwork amazed me. Over the years, she'd grown as a player and her confidence amazed me. She was going for the goal when another player got behind her and stuck her foot between Calista's legs to kick the ball, but they both went down, legs twisted together. Calista cried out in pain and didn't get up.

My heart hammered, and I ran down the aisle of stadium seats and jumped the barrier, running out onto the field.

My first concern was that she might have a gash on her. Calista was diagnosed with Von Willebrand Disease when she was younger and since it's a blood clotting disorder, she had to be really careful whenever she cut herself.

The assistant coaches tried to keep me back, but I was faster and beat everyone but the medical staff to her. She was in tears, biting her lip in pain, but I didn't see any blood.

"Calista," I said, running my hand over her forehead.

"My leg. My knee." Tears fell from her eyes.

I couldn't describe it, but when our gazes locked, it was as though we both knew. We'd find out later that Calista's leg had bent to the right and her entire knee was shattered.

I rode in the ambulance with her, waited during her MRIs and scans, listened to the doctors tell us her road to recovery. They gave her a slim chance of playing again, but luckily, we were in Chicago where some of the best surgeons were. Surgery was riskier for her than most people because of her clotting disorder but she come out of it fine.

The first eight months, she was still my Calista—unwilling to accept defeat. She'd prove them wrong. I helped her every way I could, but the harder it was for her, the more she stopped coming to my games. The more I'd come home to a dark condo. One hiccup after another in her recovery, and I felt her resentment grow every time I left to go to practice or a game. We were fighting over the stupidest shit like who didn't replace the milk or who left the clothes in the washer. I found myself staying out later after practice, even if it meant hanging out at the coffee place across the street. I'd come home when I knew she'd already be asleep.

Finally, the doctors sat us down and said that she couldn't trust her knee under the stress of playing soccer at a competitive level. She didn't cry, and when I reached for her hand, she pulled it away.

Looking back, I thought that was when she decided that she was done with me, even if she didn't say the words. She nodded, thanked them, and walked out of the room.

"Nothing?" I asked the doctor.

"I'm sorry. But the injury will consistently prove to be challenging and put her in pain, and more than likely she'll be sitting on the injured list year after year."

I thanked the doctor and naively hoped this would be a fresh start for us. That maybe now that we knew she wouldn't play, we could move on. Although I had no idea what I would do if I had been given that news. Thinking back on it, I was a selfish asshole who just wanted her to get over it so we could go back to being us.

Aubrey and Declan came to visit one weekend, and Calista and I argued so much that I ended up at a bar with Declan while Aubrey stayed home with Calista, which was now her favorite place—our bed without me in it.

One day, I opened up my drawer and stared at the diamond while it shined under the light and briefly thought maybe a wedding would give her something to do and make her happy. A new purpose in life. We could have kids without the confines of her training and traveling for games. She walked into the room, and I shut the drawer.

"I want us to go back home for the off-season." She sat on the bed.

"This is our home."

"You know what I mean."

I blew out a breath. "Like the entire off-season?" I thought maybe we could go on vacation to a beach somewhere or maybe spend some time in Europe.

"Yes. I haven't seen my cousins in a while and..." She met my gaze, and I instantly knew from the look in her eyes. We'd argued about it before. Where would we end up once our careers were over?

Hers was over, but mine was continuing, and she'd become fully resentful at this point. "I think I want to move home."

I stood up in a flash. "You what?"

"I want to move back to Lake Starlight."

I ran my hand through my hair and pulled. I had no idea what to do anymore. "You're leaving me?"

"We can do long distance."

I dropped to my knees in front of her and took her hands. "We always said no to long distance. Why can't you stay here? We've built a life here together." At least I thought we had.

"I can't do it anymore." Tears broke free, breaching her cold demeanor, and I was happy to at least see some emotion. She had been eerily calm since the news of her career ending.

"Do what?" I was desperate to know her answer, what was really going on in that head of hers.

"I'm mad, Rylan! I'm so mad!"

"I know—"

She whipped her hands out from mine and stood. "No, you don't. You don't know because you get to go and play the game you've spent your entire life training for. But the sport I loved broke my heart because after all this time, here I am, and I have no idea who I am without soccer." More tears streamed down, and my chest ached at seeing her in so much pain.

I sat on the hardwood floor of our bedroom, unsure what I could possibly say that would make it better.

"It's everything we've had in common all these years."

"I don't love you because you play soccer." My eyes burned with unshed tears.

"Played," she corrected. "Past tense."

"Calista—"

"I wish it was different, and I've stayed this entire time because I thought it would be, but every day I grow more and more angry, and all that anger is turning to you, and I can't seem to stop it from

happening. I love you and I don't want to keep hurting you, but I know I will."

Her words cut me. A gaping wound in the center of my chest. And I wondered how I would feel had the roles been reversed. Could I go to her games and cheer her on? Would I be able to start a life away from soccer while still having to be around it all the time? She'd done the work just like I did. The long hours of training, the special coaches, all the effort it took to be the best. And what had it earned her? A broken heart.

"There has to be a solution." I couldn't see my life without her. We had been through so much, and these last three years were the best of my life.

She stared out the window. "I'm not going to take any of this away from you. I'm happy for you. I am. And I'm sure this is selfish, but I keep thinking, why me? Why not someone else? Why did I have to be the one who had their dream ripped away from them?"

Her questions were valid, but I didn't have the answers.

"I'll move back with you," I said. "I'll travel during the season, keep the condo, but every long break and off-season, we'll build our life there."

She huffed and sat on the floor across from me. She nuzzled into my arms, and I moved so my back rested against the side of our bed. I held her close and kissed her temple. This was the most contact she'd allowed me in weeks.

"We both know that's not what you want."

We'd had arguments in the past. Arguments I figured we'd settle after we were done with our professional careers. In all honesty, I felt if we got married and had kids in the city, maybe she wouldn't want to uproot them and take them to Lake Starlight. She wanted them to grow up in the small town that raised her, and I wanted to bring them up in a big city where everyone didn't know everything about them and their family members.

"I want you," I said. "I love you."

She took my arms and tightened them around her. "I love you, but I'm not sure love is enough anymore."

"Love is supposed to conquer all," I told her.

We sat in silence. I was desperate to say something, anything to change her mind. But I didn't want her to stay here and hurt more than she already was.

She turned in my arms and kissed me. I needed more, I needed to be inside her. We crawled up to the bed, and I took my time undressing her, kissing and caressing her body. Maybe a small part of me knew, but I committed her body and its response to my lips to memory. Every small moan or arch of her back. I held off my orgasm as long as I could, slowly grinding in and out of her, but ultimately, I came inside her and stayed there while I softened, kissing her, hoping to convince her that we were the real thing as tears leaked from both our eyes.

This was just a rough patch for us. We could overcome anything.

I tried to stay awake long after she'd fallen asleep, desperate to come up with a solution. Eventually, my fatigue won the war, and I drifted off.

When I woke, there was a note on my pillow.

RYLAN,

LIVE *the dream for both of us. Find someone here to share your life with who wants the same things you do. You'll always own a piece of my heart. Good luck in the playoffs. I'm still your biggest cheerleader.*

LOVE,
Calista

· · ·

I THREW *off the covers and ran to the closet. Her side was bare, and I knew she couldn't have possibly done all that while I was sleeping. She'd been planning this. How did I not notice? Her vanity in the bathroom was completely void of her, as if she'd never existed at all.*

With a roar, I picked up my cologne bottle and threw it across the room, shattering across the floor. How could she leave me? Did she ever really love me?

Now, I'm staring at her wearing a wedding gown. One that shows off every damn curve I love to worship. My world tips on its axis and nothing makes sense anymore.

"Declan's outside," I say and take one last look at her before exiting.

When I get outside, I bend over for breath. If I had the ring, I might've proposed right there. I have no explanation for my reaction to seeing her in a wedding gown, but it feels... life-changing.

Needing to clear my head, I go to the tuxedo place next door. Declan is wearing his tuxedo, and it fits him perfectly.

"Why are you so pale?" he asks me through the mirror.

I sit in the big brown leather chair. "Nothing. You're good to go over when you want. Unless you're marrying Jean."

"What?" His forehead wrinkles.

"Nothing," I mumble.

I have no idea if he says anything else to me. I'm too busy thinking about Calista wearing that dress for some other bastard. A bastard who wants the same things she does. A bastard more deserving than me. A bastard who will eventually win her heart.

Get a grip, Rylan. She left you, remember that.

twenty-five

"You seemed weirded out seeing me in a wedding dress," Calista says from the passenger seat.

We're on our way to Maisie's game and I'm crossing my fingers that she gets some playing time because we've worked with her a few times and she's doing great.

"No." I shake my head to try to sell the lie I'm telling.

"You didn't say anything. You stood there, speechless."

Why is she pressing me on this?

"And Aubrey is not happy about the bite mark."

Finally, she gives me an out.

"Let me see." I shift to get a better look at her.

We're stopped at a red light, and she pulls her sweatshirt to the side. Sure enough, my mark is still visible on her. I shouldn't love it like I do. I want to mark her again for any man to see, but since we're not a real couple, I need to get myself in check.

"Don't look like a proud puppy who went outside to go potty for the first time." She shakes her head.

"Technically, the puppy and I are the same—just claiming what's ours." Jesus. So much for keeping myself in check.

A line forms at the bridge of her nose. "Remember, we're just messing around. You're going back to the city in a week."

"Trust me, it hasn't left my mind."

I press on the gas to get to Sunrise Bay faster and out of the suffocating confines of this car with her.

She seems clueless as she busies herself on her phone. Has she really been able to push me into a box that she'll seal up after I leave next week? I can picture her taping it up and shoving it into the back of her closet like a memory best forgotten. The note she left me so long ago might have said I'll always have a piece of her heart, but she's going to give away a larger portion to someone else one day. God, that's fucking depressing.

We park in the lot with a plethora of minivans and SUVs.

"I guess when you have a family, you buy one of those, huh?" I point at one of the many minivans surrounding us.

She opens the door of the vehicle. "Not me. Never."

"I've seen my siblings lose that battle. I'll say they are comfortable."

She quirks an eyebrow at me. "Are you getting domesticated on me, Greene?"

Maisie runs down the hill in her pink uniform. "Calista!" she screams and loses her footing, tumbling down the hill.

"Oh, Mais!" Calista rushes over to her.

Maisie is laughing when she lands. "I'm clumsy."

"Everyone is. This is a steep hill." Calista takes her hand, and they walk up the hill, me following.

Calista goes out to the field with Maisie. While they kick the ball back and forth, I watch from the sidelines. I forgot how much I loved watching Calista play. Her dedication, everything she poured out onto that field.

Jamison pats me on the shoulder. "How'd you do it?" He nods toward Calista.

"What are you doing here?" I ask.

He chuckles. "I'm recruiting for a girls' team. Do you know any of them?"

I nod. "The goalie is a no. Definitely doesn't want to play."

"And that's your niece with Calista?"

"Yeah, she got Calista out there again, not me." I smile, watching them. Calista lets Maisie kick the ball between her legs.

"I have a feeling you had a little something to do with that too."

I shrug. I've always wanted to be Calista's savior, but I feel like I come up short.

The whistle blows, and Calista takes Maisie's hands and whispers something. She hugs Maisie fiercely before she jogs over to us and hugs Jamison. "What are you doing here?"

"I told Rylan—recruiting, can you believe it?"

"What do you think happens to all the kids who don't get a spot on your teams?"

I was so set on being the best, I'd never thought about how many kids don't even play after a certain age.

Jamison sighs. "Unfortunately, I can only instruct so many kids. I'm sure some talented kids have slid past me. But if I had more skilled coaches, especially for my girls, I wouldn't need to worry about that." He gives Calista a look.

"Imagine how different our lives would be if we hadn't trained together," I say without thinking it over. Calista not being in my life feels like a sledgehammer to my heart.

The game starts, and Calista excuses herself and goes over to Mandi. They cheer for the team, but Maisie is still on the bench. Each second, I grow more and more angry.

Maisie is such a great sport. She cheers on her team like

Calista told her to do, and when they huddle, she gets in there even though she hasn't had any playing time. She's being a good teammate which is what Calista told her is the most important.

Noah sits in his folding chair with a pissed-off expression while my mom keeps shaking her head.

Maisie's team is up by five goals before my dad yells, "Coach, why don't you play some other players?"

"Hank," Mom says and puts her hand on his arm to calm him.

But I'm ready to scream too.

"This is ridiculous," Jamison says next to me. "They're kids."

"I know."

Near the end of the first half, the other team scores three goals back to back because our players are whining and asking for water, complaining they're tired. But the coach is just trying to pump them up and not making any changes to the lineup. By the time the whistle blows for half, I'm ready to give this woman a piece of my mind.

The second half starts, and when Maisie doesn't come off the bench, I shout, "Seriously?"

The coach doesn't look at our family, not even glancing in our direction.

Kara saunters over, looking Jamison up and down. "Mandi, we talked about the parents yelling from the sidelines."

"Shut up, Kara," Mandi says. "I pay the same dues to the park district you do, and my daughter deserves a shot out there."

"Especially since the goalie can't stop a ball. Did you see the other two goals go in? We're tied now," my nephew Crew says.

Kara gives him a dirty look.

I look to Calista, and she nods, biting her lip. Now that they're tied, we're both doubtful Maisie will get in the game. The other team calls a time-out and Calista jogs over, but before she reaches the coach, the whistle is blown again and Maisie is actually in the game.

My entire family hoots and hollers, clapping like a bunch of assholes to make it clear what they think of the fact that now Maisie is finally on the field, but it's funny as hell at the same time.

"Go, Mais!" Noah gets up from his chair, his arms raised high.

Calista jogs back to me and gives me a one-arm hug. "I shouldn't be this nervous for a nine-year-old, should I?"

I know how she feels. We've been waiting for this moment, and it's finally come. Will Maisie remember what we've taught her? And I use we lightly, since it was mostly Calista.

The ball gets kicked in, and a glance at the scoreboard tells me there're only two minutes left. The kids don't pass Maisie the ball, purposely not kicking it her way.

"Maisie is open!" I yell.

"They know that," Calista whispers. "Now I want to kick all these kids' asses." "I love that you're feisty and protective of my family." I kiss her cheek.

The other team gets the ball and takes a shot on the goal, but it bounces off the post.

Maisie's teammate just kicks it to get it out of there, and it heads in Maisie's direction.

"Lightly," Calista whispers, saying exactly what I would have.

Maisie lightly kicks the ball in the same direction as the net.

"Now go, girl." Calista's hands are clasped under her chin.

Maisie kicks the ball with her right foot then her left as she makes her way up the field.

She's got a good rhythm going.

"That's it. Keep it up." Calista walks down the sidelines.

"Excuse me," Kara squeals when Calista steps in front of her.

"Watch out behind you," Calista shouts, and Maisie swiftly moves the ball to the side, protecting it as she was taught. "Now go as hard as you can."

Maisie doesn't look at Calista once, but I can tell she's listening to her. She runs toward the net, the ball getting a little away from her, but she keeps it in her possession before her leg goes back and kicks hard.

I stop breathing for a moment, zeroing in on the ball floating in the air. The goalie shuffles from right to left. The buzzer for the timer goes off as the ball slides into the right-hand side of the net, just over the line.

"Goal!" I shout and run toward the field, but an arm stops me.

It's Calista. We step back because Maisie's teammates are surrounding her, telling her what a great job she did, giving her high fives.

I put my arm around Calista and lean in close. "Thank you. You'll be her new hero."

She looks up at me, her head on my shoulder. She shakes her head as wetness pools in her eyes. "I never thought I could love it again. Thank you."

"I didn't do anything."

"Yes, you did."

"Calista!" Maisie is running toward us, and Calista falls to her knees and hugs her tightly. "I did it. I scored a goal!"

"I saw, and it was perfect. Your uncle can't make a goal look that easy."

Maisie laughs.

"I'm so proud of you." Calista hugs her again.

I pick up Maisie and put her on my shoulder. "MVP! MVP! MVP!"

The other kids start chanting it as I carry her around the field before dropping her into Mandi's arms. Mandi's clearly been crying, and Noah shakes my hand.

"Imagine if you hadn't come home. Calista wouldn't be comfortable on a soccer field again and your niece wouldn't have gotten any playing time," my dad says into my ear and pats me on the back.

I set Maisie down and she goes back over to Calista to thank her, and my dad's words repeat in my head. If I hadn't come home for Declan's wedding, Maisie might have gotten time on the field, but she most likely wouldn't have scored. And celebrating these moments with my family feels good. Better than I thought it would.

"Pizza and ice cream at the house!" my mom shouts.

I walk over to Calista and she beams. God, I missed that. "Ready?"

"Yeah, but I can't go to your parents'. I have dinner plans with Brinley and Dion."

My shoulders sag in disappointment, but I know she has a life. I can't just expect that she'll push everyone else to the side because I'm here.

"Okay, I'll drop you off." I hold my hand out and she accepts it.

After we say our goodbyes and I tell my family I'll be there after I drop off Calista, we walk down the hill to the car.

"Calista!" Maisie screams, running down the hill again. This time, she doesn't lose her footing. She hugs Calista's legs one last time. "Thank you."

"Anytime. We can keep working together if you want."

Maisie shakes her head. "I don't really love soccer."

I act mock offended and put my hand over my heart.

"But I really wanted to score a goal." She smiles.

Calista runs her hand over her braided red hair. "Then I'm glad your wish came true."

Maisie shuffles her feet. "What's your wish? Maybe I can help."

Calista smiles softly at my niece, then looks at me. "Oh, that's sweet, but my wish is impossible."

"No wishes are impossible," Maisie argues.

"Not when you're nine, no, they aren't. But thank you, I appreciate you trying. Now, go have some well-deserved pizza and ice cream."

After one last hug for both of us, Maisie runs back to my family.

As I drive Calista to Lake Starlight, I wonder, do our wishes match?

twenty-six

CALISTA

At Dion's, I linger in the vehicle a little longer than I should before opening the door.

Rylan grabs my other hand before I get out. "Can I see you tonight?"

I look up at Dion's apartment, a flash of Rylan's and my last Christmas going through my mind. "Yeah, I'll be at the cabin around nine."

"I'll be there." He brings my hand to his lips and places a kiss on the inside of my wrist. "You never stop amazing me," he whispers.

I smile. "Give yourself some credit. You helped her too."

He nods, but I'm not sure he believes it. I think it was hard growing up as the youngest child in a blended family and the only sibling who was born to Hank and Marla as a couple.

"See you at nine."

He drops my hand and sighs. "See you then."

I get out of the car, and on my way up the stairs to Dion's apartment, all I can think of is last Christmas when he sent me the bouquet of camellias, my favorite flower. I called him up here to make it clear I didn't want anything from him, but words failed me when he kissed me...

His lips were on mine. His tongue slowly parted my mouth, requesting permission. And the traitors that they were, they opened. His warm tongue slid inside and glided along mine. I moaned and my lady parts put up no resistance, getting right on board even if it wasn't a good idea. But how could I blame them? They knew Rylan, and they knew they were going to feel really good when he was done with them.

I sank into his hold. His fingers dug into my hip, his thumb running along the waistband of my joggers. There was no denying I'd wanted this for as long as he had. I missed this feeling of safety and being taken care of—the one only he'd been able to evoke.

His lips left mine, traveled down my neck, and his hands ran up the back of my shirt. A disappointing groan leaked out of him when he found I was wearing a sports bra. I had always worn this shirt sans bra when we were together and I was hanging around the condo. But his hands slid forward, pulling up the bottom of my bra. My body waited with anticipation until his hands took the weight of my breasts and his thumbs ran over my nipples.

"Damn, Calista, I've missed you so much," he whispered.

His thigh wiggled between my legs, and I shamelessly ground my core against his strong thigh muscles.

"We shouldn't be doing this," I said, continuing to fight although we both knew I wasn't going to call this off.

"We're adults. We can do what we want." He plucked off my shirt.

Rylan long ago became a pro at stripping me of my sports bra, and soon I was bare in front of him. But there was no awkwardness because it was Rylan. The boy turned man who knew every detail of my life, my body, and my thoughts.

"Still." *I ground, and he pressed his thigh firmer up into me.*

"We made promises." I ground down on him again, my sensitive clit on fire.

With his finger, he directed my chin up to make me look at him. "That never changed anything for me. It's been hell without you."

Before I could respond, his lips were on mine again.

"I've missed you so much." My hands wrapped around his strong shoulders, and I wrapped my legs around his waist, promising my clit that she'd get the attention she needed soon. "Down the hall to the left is the guest bedroom where I'm staying."

I melted at his smile. The one he gave when he knew he'd gotten his way. But at that moment, I didn't care. I just needed him inside me.

"Are you on the pill still?" he whispered in my ear as I played with his hair that he'd cut shorter since the last time I'd seen him.

"Um..."

He got us to the bedroom, and he lowered me until my feet touched the floor. Cradling my face in his hands, he locked his gaze with mine. "I can't lie and say there hasn't been anyone else, but I've always used a condom."

I despised the thought of him with someone else. A part of me was screaming to stop this, to kick him out. The reasons we weren't together were still there. But a larger part of me said that no matter what, when he left, I'd be hurt either way. At least I'd have one more memory of him to torture myself with once he was gone.

"Same," I answered, except I was positive there'd been fewer other people on my side than his.

The jealousy that ignited in his eyes shouldn't have made me happy. Rylan had always been clear about his feelings for me since we'd reached adulthood.

"Fuck, I hate the thought of some asshole having his hands on what's mine." His fingers hooked in the waistband of my joggers, and he yanked them down. I stepped out of them, leaving myself in a pair of blue thong panties.

"You have too many clothes on." I slid my hands up the hem of his shirt until he grabbed it by the back neckline and pulled it off the rest of the way.

God, of course, he was more chiseled than I remembered. That was always the case with him. When we weren't together, when I wasn't a distraction, he'd always get stronger, trimmer, faster. Not that he ever mentioned it, but I was sure his coaches and trainers had noticed.

I flicked the button of his pants and slid the zipper over his prominent bulge.

"I love your hands," he groaned.

His pants opened, and I pushed them down his legs. While my hand slid down the waistband of his pants, his hard dick rested heavy in my palm. Another strangled groan came from him, and I bit my lip to keep from smiling. I loved hearing his noises.

I had no preparation before his lips met mine again, his tongue not requesting permission like moments before but plundering. We fell to the bed, and he lay on me, my hand continuing to pump his cock.

"I'm going to blow if you don't stop."

"Well..." I gave him a cheeky smile.

He removed my hand, shimmying out of his boxers and sliding down the bed. "Hell no. I wanna come deep inside you. Remind you who you belong to." His hands glided up my bare thighs and he peeled my thong from my body before nestling between my legs. "After you come first of course."

The devilish glint in his eyes made promises I knew he'd deliver on. One swipe of his tongue and my hands flew to his head, my fingers twisting his hair as my head fell back to the pillows. He continued his assault on my clit, sucking and twirling and making me lose control.

"More," I begged.

Knowing my body so well, he teased me with the tip of his finger. "This?" He thrust it inside me, curling it so it brushed my G-spot.

"Yes!" I cried out, arching my back.

"More? Tell me how many fingers you want, baby."

"God, yes, another."

He pushed in another finger and arched them inside me while his tongue and mouth continued to devour me.

"Oh, Ry, oh god, I'm coming." My back lifted from the mattress.

He held my pelvis down with his free hand, making sure I rode the orgasm to its finish. As I crashed from the intensity, Rylan sat up and licked his fingers, his eyes on me as he made his way up my body casting small kisses along my bare skin.

"I want to worship you. You have no idea what you do to me." His thigh separated my legs, and he nestled there, the tip of his cock pushing past my opening.

"Please, Rylan."

"You know I can't handle it when you beg."

"Bullshit." I wiggled under him, and he laughed, thrusting into me instantly.

My body lit up from the inside and my arms clung to him. He pumped into me over and over, unrelenting in his desperation to claim me. I dug my nails into his shoulder blades, scratching him.

"Fuck!" he shouted, sweat dripping from his forehead onto my breasts. "Goddamn, you feel too good." His arms moved under my shoulders and around while he thrust and hit that spot—the gold mine he knew was there, waiting to be pillaged.

"Don't you dare stop," I warned, barely hanging on.

SWEAT DROPPED *from his forehead onto my face. The salty taste was familiar from when we'd go at it after working out.*

"Never. Never. Never."

I could tell he was getting closer, and he drew it out, circling his hips and drilling me again so that it pushed me over the edge.

"Ry!" I screamed.

His heavy breathing echoed in my ear, and he growled as he pumped slower into me until his cock pulsed, spilling his release inside me.

Tears threatened to fall, but I sucked them back as hard as I could.

He collapsed on me. When he regained his breathing, he inched up on his elbow and slid a piece of my hair behind my ear. "You're gorgeous."

We both knew this changed nothing, but neither of us wanted this to end, so we stayed where we were, soaking up the feeling of being together again until he grew soft inside me. Afterward, we cleaned up and got dressed.

"I always did hate seeing you get dressed again," he said, zipping up his pants and reaching for his T-shirt.

"All good things must come to an end." I smiled and meant it as a joke, but he didn't smile back.

He sat on the bed as I put on my shirt. When I was finished, he took my hands, and I reminded myself that I needed to remain strong. Nothing had changed. He was going back to Chicago.

I pulled my hand from his and placed my finger on his lips, shaking my head. "It was nice. Let's just leave it at that."

He looked crestfallen, and I wanted to take my words back, but I couldn't.

"Thank you for the flowers. In hindsight, I wish I would've just enjoyed them."

"I wanted to make you smile."

I ran my hands down his stubbly cheek since it seemed he'd taken a break from shaving. "You never understood my love for that flower. They made me smile because you gave them to me. Because you were thinking of me when you bought them."

"They don't make you smile anymore?"

I could've lied. I should've lied. But I could never lie to Rylan. "No, they do."

"Good." He tucked a strand of hair behind my ear, and we stared into each other's eyes for what felt like forever.

Finally, I worked up the courage to say, "You should go."

He nodded and placed one last gentle kiss on my lips. "Merry Christmas, Calista." His voice held so much more emotion than a few days earlier.

"Merry Christmas, Rylan." I closed my eyes, willing my tears to stay put until he was on the other side of the door.

He took my hand, and we walked out of the guest bedroom.

"Well, well, well. When I let you stay with me, sis, I didn't think you'd be fucking people." Dion stood up from the couch and put out his hand. "Good to see you, Ry."

Guess he'd come home at some point while we were in my room. Great.

"Rylan was just leaving," I said.

"Good to see you, Dion." Rylan shook his hand and nodded. "Have a great holiday, Baileys." We walked out the door, and he squeezed my hand at the top of the staircase. "Bye."

"Bye," I said, and he released my hand and walked down the staircase, never looking back.

twenty-seven

CALISTA

The ceremony went off without a hitch and Glacier Pointe Resort did an amazing job of decorating their ballroom for the reception. Aubrey cried during the slideshow, which meant it was a success. Everything has been perfect up to this point and now it's time for the bouquet and garter toss.

We all watch Declan take off Aubrey's garter with his teeth while she giggles. He holds it up in the air like a prize and gyrates to the beat of the music, telling all the single guys to come forward. Instead of all the young guys, all the men from Northern Lights Retirement Center come into the middle of the dance floor.

"Oh boy, you're not gonna go out there?" I ask Rylan.

He chuckles. "No thanks."

"No marriage for you?" He stares at me for a long moment, and I say, "Forget I asked."

Declan turns around so his back is to the group.

"Hold on, Declan, I just have to lock Ollie's wheelchair." Alice finishes and gets out of the way.

"Who's your money on?" I ask Rylan.

"The guy stretching on the far right. He seems to be the most mobile."

"I'm going with Petey with the cane. He can use that thing to beat off anyone in his way."

"What's the wager?" Rylan crosses his arms.

"Whoever loses has to… give the other one a massage?"

He smirks. "Naked?"

"Well, obviously." I roll my eyes good-naturedly.

"Done."

I put out my hand. "Shake on it."

His hand slides into mine, and we seal the deal.

Declan makes a dramatic event out of the garter toss—because Aubrey wasn't wrong when she said he always wants the laugh. He positions it like a slingshot over his head and lets it go. Rylan's guy walks slowly in the direction it went, and I guess all that stretching was for show because I'm sure a turtle could beat him. And then my guy lifts his cane higher than anyone can reach. The garter hits the end of it and slides down toward the handle.

"You can suck it, Ricky!" Petey says.

"You win," Rylan whispers. "Let's go."

"Nope, we have the bouquet toss. Maybe you can redeem yourself."

He's been staring at me intensely lately, and although I love his eyes on me, it's making me uneasy. For the first time, I have no idea what's going on behind those hazel eyes.

"Okay, ladies!" Aubrey stands on a chair. Actually, she's straddling two chairs, one leg on each.

Again, most of the younger women aren't on the floor, but Alice, Jean, and a few others are. Aubrey turns around, careful not to trip on her dress.

"I'll double my bet that Aubrey falls off the chairs," Rylan says.

I put out my hand, and he winks.

She tosses the bouquet, and the women watch it like a first time T-ball player in the outfield, unsure where it's going to land. It lands in Alice's hands, and she raises it like a huge prize.

"Grandma?" Aubrey says, not seeming as excited as her grandma that she caught the bouquet.

Declan helps Aubrey off the chair unscathed.

"No luck today, Greene," I say.

"I guess that's you naked under my hands, bathed in oil twice." He shrugs.

I narrow my eyes at him. "Somehow, I think neither option was really a loss."

"Okay, time for Petey to put the garter on Alice!" the head of the band announces.

Aubrey puts up her arms, waving off the instructions.

"Sit on down, Alice girl." Petey lowers himself to the floor slowly, and Alice sits on one of the chairs Aubrey had been standing on.

"Oh my god," I say, with my hand over my mouth.

Aubrey searches me out and widens her eyes. She wants me to do something, but I'm not sure what I can do. This whole scene is already in motion.

I rush out from the sidelines and open my mouth, but nothing comes out.

"You two don't have to do that," Rylan says at my side.

"What? You think we can't? Who's this guy?" Petey looks at Alice.

Alice shoos us. "Go. We're not invalids."

We step away. Declan is laughing so hard, Aubrey elbows him in the side.

"Babe!" he screeches.

The entire audience watches Pete put the garter over Alice's tan orthotic pump, then he lowers his mouth and drags it up her thigh with his teeth.

"Shit, they did it," Declan says. "I'm scarred for life."

Petey must do something with his mouth when he's between her legs because she hits him on the back, laughing.

The band announces it's over and everyone claps except for Declan, who's staring with his jaw wide open.

"Close your mouth, honey." Aubrey puts her hand on his jaw and moves it into place. "Let's go cut the cake and get these people's minds on something else."

She drags Declan away and I finally let my laugh loose.

THE NIGHT IS COMING to an end. The retirement gang had gone back to the home earlier, and a lot of the other guests had already left.

Declan is perfectly healed from his groin injury now, as evidenced by the way he whirls me around the dance floor while "Happy" by Pharrell Williams plays over the speakers.

"Slow down, bucko," I say, gripping his bicep as he spins me.

"Sorry, I just can't believe it. She married me, Calista!" He slows us slightly, but the man must've taken dance lessons because I'm constantly being spun out and pulled back into him.

"I was there. You're one lucky bastard."

He leans forward, champagne on his breath. "I know."

"So I don't have to give you the 'if you hurt her, I'll kill you' speech?"

He points at his feet as they move across the floor, and

when the song changes, he takes me by one hand, his other on the small of my back. "She's my world. I'll never do anything to hurt her."

I smile, knowing it's the truth. The man has been in love with her since she first told him he'd better ask her out before she decided to go out with someone else.

"What about my boy?" he asks.

I catch Rylan's eye as he leans against the bar, watching us. "Your boy is going back to Chicago."

He shrugs. "I heard."

Rylan's been so affectionate the past few days, and he keeps saying little things about small-town life. They aren't negatives like I'm used to. I can't help but wonder if maybe he's changed his mind about staying until the season starts.

"So that's it for you two?" Declan asks.

I look back at Rylan, and he tips his drink to me. "Another chapter in our book. Yeah. That's it."

"You guys are a terrible romance novel," Declan says with a shake of his head.

I never thought about that, but he's right. "Yeah, I guess we are."

I look over again, and this time, Rylan isn't there. Declan is spinning me so much I get dizzy.

"Where did you learn to dance?" I ask.

"Aubrey found a coupon for some place. I know, I'm a natural, right?"

"Does a natural dance come with a warning? 'May get whiplash.'"

He laughs, thinking I'm joking. I smile when I see a tall figure behind Declan, tapping him on the shoulder.

"I've let you borrow my girl long enough," Rylan says.

Declan slides out of my hold. "I have to find my bride. God, I love being able to say that."

He circles around, but before I'm in Rylan's arms, Declan's already distracted by some family member wishing him congratulations.

"If I Ain't Got You" by Alicia Keys plays, and Rylan offers me his hand.

"Depends. Do you have the same moves as your best friend?" I nod toward Declan.

He laughs. "Sadly, no."

I place my hand in his. "Then I'm all yours."

Rylan smiles, drawing me in and holding me close. His scent is as intoxicating as ever.

"You look very dashing tonight in your tuxedo."

He spins me. "You look gorgeous, and if I went into specifics about what this dress does to me, your dad would probably knock me out."

I laugh, and when I pick up my head, he's staring at me. "What?"

"I just want to be with you tonight. Calista—"

I place my finger over his lips. "Rylan, you will not give up your dream for me. You're healthy and have years left of your career. Maybe things will change in the future. Maybe I'll come to Chicago and visit."

His eyes light up and I hate that I might have given him false hope. We don't work like that. We can't do casual for longer than this week. I can't pop into town for a booty call just to leave on Monday morning with a wave and "Until next time" on my lips. We burn too hot for that.

"I don't want to talk about it right now. Let's enjoy our best friends' wedding."

He nods and pulls me closer. He spins me around, not as suave as Declan, but I'm okay with that.

"Can you keep a secret?" he whispers, looking around as if

someone could be listening. Then again, who knows around here?

"Do I want to know?"

"I'm not sure."

I give him a weird look and he shrugs. "What?"

"We would have been first." He smiles as though he's happy the secret's out and I should be ecstatic about it, but I have no idea what he's talking about.

I look into his eyes. "First for what?"

"I had the ring. I still do."

My heart clenches and wetness pools in my eyes. "Are you saying you were going to propose but didn't?"

Rylan's a smart guy. I don't understand why he would tell me this right now. Especially when he's getting on a plane tomorrow to head back to Chicago.

"That's exactly what I'm saying."

The temperature in my veins rises. "Why are you telling me this now?"

He shakes his head. "I don't know, but I just… it's the only thing you didn't know about me."

"When?" I stop moving and my breath struggles to leave my lungs. "When were you going to propose?"

"I'm sorry. I didn't think it would upset you. I just… it was selfish for me to tell you."

"Rylan, when?"

"The night of the accident. Your accident."

A strangled whimper escapes me and I close my eyes, tears streaming down my face. "Excuse me."

I rush out of the venue, unable to face the idea of what would've, could've, and should've been.

twenty-eight

RYLAN

"Fuck!"

"What did you do?" Aubrey blocks me from leaving the reception.

"It's between us." I sidestep her and rush out after Calista.

Looking to my right, I spot her going out the back patio doors. I jog over to her. It's freezing. The venue has hung up string lights across the patio and she stands at the edge, staring at the sky.

"Why did you have to tell me?" she says without turning around.

"I think I just... I don't want to say goodbye tomorrow. And maybe if you knew, you'd come back with me."

She turns around, holding her arms over her chest. "So, you decide to tell me that I not only lost my career in one night, but because of the depression I fell into, I lost my future with you too?"

"No. It's the exact opposite. Your future with me was never a question." I rest my coat over her shoulders.

"If I hadn't had the injury, you would've proposed to me that night and we'd probably be married by now."

"I thought you'd be happy that I was going to propose." I can see now that it might have been a real dick move to tell her my plans.

"Why?" She wipes her eyes. "Because once I was damaged goods, you didn't know whether you wanted me or not?"

"Fuck no, Calista." My voice rises and I look around, stepping closer to her. "We were slipping. At first, I didn't want to propose when you were healing and getting better. You were focused on being able to play again and I was right there cheering you on. And then when we got the news that you wouldn't play again, I wanted to wait until you'd mourned that loss, but then you left me. You were never damaged goods. You have always been the only woman who owns my heart."

She wipes her face again. "But to know that I lost everything I ever wanted in my life in five seconds..." She stares at the sky. Her makeup is completely smeared from the number of tears cascading down her face. I want to hug her, but I'm afraid she'll push me away.

"I never should have told you," I murmur.

"Probably not."

Screw it all to hell. I tug her into my arms. "If you knew how much I love you. How much I hurt. I've tried forever to get over you and I can't. God, Calista, it was a selfish move on my part to tell you, and I'm sorry."

She draws back and her hands touch my face. "We have to end this. We can't keep doing this to one another."

I hold her tight. "I can't lose you. I don't want to think about never having you in my arms again."

"It's the only way. We have to get off the roller-coaster ride. We both agreed that this would only last until tomorrow."

I swallow past the painful lump in my throat. "What are you saying?"

"I want one last night with you. One night without thinking about the future or what this means. Just one night where we push that aside and it's just us."

I hold her head, my thumbs brushing away her tears. "Isn't it going to hurt twice as much tomorrow?"

She nods. "But then you're gone, and I'm here and we both have to move on with our lives."

I lower my lips to hers. She clutches my shirt as if I'd try to get away.

"Take me to the room, Ry," she whispers.

My hand glides down her arm, and I lead her inside and over to the bank of elevators. We slide in unnoticed, and I press the button for the top floor.

We reach my floor, and she leans on the wall while I open the hotel room door. Once it's open, she slides through. In one motion, I shut the door and press her back to it, then cover her with my body.

My fingers find the zipper of her dress and I lower it painfully slowly. My bite mark is faint after her makeup rubbed off during the night. The dress falls to the floor, pooling at her ankles. She steps out of it, and I kick it out of the way. She's wearing only a black strapless bra and matching panties.

"Are you trying to kill me?"

She smiles and undoes the buttons of my tuxedo. "Touch me, Rylan."

My fingers dip under the waistband of her panties and she moans, her back arching off the door.

"You're so gorgeous," I say, my fingers dipping lower.

She pushes off my tuxedo jacket, undoes the bow tie, then slides off my shirt. Then she dips her head, her tongue sliding up my abs. "I told you I was going to lick them."

"I'm all yours."

I open my arms and she fiddles with my belt and zipper, my pants falling to join her dress on the hotel room floor. I quickly undo her bra and it floats to the floor. I toe out of my shoes and take off my socks.

Falling to my knees, I inch my hands up her thighs, parting them. Taking one finger, I run it over her wet panties. Her head hits the door with a groan.

"More, baby?"

Her gaze finds mine. "Yes more."

I hook my fingers on either side of her panties, dragging them down her toned legs. When she steps out of them while still wearing her heels, I hold up the panties.

"Mine." I toss them by my jacket. Nestling my face between her legs, my tongue swipes along her slit. Her hands reach for my head to hold me there, but I'm not going anywhere until she screams my name. "You're soaked."

I run my finger along her slit, eventually sliding into her opening. I pull my finger out and bring it to my mouth and suck. "I love the way you taste."

"Please," she begs.

I get her legs on my shoulders, my hands on her ass and thighs, holding her weight as my tongue worships her pussy. I suck her clit, circle my tongue, run it along her folds, and slide it inside her opening. She's moaning and grinding. My nose to my chin is covered in her and I could die a happy man right now.

"Oh god." Her fingers thread deeper into my hair and tighten. "I'm gonna come." I continue my assault until she squeezes her legs around my head. My tongue fiddles with her clit until her head hits the door and she screams, "God yes!"

I wait until her orgasm has subsided before drawing back

and setting her gently on her feet, making sure she can stay upright. Then I stand, pick her up, and carry her to the bed.

"Your turn," she says and flips onto her back, hanging her head off the bed. "Come here." She grabs my cock in her hand, leading it over to her mouth.

"You don't have to."

"I want to. I love it."

She kisses the tip of my dick before I get close enough so she has access to lick around my tip and cover it with her mouth. She pumps me while sucking on the head and I don't want to come, so I try not to enjoy what she's doing. But then she deep throats me and I thrust into her mouth, staring at her naked body spread across the bed. I can't spend our last night not being deep inside her, looking into her eyes, while I spill inside her.

"Get up," I say in a rough voice, and it takes all my self-restraint to do so.

She comes off my dick and quickly sits up and turns around to face me. "What?"

"I want to be with you, not have you choking on my dick." I cradle her face. "But it felt fucking great, baby."

Her forehead creases. "Why would you want me to stop?"

"Just relax." I get on the bed, bring her to my side, and turn us over, my thigh opening her legs. I slip inside her wetness, and she moans, her hands caressing my face.

"Oh, Rylan," she says.

This is what I want. Her staring into my eyes like I hung the moon for her, like I'm her Prince Charming come to life.

I thrust inside her and she clings to my biceps. "It feels so good."

"It always feels good with you." Our eyes lock as I lower my body, sliding up and down.

Her hands run through my hair, over my back and my ass.

"I love you," I say, and for once, she doesn't place her finger over my lips. "It's always been you."

She kisses me, her tongue sliding into my mouth.

When I pull away, I bury my head in her neck. "I have to know. You love me, right?"

"Oh, Rylan." She pushes my face up. "Always. You're mine."

I smile, and our lips crash together again. I circle my hips and I'm hanging on by the thinnest thread. Finally, her thighs tighten around my waist, and she comes quietly, her body shaking.

Moments later, I still inside her as I come, lost in her eyes.

I brush her hair out of the way and kiss her, trying to convey everything I feel through it. Because I want her to remember us like this. Not as the couple who couldn't get their shit together, but two people who loved one another so hard, they couldn't stay away, but at the same time, couldn't find a way to stay together.

When I'm soft, I slide out of her and get her a washcloth from the bathroom. Her eyes are already drifting closed when I return to clean her up. I want to beg her not to fall asleep so we can continue to share these final moments together, but it's been a long day.

After I clean myself, I return and find her fast asleep on her side. I slide her under the sheets and sit in the chair across the room. After pouring myself a whiskey from the minibar, I turn off the lights and watch her sleep.

A few minutes later, she rolls over. When I'm not there, she looks around and finds me in the chair. "What are you doing over there?"

"Watching you."

"Come warm me up." She pats the side of the bed.

I sip my whiskey, carry the glass over with me, set it on the nightstand, and slide down next to her. She wraps my arms around her as if she's afraid I'll leave before she's ready.

MORNING COMES TOO FAST, and I get up, staring at her dark hair strewn across the pillow. I turn on the shower since my flight leaves in three hours. I scrub her off my body as if it's a cleansing ritual and dry off with a towel before wrapping it around my waist.

She's up, dressed, and checking her phone when I come out.

"You could've joined me," I say.

She smiles, and it's clear our time is up. The sun has risen, and that means there are no Rylan and Calista anymore. "I'm going to leave."

"You can stay here. I have to leave for the airport anyway."

She shakes her head. "I think I have to be the one who leaves first." She walks over to me. Her hands land on my chest and she rises on her tiptoes and kisses me briefly. "Work on your footwork this off-season. You're opening up too much and they're getting a toe in. You used to be faster than anyone, but now you have the young ones coming after you. Remember to protect the ball."

She kisses me once more. "Come home and visit your family. They miss you, and whether you believe it or not, they love you. I know you always thought because you were so much younger you didn't have the same relationship with them as they had with each other, but they love you, Rylan. They want to be part of your life." She kisses me again. "Last, you are way too good of a guy to not love someone. Open yourself up to it."

When she rises on her tiptoes again, I grab her waist and keep her there. "I'll only ever love you."

She smiles, but it's a sad smile. "One day you'll meet someone, and I'll be that girl you loved once upon a time." She settles down on her feet. "I have to go." She's all business, putting her purse over her shoulder and grabbing her suitcase. "Bye, Rylan."

She smiles, turns, and walks out of the room, leaving me standing speechless while my heart falls from the gaping wound in my chest onto the floor.

twenty-nine

RYLAN

Calista left me in the hotel room a week ago. Now I'm back in Chicago, filming and shooting my endorsement deals and trying to get on with my life, which has felt pretty impossible.

I'm on my way back home when I notice a new Chinese restaurant that's opened up on the corner across from my building. Deciding to try it, I stop in. It smells hopeful.

The employee comes to the register to take my order, and she doesn't know who I am. Of course she doesn't. Not because she doesn't follow soccer but because she didn't grow up in my cluster of small towns. While I was at home, I got used to waving, nodding, and saying hello to people as I passed by. Some said they were sorry I didn't make it further in the playoffs. Others wished me luck next year. I always thought that was annoying in the past, people in my business when they didn't need to be, but it didn't feel quite the same this last visit.

"Orange chicken, and two egg rolls, please."

The friendly lady writes down my order, cashes me out,

and tells me it will be ready in ten minutes. I sit at their bar area and watch television while I wait.

Ironically, it's a sports channel and they're talking about my team. How we need some young blood and that I'm too slow. Exactly what Calista told me. I laugh, thinking about the fact I have all these coaches and they're either too scared to tell me I'm getting to be the old man or they don't see it.

I pull out my phone and open the Buzz Wheel app. I scroll through the last thirty days since that's how long the posts stay up these days. I missed the one from the wedding night. Someone took a picture of us on the patio with the title "Looks Like Sunrise Bay Boy and Lake Starlight Good Girl Aren't Going To Work Out" with a sad emoji. All the comments reflect on how they wish we could be together. Some asked what was keeping us apart and questioned whether we truly loved one another.

I close the app. Luckily, the woman comes out with my food. I thank her and cross the street back to my condo.

My cell phone rings, and I take it out, seeing Mandi's name. I slide my finger over the screen and put it on speaker. "What's up?"

"Uncle Rylan, I scored another goal!" Maisie shouts.

"You did? I thought you didn't like soccer?"

She laughs. "Mom and Dad said I have to play for the rest of the season, but I kind of like it better now because we're playing inside and it's not as cold."

I chuckle.

"And I stole the ball from a player too."

"Man, I better watch out. You'll be coming for my position soon." I skirt past a man texting, walking straight ahead and not even looking up.

She laughs. "Is Calista with you?"

"No, I'm in Chicago now."

"So?"

"Maisie…" Mandi says in the background.

"Why can't Calista be in Chicago?" Maisie asks.

I reach my building and nod at the doorman as he opens the door for me. Once I'm inside, I wait by the elevator, knowing my call will drop if I get on.

"Mais!" Mandi's voice grows sterner.

"Calista lives in Lake Starlight." I take the phone off speaker and bring it to my ear so anyone passing by doesn't have to listen to my conversation.

"I thought you loved her?" Her innocent voice sounds so confused.

"Mais! Noah, she will not give me the phone." Mandi's in full panic mode.

"Maisie, give the phone to your mom." I hear running and stomping on stairs before a door slams. "Maisie?"

"I locked them out." She giggles.

I shake my head. "Why?"

"Because you sound sad."

My chest warms at how sweet my niece is. "I'm not," I lie. "It's just me here, that's why." I look at the bag of orange chicken. It has promise.

"You're lonely? I get that way sometimes cause it's only me and all my cousins have brothers and sisters. They have people to play with and I only have me."

I laugh. "I'm not lonely. You'll find out when you're an adult. Sometimes it's nice to be by yourself."

"All the time?" She sounds skeptical.

"I'm not alone all the time. I have friends."

"Oh."

I hear her parents knocking on the door. "I don't want you to get in trouble. You should probably unlock the door."

"You love her, right?"

"Who? Calista?"

"Yeah."

I can't lie again to this little girl. "I do."

"Then why aren't you together right now?"

I chuckle. "It's adult stuff."

"I don't want to be an adult. Sounds complicated." There's more noise in the background. "Oh, they got in. Gotta go. Love you, Uncle Rylan!"

The line dies and I press the elevator button.

By the time I've reached my condo, Mandi has sent an apologetic message for Maisie poking around in my private business. She says she knows I don't like when my siblings involve themselves in my personal life.

I plate the orange chicken and rice, then head to the family room to watch something on Netflix. One bite of the orange chicken and I spit it back onto the plate. The egg roll isn't any better. I dump it all in the trash. Nothing compares to Wok For U. I don't know why I even bother.

Mandi's words repeat in my mind about how I don't like them to insert themselves into my life. I always felt as though they didn't care to or that they were doing it out of obligation. By the time I was grown enough to form any real relationship with my siblings, they were adults, busy raising kids of their own.

I walk to my bedroom, open the bedside drawer, and take the ring out of the box. I have no idea why I've kept it. I didn't want to be that guy returning a ring to the store, that was for sure. But I think a part of me always thought we'd get back together eventually. But there was a finality this time, more so than any other. I blow out a breath and lie on my bed.

My eyes drift closed, and I have the same dream I've had all week—Calista in that wedding dress and an unknown groom waiting for her at the end of the aisle. I'm chained to a chair, having to witness her walk down the aisle with that smile. She stops in front of me and puts her hand on my face. "It's okay, Rylan. Everyone has a number one in their life."

She turns almost robotically and walks down the aisle. The guy strips her of her dress and says they're going to consummate the marriage right there for everyone to witness.

She screams no and I try to free myself of the metal binds, but I'm not strong enough. The guy's face turns into a monster with a lot of teeth and the white fabric of her dress flies everywhere when he drops his mouth on her.

I wake up in a cold sweat.

The buzzer of my condo goes off and I frown. I wasn't expecting anyone. I get off the bed and deposit the ring back in the drawer.

I open the door and my dad strolls in with his luggage. "About time. I've been ringing that thing for five minutes."

"Dad?" I push a hand through my hair and look after him, holding the door open. "At least when your brothers had their heads up their asses, I only had to travel five minutes down the road." He opens my fridge, takes out two beers, opens them, and sits at my table, patting the place across from him.

I look out the door again.

"Only me. Sorry to disappoint."

"I just figured Mom..."

"Nope. Come and sit, son."

I close the door and slide into the seat across from him.

He slides the beer my way. "I think when it comes to you and Calista, I've ridden in the back seat long enough. I thought you two would've figured your shit out by now."

"Dad—"

He raises his hand. "No, Rylan." He rarely uses my full name, so I sit up straighter. "I've sat back long enough, and now your mother isn't talking to me because she doesn't think

I need to be here. She's wrong. But I'm not going to tell her that." He squares his gaze at me and I'm wondering who this man is.

"What?" I ask meekly.

"When you decided that soccer was your sport, I didn't understand. We were a football family. All your brothers played quarterback and I assumed you would too. But I supported you, as did your siblings. We drove you to your practices and tournaments. We bought your equipment, got you extra coaching, and cheered you on at all your games. And you were good. You excelled beyond our wildest imagination. But you aren't my first son who made their sport professionally."

Here we go. Time to compare me to Xavier.

"Yes, the seasons are different, but you have time off throughout the year. Do you know how many times I've heard your mom cry after a phone call from you?"

Guilt weighs down my shoulders, and they sag. "I'm sorry."

He takes a long pull from his beer. "I'm sorry, it was a bad flight and I'm irritated."

"Okay."

"When your career ends, who do you think will be by your side? Who's gonna celebrate with you? Your teammates? Maybe. A few friends? Probably. Will the people who love you for you, not for your talent, be standing here?" He gestures around my condo. "Sure, your mother and I will be here because our love for you is unconditional. You can be an asshole to us, and we'll still love and support you. But you rarely answer your siblings' phone calls. You don't come home when you're able to visit, and during off seasons we get a week... maybe."

"I was just home for three weeks," I argue.

"And did you see how happy your mother was? How happy everyone was? And let's be honest, you spent as much time as you could with Calista." I open my mouth, but he raises his hand. "We know you love her, but here you are." He looks around my apartment. "And she's not here. Why is that?"

"Because she doesn't want to live in Chicago."

He nods and drinks his beer again. I haven't had a sip of mine.

"When Calista got hurt, I remember calling you after your games and a lot of the time, you'd be out on the town. I'm curious, did you purposely stay out late?" he asks.

"Not at first."

"You pushed her instead of giving her time." He doesn't ask; he's sure of it.

"She didn't want to come to my games. What was I supposed to do?"

"Help her. Have her see a therapist? She can't go her entire life and never see someone play soccer again. Get her help? Be patient? Ease her into it? But I have a feeling when she got injured, you just let her fall apart in this apartment."

"No! I tried everything I could to help her." Tears pool in my eyes. "I love her, Dad." I scrub my eyes with the heels of my hands. "It was a nightmare. I would do anything to have her here with me. I told her as much. She doesn't want to live here. What am I supposed to do?"

My dad's expression softens as I wipe my face with my T-shirt, all the events of the last few weeks catching up to me and feeling like too much to bear.

"Your mom and I talk. We come to decisions together. You can't have a life together when one person is always living out their dream and the other one has constantly sacrificed for it."

"Do you think I would expect her to live an unhappy life so I can play?"

He shrugs. "I don't know, because you don't tell me

anything. You keep it all hidden inside, and I'm pretty sure you keep a helluva a lot to yourself when it comes to her too."

I sip my beer to try to ease the painful, burning lump in my throat.

"Talk to me, son. Help me understand."

I shrug. The words push against my lips, but I don't know whether I should let them escape. My dad silently watches me until I can't take it anymore and I let it all out.

"I never felt like one of them! They were older and had years of memories of living together that I didn't. They were all bonded long before I came along. I felt like a tagalong and a nuisance. The way Mom would make them come to my games." I cringe, remembering seeing my siblings there and feeling as though they probably would rather be anywhere else.

My dad shakes his head. "No one made them come to your games. They came because they wanted to."

I shrug. "I don't know, I just never felt like one of them."

"When your mom got pregnant with you, it was a surprise, which I'm sure you know, but we wouldn't have traded it for anything. We were ecstatic, as were your siblings. You're the product of our families blending together. You're a piece of both me and your mom. I love our family, and sure, we had to depend on your siblings to help us with you sometimes, but none of them felt obligated to do so. But hiding out for the rest of your life isn't going to make you feel any closer to them. You're all adults now. You're all on the same level."

"I know," I say, but I think I never really considered the fact that now I'm an adult like them. Sure, I'm still younger, but the differences in our stages of life aren't a gaping canyon between us anymore.

We each take a pull of our beer.

"And when it comes to Calista, it's your decision, but I

want you to think hard about what I asked. If you retire tomorrow, who will be there to celebrate your success? Who believes in you the most? Who will still be there a year after you retire? There's always a way, Ry. Your mom and I were able to blend two families who didn't like one another and make them a close- knit family who are there for each other. You and Calista need to figure it out together, because neither of you is happy right now."

I sit up straight. "Did you see her?"

"No, but I don't need to. Seeing you, I imagine she must be the same. It's been years since her injury. She might be able to give something a try now. But soccer isn't going to hold your hand when you're on your deathbed, son."

"Jesus, Dad." I scowl at him.

"Yeah, I've never had to get that morbid with any of your siblings, but I really want to hammer the point home." He finishes his beer and gets up from the table. "Now, call me more often." He walks over to his suitcase and wheels it toward the door.

"Where are you going?"

"Your mom is at the hotel. We're gonna have a little weekend getaway."

"Seriously?"

He lifts the suitcase. "Had to scare you. It's empty." He laughs and holds out his arms. I hug him tightly.

"I love you, son. The entire family loves you."

Then he's out the door as though it was all a dream. It wasn't, was it?

CALISTA

One week has passed, and I miss Rylan like crazy. I'm not sure our last night together was a good idea because all I see when I close my eyes is him staring at me in my black panties and bra. All I feel is him inside me, thrusting and telling me how much he loves me.

I pack up the slides of us and go to store the box in the cabin's bedroom closet. If I'm going to spend more time here, I want to get this place cleaned up. The only real storage is the bedroom closet. I open up the folding doors, but I sit down when I see that there's no room for anything else.

Foam presentation boards are stacked on the floor inside the closet, and I lift one. In black cap letters, MISSION #1 is written across the top.

A picture of Uncle Austin is on the left side and Aunt Holly is on the right. In the middle, under the heading "Modus Operandi," is a list: make sure the tryst is reported in Buzz Wheel, enlist the help of Jack in getting her to Founder's Day, and on and on.

I put the board back and examine the next one. Every one

of my aunts and uncles on my dad's side has their own "mission," then all of Rylan's brothers and sisters.

Is this what my great-grandma used this place for after Great-Grandpa died? Headquarters for the geriatric matchmaking crew?

I see one lone board on the other side of the closet. I pick it up, and it says FINAL MISSION: Rylan and Calista. Tears well in my eyes. The notes on the board say things like "you have to be ready to act fast, as soon as Rylan comes into town, it's game time" and "they're both stubborn but don't take no for an answer."

I read through the list...

Give Calista the cabin.

Make them do the slideshow, but have Pete do one of them.

Get anyone you need to involved.

Make sure Rylan sees her in a wedding gown.

Oh my god, were they really able to accomplish all this?

There's a knock on the door, and I rush over, hoping it might be Rylan. No one else knows about this place except for Alice and her peeps. I look through the curtain, and I'm surprised to see my mom and dad.

I unlock the door and open it. "Hey, what are you doing here?"

"Hey, sweetie." My mom puts her hands on my cheeks and kisses my forehead.

"How did you guys find me here?"

My dad rolls his eyes. "We all know about this place. We're just respecting G'Ma D's wishes in passing it on to her great-granddaughter."

"Oh."

"Don't worry, we're all in agreement. No one disturbs whatever you do here."

"You'll never believe what I found." I rush back to the closet and pull out their mission board. "Look."

My mom sits on the couch, her hand flying up to her mouth. "Oh boy. Look how young I looked." She sounds wistful.

"You're still just as beautiful." My dad kisses the top of her head.

"I was a crazy mom who showed up to town with a baby on my hip."

My dad leans in to look at the board. "And thank God you did, because look how lucky we were to live a blessed life."

Mom laughs. "Oh boy, he's being sentimental. Get ready, sweetie."

"Aren't you surprised at the board?" I ask.

My dad huffs. "How else would they keep it all straight? They were eighty-year-old matchmakers."

"But what if they hadn't interfered? Maybe you and Mom wouldn't have—"

My dad shakes his head. "No, Calista. They helped, don't get me wrong, but I didn't fall in love with your mom because of my grandma. She probably helped us get out of our own way though, like we're about to do for you right now."

I frown.

My mom places the board on the coffee table, her hand running over the picture of her with me at eighteen months on her hip. A tear slips down her cheek.

"What do you mean? Why are you crying, Mom?"

"Sit down," my dad says.

I sit on the couch beside my mom, and my dad takes a seat on the opposite side of her.

"Your mom and I always wanted to let you all make your own decisions. We wanted you to make your own mistakes and find solutions to them, but you're on a record player that's stuck on the same verse, not realizing you have the power to move the needle."

Mom puts her hand on my dad's knee. "Do you love him, Calista?"

"Rylan?"

She gives me a look as though wondering how I could think she meant anyone else.

"Yeah." My voice cracks.

"Let us tell you a story then," my dad says. "When your mom came here, she didn't know if this was where she wanted to live. Lake Starlight is drastically different than Seattle. I'd just opened my restaurant and returned from Europe to restart my life here. I'm fortunate your mom fell in love with our small town and wanted to stay. But we're also lucky that neither of our jobs took away our choice."

I shake my head. "I can't."

"You can," my mom says. "You're thirty, Calista, and you've been babied enough on your injury. You've had time to mourn your career, and now it's time to go out there and live your life again. I don't care if it's with Rylan or not, but you are not going to hide in this town doing your family's bookkeeping and taxes for the rest of your life."

"Jeez, Mom," I say.

She shakes her head. "You're just letting the years waste away. I thought when Rylan came back and got you to teach his niece soccer, it would open your heart again. But damn it, you seem almost happy to keep it stitched twice to keep people out."

She's wrong, because no matter how hard I try, Rylan always finds an opening to seep into. "That's not it."

"Then enlighten me." She crosses her legs and waits for me to answer. I open my mouth and shut it.

"Exactly. With commitment to someone comes sacrifice. If

you love him like you say you do, like I think you do, I see no reason why you can't suck up a couple years in Chicago while he finishes his career. If you don't love him enough to do that, then I have news for you, sweetie—you don't really love him."

I blink a few times. My mom isn't usually so brutal or blunt. "My career ended in a blink. I wasn't prepared. I didn't want it to end. It wasn't my choice." Tears spring from my eyes again.

She wraps her arm around my shoulders. "It doesn't have to be your only dream, baby. I'm not sitting here saying it doesn't suck what happened to you. After all the years you put into it, and it ends that way. And it sucks that the man you love most in this world—"

My dad clears his throat, and we laugh.

"I'm not joking. She loves me more than him, right?" Dad eyes me, and I give him a soft smile.

Mom says, "It sucks that he plays soccer professionally. But he also wouldn't be the love of your life—"

My dad clears his throat again. Raising both hands, he says, "Just sayin'."

"He wouldn't be that man if he didn't play soccer. You two found this connection on the field first, and your love evolved around that. But sometimes dreams don't work out, so you have to make a new one. You're thirty and I'm not pushing, but do you want a family one day?"

I nod, sucking back my tears.

"If you stay here, you're going to find some man you kind of like and maybe can learn to love enough to marry and raise a family with. But he'll never be what Rylan is to you. I bet you have visions of hot sex and not being able to keep your hands off one another, not the kind of marriage where you're scheduling sex in once a week."

"Harley!" Dad shouts.

"You don't have to answer that, but don't stay here and settle for mediocre. Go. Live your life with the person who matters most to you."

"Again, me!" My dad holds out his arms and looks at us as though he doesn't understand what we aren't getting.

Mom shakes her head. "I'm sorry if you think I'm being hard on you. And I understand why you came running home years ago, but now it's time to take responsibility for your life and start living a new dream."

God, everything she's saying makes so much sense. I can't believe I couldn't see it for myself. I'm starting to understand why my great-grandma felt like she had to step in so much with all her grandkids.

I glance at my watch. "Can you take me to the airport?"

"Brinley already packed your suitcase. Thank Uncle Wyatt. His plane is waiting in Anchorage for us."

"Thanks." I kiss her cheek, then my dad's.

I rush to grab my purse and put on my shoes, then I'm locking up the cabin, thinking of how Rylan would be surprised if he could see me doing so without a reminder. I hear my parents talking by the car.

"You stole my thunder," Dad says.

"She's your baby girl. You would've gone too soft on her."

"Probably. I am the man she loves the most though."

Mom laughs. "Oh, babe, I hate to break it to you, but you're being replaced."

I make my way down the steps and over to the truck.

"I'm not, am I?" Dad asks me as I'm about to jump in the back seat.

"Never, Daddy. It's a different kind of love." I kiss his cheek and hop in. "Now hurry please."

DAD DOES me a solid and gets me to the airport in no time at all, and my mom tells me how proud she is of me and expects an update as soon as I manage to get out of Rylan's bed. My dad groans and she tells him to get over it.

I arrive in Chicago at ten thirty at night and hail a cab to Rylan's condo. I get into the building by following someone else. The doorman isn't there, so I figure he must have gone to the washroom or something, but I'm not complaining.

My stomach is a mess as the elevator rises. It dings and the door opens.

With a deep breath, I walk down the hall to Rylan's condo and ring the bell, praying like hell that for once we get it right.

RYLAN

"Fuck." I run my hand over my face again. I have that damn nightmare every time I fall asleep now. You'd think after my talk with my dad and the fact that I've already set in motion what I need to do, it would go away.

The ringer to my condo buzzes. Please tell me it's not my mom here to give me more advice on the matter. My head is finally on straight.

I walk down the hallway shirtless in my pajama pants and look through the peephole.

No way.

I hurry up and open the locks, blinking to make sure Calista's really here.

"Are you a dream?" I pull her into the condo, her small suitcase trailing behind her. Then I look down the hallway toward the elevator. "Is the monster chasing you?"

"What?" Her forehead creases.

"I thought it ate you." My hands touch her everywhere as my eyes take her in. Last, I check her left hand. No ring.

"Rylan." She puts her hand on my forehead. "Are you okay?"

I pull her toward me. "He was stripping you and mauling you. I couldn't get to you. I was chained up."

She laughs into my chest, and I hold her tightly.

"I think you're still sleeping," she says, placing her hands on my face.

"No. It's just this nightmare that's been plaguing me for the last week. What are you doing here?"

She draws in a deep breath, seeming to gather her courage. "I'm here to apologize. I'm here to tell you I love you and I've been a fool for far too long and I want us to work. Whatever that means."

My smile spreads slowly, and I feel as if a thousand-pound weight has been lifted off my chest. "Really?"

She nods.

"Me too, baby. God, I've missed you so much. I love you. I was an idiot to come back here." I pick her up, and her legs wrap around my waist.

"Take me to our bed," she says.

"My fucking pleasure."

I walk us to our room and deposit her carefully on the bed. She quickly strips down and gets on her knees, pushing down my pajama pants.

"Okay, first time fast, but the second time, we take it slow."

She climbs me, hanging off my neck. "Whatever you say, Mr. Greene. I'm yours."

"Forever?"

"And ever."

"And always."

I lower her to the bed and slide into her. Her back arches and she moans.

"I love you," I murmur right before taking her left breast in my mouth.

"I love you more."

AFTER AN INCREDIBLE NIGHT OF SEX, I slip out of the bed the next morning and head to the kitchen. I start the coffeepot and look in my fridge where I have... nothing. I order breakfast from the restaurant down the street and I'm just getting her a cup of coffee when my doorbell rings. I answer the door, and the courier looks down at me.

"Sorry, the girlfriend surprised me last night." My dick is swinging back and forth in full view of this poor guy. He should be happy I don't have a hard-on what with my thoughts on Calista again.

After I sign, he hands me the envelope. I go to the couch and open the envelope. I don't think twice about it, grabbing a nearby pen and signing my name in all the flagged areas, initialing all the places I have to. The woman sprawled out in my bed is worth more than this any day of the week.

"Hey, you. I don't like waking without you." Calista comes out wearing my shirt and, if I'm lucky, nothing underneath. She rubs her eyes and her hair is a mess, but it's one of her best looks. She climbs onto my lap and straddles me. "Why aren't you in bed?"

"I was just ordering us breakfast, and I made you coffee."

"Coffee?" Her eyes light up.

I reach over to grab it.

She leans along with me and glances at the papers. "What's that?"

"Nothing."

"It doesn't look like nothing." She grabs the stack of papers.

Her eyes catch on the title at the top—Release Contract. Then she scans the rest and frowns. "Ry?"

I kiss her neck, pulling her toward me. "I've asked to be released from my contract. I'm retiring." I suck on her earlobe.

She puts her hand on my chest and pushes me back. "No, you aren't."

"Yes, I am." I try to grab the papers while I pull her closer. She isn't wearing anything under my T-shirt, and with all the friction of our movement, my dick salutes her.

She moves the papers so I can't get them. "Calista, give me the papers."

"You're not retiring. You're in great shape. You have no reason to retire."

I stop accosting her neck. "You're more important than my soccer career. I choose you."

Her shoulders slump.

"What?" I pull back to look at her.

She's frowning. "My mom's words to me just rang too close to home. I hate when they're right."

"Talk to me, Calista."

"It was never a choice. Or at least it shouldn't have been a choice you had to make." She holds the papers up, then tears them in half. "You play. I'll move here. I wasn't ready before to face being around everything that reminded me of what I lost, but there's no one I'd rather watch live out my dream more than you. I'll find a new dream, but..." She pokes me in the chest. "Every off-season, we go home. You do your training there. Agreed?"

I nod. "And when I'm old and washed up, you choose where we live, no complaints from me."

"Why didn't we do this years ago?" she asks, sounding a little melancholy.

"Because you're stubborn."

Her eyes narrow. "Because *we're* stubborn. We're a team now."

I chuckle. "Come on then, teammate, I have a few things to show you." I stand, lifting her with me.

"Coffee!"

I lower her, and she picks up the coffee cup off the table.

Back in the bedroom, I lower her to the bed and get on my knees.

"Calista, thank you."

"Don't make me cry again. I was stupid all those years ago. I just couldn't see past my own pain." She pauses as though she wants to say more, so I stay quiet. "I might start seeing a therapist to talk about how my injury affected me mentally. I think that could be good for me."

I squeeze her hand. "I think so too. But I would've retired for you."

A tear falls down her cheek. "I know."

"I want you to know that before you showed up here, I was coming for you. I just wanted to sign those papers before I hopped on a plane."

She places her hand on my cheek. I'm suddenly so over-whelmed by my love for this woman that I know what I have to do. I stand and grab the ring out of the drawer.

"Will you marry me?" I hold the ring out to her. "I want to get off the roller coaster and on the merry-go-round."

Her eyes widen. "We don't have to rush into this."

"Yes, we do."

"Why?" she whispers.

"Because we've wasted too much time already and I want to start our life together."

"Okay." She grins. "Well, slide it on."

I don't waste any time sliding the platinum band with a four-carat diamond onto her left ring finger.

She lifts her hand. "Had I known this was the ring in the drawer, I might not have left." She laughs and I climb on her, tickling her ribs. She squirms. "I'm joking."

I kiss the palm of her left hand and where the ring rests on her finger. "We should have—"

She places her fingers on my lips. "No regrets. We only look toward the future. Okay?"

"Deal. What do you want for the rest of your life?"

"You. Just you."

"That's it?" I arch an eyebrow.

"And maybe a few kids and a dog?"

"Sounds perfect to me." I kiss her, swearing I'll never stop for the rest of my life.

epilogue

CALISTA

Almost One Year Later...

"Now you've seen me in the dress!" I whine as Rylan continues to cover my eyes even though I have a blindfold on. "Plus, my hair and my fake lashes."

"I already saw you in this amazing dress, and it's been torture having to imagine unzipping you out of it for months." His hand slides down and gives my ass a light slap. "Second, you're beautiful."

We waited until his season ended, but he planned the entire wedding. I didn't lift a finger, and I was okay with that. We've kept it to just our immediate families—which are still over forty people—plus Declan and Aubrey and a few players and their wives.

"What kind of music is that?" I ask.

Rylan blows out a breath. "Can you please be patient? Now

this is where I leave you. Your dad is right here." He positions my hand on what I guess is my dad's arm.

"Hey, sweetheart," my dad says.

"See you in a few." Rylan kisses my lips.

"Rylan, you can't kiss me before the officiant says you can!" All I hear is his echoing laughter getting farther away.

"Dad, what's going on? Who does this to their bride on their wedding day?"

My dad chuckles. "The love of your life apparently."

"Stop having hurt feelings. You'll always be my daddy."

"Uh-huh."

"Tell me what's going on," I whine, sick of wearing this blindfold.

"Nope, that ruins the surprise, and your mom is head over heels putting that boy on a pedestal. If I ruin this surprise, she's gonna throw me in the Hudson."

I laugh and decide to wait patiently.

"Okay, the boy says I can take off your blindfold. You ready?" "I am."

My dad gently lifts the blindfold, and I blink, hoping my fake lashes are still in place. A smile spreads on my face. I'm at the end of a long red carpet with Rylan standing at the very end—by the entrance of a merry-go-round.

"He rented out the entire place," my dad says and squeezes my hand.

My family members line the carpet, and there's a big tent with tables set off to the side.

The carousel is in the Brooklyn Bridge Park. We went by this place before and I made him ride it with me. Or did he take me here knowing I'd make him ride it? Oh, he tricked me!

I walk down the red carpet with my dad to the sounds of a string quartet. When I get to the end, Rylan thanks my dad and takes my hand.

"I don't think your dad likes me," he whispers.

"He's just going through something."

Before the officiant can talk, Rylan clears his throat and addresses our guests. "I just want to say something before we get started. As all of you know, this has been a long time coming. Too long. Some of you might think I planned this to be romantic and others might think it's adorably unique, but the reason I rented out this space and this carousel is because Calista once told me she felt our love was like riding a roller coaster. She never knew when we'd hit a sharp turn or go into a dip. She craved the stability of a merry-go-round. So today, I offer her that future as she agrees to marry me." He locks eyes with me and squeezes my hand. "This is where we step off the roller coaster."

A few of the women ooh and aah and I fall even more in love with him if possible.

The officiant clears her throat, and we go through the I dos and the exchange of rings.

Once we're pronounced husband and wife, Rylan leads me onto the merry-go-round, and because I can't straddle an animal in this dress, we opt for one of the benches. That turns out to be perfect, because I can kiss my husband privately while everyone else finds a seat.

All the kids and adults get on and pick their animal or stand and hold on to a pole.

"This is so amazing." I slide under his arm. "You're too good to me."

"You're too good to me. This year has been beyond my wildest dreams." Rylan kisses the top of my head.

He had a great year professionally and his team made it to the playoffs but got knocked out by the third round. Still, it's further than they made it last year.

I'm seeing a therapist now to deal with my grief over losing my dream, and I've become more active with the park district's girls' soccer program. A high school recently reached out to me about coaching their girls' team all year round, but I like to travel with Rylan, so I'm not sure I'm ready for that commitment. Plus, I just went off the pill. We're hoping I'll get pregnant soon. God knows my mom didn't have any problems in that regard.

"Me too." I kiss his lips. "Now can we go to the hotel and consummate this marriage?"

"Good news for you, my groin is perfect." He smiles and I laugh.

"Are you ready to go back to Lake Starlight?"

We're going on a two-week honeymoon, then true to his word, we're going to Lake Starlight for the off-season.

"Yeah, I'm excited actually. Maisie is really loving soccer, and I guess Peyton is the fastest on the football team. Plus, you and I will get uninterrupted time."

Rylan's made a big effort with his siblings and his nieces and nephews this year. We flew home for a couple birthdays, and he's getting to know them better as individuals. No more gift cards from Uncle Rylan for Christmas.

"I'm excited too."

The ride ends and we get off to thank our guests and mingle, but Rylan's gaze is always on mine from across the tent. At the end of the evening, after most of our guests have gone to their hotels, Rylan asks me for one last ride.

I accept his hand as he leads me on.

"I can't promise our life will always be this smooth and easy. We're gonna hit bumps, but what I promise is that I will never, ever leave your side, Calista Bailey-Greene."

I tear up. "Me either. You're stuck with me."

"There's no one I'd rather be stuck with." He holds me so

my back is to his chest, and his hands cover my stomach. "Is it bad I can't wait until your belly is swollen with my child?"

"You sound a little possessive, Mr. Greene."

"When it comes to you, I am."

I tilt my head back, and he kisses me. "That's okay. I like it."

After we get off, we go to a hotel, where he carries me over the threshold and makes love to me all night.

Every day I'm surprised by how much better our life is when we're sharing it together.

THREE WEEKS LATER, we fly into Anchorage and Brinley picks us up.

"Hey, lovebirds," she says.

Rylan climbs in the back and I sit in the front. We have to go get my stuff from the apartment I shared with Brinley because she has a new roommate moving in.

"We'll swing by the apartment to grab your stuff before I drop you off. It's only, like, three boxes."

"You could've dropped them at my mom's."

She waves me off. "It's fine. She's not going to be here for a little while anyway."

"How did you meet her?" I ask.

"Through the paper." I open my mouth to say something, but Brinley adds, "Now, before you argue, I did hire someone to look into her. No criminal record. Good credit report. Like, no debt. Not sure why she needs a roommate to be honest."

"That's all good. I still don't like the idea of you living with a stranger." I glance at Rylan, who's on his phone.

He said he won't entertain any family members living with us—ever. I brought it up a few times in Baja and he said he'd buy them a place before anyone lives with us. Which I get. We just got married, and he wants us to walk around naked. That's easy to say when you're an Adonis like him.

"I'm fine. I come from tough stock."

We laugh. It's true, Aunt Savannah is a hard-ass and Uncle Liam definitely holds his own in a fight.

"What's her name?" I ask. "Um... Carrie."

Before I realize it, we're in Lake Starlight, and Brinley parks along the curb.

"Did we miss anything?" I look around, but everything looks the same.

"Nope. It's been quiet." She gets out of the car, and we go up the stairs to my old apartment.

Rylan scopes it out since he never spent any time here, then picks up the boxes—eager to get to the house we rented, I'm sure. The sound of a motorcycle makes the windows shake, and it must stop right in front of the building because it's so loud. The sounds of footsteps on the stairs come next.

"Did someone new move in next door?" I ask.

Brinley shakes her head, seeming just as confused.

Meanwhile, Rylan walks to the window. "Smokin' Harley down there."

A knock sounds on the door and I go over to answer it.

A handsome tall man with a T-shirt and jeans and tattoos all down his arms stands there, looking around. "Hey, I'm Carey." He holds out his hand to me. "Are you Brinley?"

I shake my head and point at my blonde cousin.

He walks over to her with his hand out. "Nice to finally meet you."

"I thought it was Carrie with an i-e?" Her face is pale, and her eyes are wide.

Guess she should've gotten whoever she hired to confirm that Carey was a she, not a he, too.

"People get that wrong all the time. Ends in an e-y actually. Which room is mine?" He spots Rylan across the room and nods at him. "What's up, man? Carey."

"Rylan."

"Point the way, and I'll be out of your hair," Carey says.

He seems friendly enough, but the tattoos and leather jacket in his hand... this is not Brinley's style. Sawyer wore a suit to work every day. Not that she's looking at this guy as a possible romantic partner, but I want her to be comfortable in her own apartment.

"Um. Just around the corner to the right is your room." Brinley looks at me with wide eyes when he disappears down the hall.

"Nice guy. Let's go." Rylan comes to stand next to me.

"You can't leave me here. She is a he!" Brinley whisper-shouts.

"Actually, he's always been a he. Sounds like a mix-up with the paperwork," I say, which earns me a not-so-nice look from Brinley. "We can stay a little longer, right, babe?"

Rylan groans. "Fine." He drops the boxes and goes to sit on the couch.

"What do I do?" Brinley brings her nails to her mouth.

We both look in the direction Carey went. "I have no idea."

The End

cockamamie unicorn ramblings

We finally delivered Calista and Rylan's story and we hope you loved it as much as we loved writing it! This one was an emotional journey and a true labor of love. You all wanted it so much and we wanted to make sure we did it right for you and gave this very special couple the story they deserved. We hope Calista and Rylan wiggled their way into your heart.

Teasing a couple through a nine-book series beginning when they're ten years old and ending when they're seventeen is hard work (The Baileys series). Then incorporating them throughout The Greene Family series was an even bigger challenge. Especially when we didn't really have their story set in our heads completely. LOL

Now, let's address the proverbial elephant in the room—our grandma gang. We know some of you might be upset about the passing of Dori and Ethel. We're upset! Please know we didn't make the decision lightly. We almost didn't write this series because we didn't want our favorite senior citizens to have to pass on, but we all get older and since they'd have to be well into their 100's by the time this series was done we made the decision to have had them pass before the Lake Starlight series began. The last thing we wanted is to have them pass on mid-series and to have to write about more specifically about their passing. So, we made the tough, excruciating, hardest ever decision that we had to regarding one of our stories. But you'll get a little of them in every book, we promise.

Now here's the part we the time we tell you what changed from conception to final copy and this time we kept a list!!

1.   We weren't sure how involved we wanted Calista and Rylan to have been in the timeline prior to this book until Chevelle's book where we had them coming upstairs from the basement. Even then we didn't know if we ever wanted them to embark on an actual relationship. But after writing Greene Christmas and seeing them on the page, it just felt like they had at one point.

2. Originally, Rylan was coming home for Grandma Dori's funeral, but we liked the wedding angle better and the fact that we could bring in Aubrey and Declan from Fisher's book (The Greene Family #5).

3. Midway through the book, their venue was going to flood or catch on fire and Calista would open up the cabin and acreage to hold the event for them. (Good thing we changed this because it would've been a frigid outdoor wedding, but hey, Cam and Chevelle made it work in My Brother's Forbidden Friend LOL).

4. We went back and forth over when we wanted them to actually sleep together. At one point it would only be after Aubrey and Declan's wedding, but once we were writing, there was way too much sexual tension for us to hold off that long.

5. Rylan was going to bring a date to the rehearsal dinner because it was previously planned and then send her home before the wedding after Calista conveyed her jealousy, but that didn't feel right.

We're so happy with the way it did turn out and feel like their story has now gone full circle and we've left them in the happiest of places. Thank you so much for wanting their book!

As always, we have a lot of people to thank for getting this book into your hands...

Nina for her early read of this one and the entire Valentine PR team.

Cassie from Joy Editing for line edits.

Ellie from My Brother's Editor for line edits.

Rosa from My Brother's Editor for proofreading.

Hang Le for the cover and branding for the entire series.

Wander Aguiar for his awesome job of photographing our muses Calista and Rylan.

Bloggers who consistently carve out time to read, review and/or promote us.

Piper Rayne Unicorns who give us a safe space online to chat and show us love on the daily!

Readers – this book exists because of you! You made it clear that you wanted Rylan and Calista's story, and you kept asking for it over and over again. Thank you for loving our Alaska families like we do! We have so much more in store for the Bailey grandkids and we can't wait to explore all their lives a little more.

We're pretty sure you can guess which Bailey grandkid is getting their story next... Brinley Kelly, the daughter of our most beloved couple from the Baileys series, Savannah and Liam Kelly. We didn't give you too much to go on, but we can tell you, the apple didn't fall too far from her mother's tree!

Xo,
Piper & Rayne

about piper & rayne

Piper Rayne is a USA Today Bestselling Author duo who write "heartwarming humor with a side of sizzle" about families, whether that be blood or found. They both have e-readers full of one-clickable books, they're married to husbands who drive them to drink, and they're both chauffeurs to their kids. Most of all, they love hot heroes and quirky heroines who make them laugh, and they hope you do, too!

A Greene Family Summer Bash

My Sister's Flirty Friend

My Unexpected Surprise

My Famous Frenemy

A Greene Family Vacation

My Scorned Best Friend

My Fake Fiancé

My Brother's Forbidden Friend

A Greene Family Christmas

The Modern Love World

Charmed by the Bartender

Hooked by the Boxer

Mad about the Banker

The Single Dad's Club

Real Deal

Dirty Talker

Sexy Beast

Hollywood Hearts

Mister Mom

Animal Attraction

Domestic Bliss

Bedroom Games

Cold as Ice

On Thin Ice

Break the Ice

Box Set

Charity Case

Manic Monday

Afternoon Delight

Happy Hour

Blue Collar Brothers

Flirting with Fire

Crushing on the Cop

Engaged to the EMT

White Collar Brothers

Sexy Filthy Boss

Dirty Flirty Enemy

Wild Steamy Hook-up

The Rooftop Crew

My Bestie's Ex

A Royal Mistake

The Rival Roomies

Our Star-Crossed Kiss

The Do-Over

A Co-Workers Crush

Hockey Hotties

My Lucky #13

The Trouble with #9

Faking it with #41

Sneaking around with #34

Second Shot with #76

Offside with #55

Kingsmen Football Stars

You had your chance, Lee Burrows

You can't kiss the Nanny, Brady Banks

Over my Brother's Dead Body, Chase Andrews

Chicago Grizzlies

Something like Hate

Something like Lust

Something like Love

Standalones

Single and Ready to Jingle

Claus & Effect

9 798887 142272